Brian McGilloway is the author of eleven crime novels including the Ben Devlin mysteries and the Lucy Black series, the first of which, *Little Girl Lost*, became a *New York Times* and UK No.1 bestseller. In addition to being shortlisted for a CWA Dagger and the Theakston's Old Peculier Crime Novel of the Year, he is a past recipient of the Ulster University McCrea Literary Award and won the BBC Tony Doyle Award for his screenplay, *Little Emperors*. His novel *The Last Crossing* was Highly Commended at the 2021 Theakston's Old Peculier Crime Novel of the Year. He currently teaches in Strabane, where he lives with his wife and four children.

Praise for Brian McGilloway

'**Poetic, humane and gripping** . . . reminded me of Bernard MacLaverty's early work. Yes, it's that good'

Ian Rankin

'**Moving and powerful**, this is an important book, which everyone should read'

Ann Cleeves

'[A] superb book . . . **thoughtful and insightful**, wrenching and utterly compelling. It says something truly profound and universal about love, loyalty and revenge . . . If you want to understand Northern Ireland, or any society that has experienced conflict, put it on your list. And **the writing is exquisite**'

Jane Casey

'An **extraordinary** novel from one of Ireland's crime fiction masters'

Adrian McKinty

'A gentle, reflective book about a violent situation seems like an oxymoron but that's what Brian McGilloway has achieved with *The Last Crossing*. **An eye-opening read**'

Sinead Crowley

'This IS important. This book is the peak of what crime fiction can do. Brian **McGilloway writes like an angel**'

Steve Cavanagh

'As **heart-stopping and thrilling** as it is exquisitely written and prescient. A work of fiction which looks unapologetically at the legacy of our troubled past'

Claire Allan

'**Utterly stunning** and beautifully written'

Liz Nugent

'A cool, controlled, **immensely powerful** novel. McGilloway brings a forensic and compassionate eye to bear on the post-Troubles settlement in this thoughtful, morally complex book'

Irish Times

'**Outstanding.** From its harrowing opening scene to its equally violent conclusion, this is an **utterly compelling** story of how Northern Ireland's violent history has affected generations'

Irish Independent

By Brian McGilloway

The Inspector Devlin series

Borderlands

Gallows Lane

Bleed a River Deep

The Rising

The Nameless Dead

Blood Ties

The D.S. Lucy Black Books

Little Girl Lost

Hurt

Preserve the Dead

Bad Blood

Standalone title

The Last Crossing

THE EMPTY ROOM

BRIAN McGILLOWAY

CONSTABLE

First published in hardback in Great Britain in 2022 by Constable
This paperback edition published in 2023 by Constable

1 3 5 7 9 10 8 6 4 2

A CIP catalogue record for this book is available from the British Library.

ISBN: 978-1-47213-329-8

Typeset by Hewer Text UK Ltd, Edinburgh
Printed and bound in Great Britain by Clays Ltd, Elcograf S.p.A.

Papers used by Constable are from well-managed forests and other responsible sources.

Constable
An imprint of
Little, Brown Book Group
Carmelite House
50 Victoria Embankment
London EC4Y 0DZ

An Hachette UK Company
www.hachette.co.uk

www.littlebrown.co.uk

For David Headley

'Alas, how terrible is wisdom,
when it brings no profit to the man who's wise.'

Sophocles, *Oedipus Rex*

'Only Elpis was left within her unbreakable house, she remained under the lip of the jar, and did not fly away. Before [she could], Pandora replaced the lid of the jar. This was the will of aegis-bearing Zeus the Cloudgatherer.'

Hesiod, *Works and Days*

Three Days

Chapter One

The sky was bleached white the morning Ellie went. The cloud cover, low and heavy and unrelenting, seemed to trap its light and disperse it, draining from it all colour, all hint of warmth or heat or joy. I could see it through the crack caused where the curtain caught on the radiator and hadn't been pulled wholly closed. The vertical blinds offered a gap-toothed smile as three of the middle strips lay curled on the sill, their plastic fittings snapped and not yet replaced.

Eamon had woken early, rolling himself off the bed with a movement that caused the springs to creak in complaint as first they dipped then rose again in his wake. He'd been awake for a few moments; I'd felt him turn from his usual position, facing the far wall, shuffle closer to me, his hand snaking up inside my T-shirt. He pressed himself against me, waiting in vain to see if I would respond, then gave up and went downstairs.

Alone now, I allowed myself the luxury of moving to the centre of the bed, pulling the duvet after me, feeling the heat seep into my bones, imagining myself filling with light that would take away their ever-present aches.

Eamon was rattling around in the kitchen, making no effort to be quiet, no allowance for the sleepers of the house. I could chart his movements by the bangs and clatters and the evidence of previous scenes he had left for me to clean on countless other mornings: the cupboard for a bowl; the casual pour of cereal, which would leave cornflakes scattered across the floor; the suck and thud of the fridge door opening and closing; the sloshing of the milk, spilling on the counter top where he would leave the milk carton unlidded; the prangs of the toaster; the click and low rumble of the kettle; the chiming of the porcelain as one mug struck another as he pulled it from the wooden tree next to the teapot; the rising, quieting pitch of the water filling it; the stir and double tap of the spoon on the mug's rim; his smack and sigh of satisfaction as he took his first sip.

I found some strange comfort in that game, played it most mornings when Eamon was going to work, then tested myself by imagining where in the kitchen he'd have left lying the various items he used for me to clean. There was something satisfying in each minor success, some validation that I knew my husband, knew my family, that I was a good wife, a good mother. Such small victories. As if they mattered.

I must have dozed for he appeared at the end of the bed seemingly seconds later, but the light had changed in the room, and my cheek was slimy with drool. I wiped at it with my sleeve as he bent to kiss me, leaning his weight on the bed, on me. His breath was warm and yeasty from last night's beer.

'I'll see you on Monday, love,' he said.

'What time's your crossing?' I sat up, gathering the duvet around me.

'Eleven. Best get a head start, what with all the checks and that.'

I glanced at the alarm. Seven thirty a.m. He'd woken early, maybe in the hope of sex before he left. With that unfulfilled, he was going on to work. I felt a little guilty at my earlier pretence so kissed him, hard and open mouthed, like a promise.

'Take care on the sea.'

He chuckled, low and scoffing. 'That's beyond my control. I'll ring you later. My Bluetooth is broken so don't be calling me when I'm driving. Tell Ellie I'll see her on Monday.'

He stopped in the doorway and turned. 'I'm sorry about last night. You know how I get before I head off. I hate being away from home.'

'I'm sorry, too,' I said. 'Be careful on the road. Come home safe.'

'I will,' he said, his hand raised in a gesture of farewell as he trudged off down the stairs.

With that, he was gone, the room suddenly silent and wide. I stretched, heard the door shut tight. A moment later, I heard the deep rumbling of his truck engine, shaking itself to life. Scraping open the drawer next to the bed, I fished under my pants and tights for the box of cigarettes I hid there, grateful to have three whole days of freedom to smoke in my own house.

After we married, Eamon told me he didn't like me smoking inside, because of his chest, he said. His allergies. He spent enough time cramped in the cab of his truck, crossing Europe, he said, without having to feel he was suffocating in his own home. Besides, he always added, it was better for me to quit, better for my health, for Ellie's.

But when he was away on a long haul, I had two,

sometimes three days to indulge myself. On such occasions, I could sicken myself. Even on my worst days, before marriage, I'd not have had one before my morning cuppa, but today, I moved across to the window, peering through the gaps to watch his tractor unit disappear around the corner of the estate, offering a hoarse blast of farewell to Harry, the guy who lived on the corner, Eamon's mate, who was just now getting into his own builder's van. He glanced across at the house and I felt sure he spotted me at the window, sure enough to retreat behind the curtain until he was gone.

I opened the window a crack. It was so long since I'd last smoked that the first drag left me immediately lightheaded and nauseated. But it passed. And I felt I had found a brief moment of peace.

Above the estate, crows circled and wheeled, stark against a sky the colour of old bone. Beyond that, though, the world was still, all traffic silenced at this distance, all movement frozen save the frantic shifts and turns of the birds. Even the lawns in the small yards I could see and the common, a green area encircled by the estate, seemed drained of colour somehow, the grass sun-bleached. I had a sense that the earth had been asleep all along and was only now rousing itself to wake and, for some reason, that morning, that thought brought no comfort.

My smoke finished, I pulled my dressing gown about me and went down for breakfast. As I passed Ellie's shut door, I could see the daylight bleeding around the crack of it and thought she must have forgotten to pull her curtains the previous night. She'd gone to a friend's party for a few hours, she said, and hadn't been home when I went to bed.

I opened her door an inch, just to check that she was okay. Her bed lay empty, the duvet undisturbed, her teddy bear, Leo, still sitting sentry on her pillow, staring at me glassy eyed.

That was the moment, I would later realise, by which all other moments in my life would now be defined, the moment that would give them all, for good or bad, their meaning. The moment I discovered I'd lost my daughter.

Chapter Two

My first thought was that she'd stayed over with Amy, her friend from school. She'd told me she was going to a party with her the previous night. She'd never stayed out all night before, though had asked once or twice to sleep over in her friend's house on the next estate. I'd always refused. 'What can you be doing in someone else's house you can't do in your own?' I'd asked rhetorically, both of us well aware of all that you could do at the age of seventeen, away from the restrictions of home.

Ellie had huffed a bit about it, pouted and fussed and claimed everyone else was allowed to do it, why couldn't she, but she'd never really challenged it and I suspected it was because she liked her comforts, liked her own bed, the security of her things, her pictures, Leo watching over her as she slept, his fur threadbare in places now from being hugged.

I tried her mobile, but it went straight to voicemail. I left her a message, asking her to call, telling her I'd assumed she'd run out of charge because she'd not come home to charge the phone.

I'd been surprised at the ease with which she had accepted the embargo on staying out all night, indeed had half expected some act of rebellion before now, would have grudgingly accepted it as an indicator of her growing independence. Still, on that morning, as I waited for Brenda, Amy's mother and my closest friend, to answer the phone, I worked myself into a pantomime of anger, ready to play my expected part.

'Yes?' Brenda's voice slurred with recent sleep.

'Brenda, is my Ellie there?'

'I'm not sure, Dora. I don't think so. Let me check.'

I heard the business of movement and the muffling of a hand on the mouthpiece of the phone, then, in the background, heard the soft tones of a girl's voice somewhere, which I took to be my child's. My relief at having located her so easily gave way to a slow build of annoyance at what she'd done when the girl's voice on the phone surprised me.

'Mrs Condron?'

It took me a second to realise it wasn't Ellie.

'Amy?'

'Yes?'

'It's Ellie I wanted to speak to,' I said.

'Ellie?'

The silence lengthened as I realised the cause of her confusion.

'Is Ellie not with you?'

'No,' Amy said. 'Why would she be?'

'She's not come home,' I said. 'She was out with you last night at a party. I thought she might have stayed over.'

'No,' she repeated, and I was unclear just which element of all that I'd said she was challenging.

'She was with you last night, wasn't she?'

I could hear Amy's breathing, ragged, fuzzing in the receiver.

'She didn't stay here,' she offered.

'Then where is she?'

'I don't know,' the girl said. 'She wasn't here anyway. Maybe she . . .' The comment seemed to die in her throat and I heard a voice in the background, presumably Brenda's. 'She thought she might have stayed here,' Amy said to her.

A mutter.

'I don't know,' Amy said. 'She didn't tell me . . . I don't . . .'

It became apparent that her attention was focused more on her mother than on me.

'Do you know where she might be, Amy?' I asked, raising my voice to draw her attention.

'No,' the girl said. 'Did you try her mobile?'

'It went to voicemail.'

'I don't . . . I'm not sure,' Amy said. 'I can Snap everyone, see if anyone knows where she is. I'll call you when I find out.'

I thanked her and hung up, worry starting to gnaw at my innards, my imagination casting to the most extreme reasons for Ellie's not coming home, almost as if thinking the worst would somehow ward against it actually happening.

I made a cup of tea and lit another cigarette, then tried Ellie's mobile again and left another message.

Beyond the kitchen window, I could hear the street come to life: the slamming of front doors; the spluttering of car engines; somewhere the sound of a baby crying, which caused my stomach to constrict, as if in protest at the warm drink.

I replayed, in my mind's eye, our conversation of the previous evening. She'd come into the living room while I was watching *EastEnders* and ironing Eamon's T-shirts; he liked the crispness, he said. She was wearing a tan leather skirt and a brown top under a faux-fur waistcoat. Her hair was straightened and hanging round her shoulders.

'I'm off to Amy's,' she said. Or did she? I replayed the conversation, but this time she said 'Mary's'. She had a friend called Mary, so it was possible, but I'd no number for her. I assumed Amy would know her, though; would include her in the Snap she was sending. But it might have been someone else entirely. I realised that, all the time she'd been talking about these friends from college and they had come alive for me through her telling of their stories, I didn't know who they were or how to begin finding them.

'Don't be late, love,' I'd called.

'I won't.' She half closed the door, then opened it again and leaned in, her hand gripping the edge, her fingers tanned, her nails painted, which colour I can't for the life of me remember, for each time I do, they change from blue to red to black.

'What time is Eamon leaving in the morning?' she asked. 'Eamon' never 'Dad'. That's not who he was to her.

'The usual. Have fun, love,' I added, glancing up at her and smiling.

She raised her chin a little in acknowledgement of the response. 'See you,' she said.

And with that she was gone.

That was the final memory God or the universe or simple accident gifted me. 'See you,' as she slipped away out the door.

'Do you have your key?' I called after her, but she was already out of earshot.

Chapter Three

The police officer who took my call, initially, seemed disinterested. She's probably out with friends, he said. Nine times out of ten, too much drink has been taken and the missing teenager will roll into the house, sheepish and worse for wear, by lunchtime. Still, he said, best give us a description, what she was wearing, where she was going.

'I think she said she was going out with her friend, Amy, but Amy says she wasn't with her last night.'

There was a pause. 'Could there be a boyfriend on the scene? Or a girlfriend? Someone secret she didn't want you to know about?'

How would I know if it was a secret? I wanted to scream.

'None that I can think of,' I said.

'Is this out of character for her? Staying out for the night.'

A roll call of suspicion and implication. Was she a good girl? Did she sleep around? Could you trust her? My immediate response was annoyance. Of course I trusted her; she was my child. Was she a good girl? Yes. to me. Could she have slept around? She was still a child who cuddled her teddy bear as far as I knew.

'Totally. She never stays away from home. We don't allow it.'

'Has she taken anything with her? Toothbrush? Money? Anything that might suggest she'd planned on staying out?'

I realised, with frustration at myself, that I hadn't thought to check and so went back upstairs to look, taking the steps two at a time, my dressing gown hem bunched in one hand, the phone in the other. Her toothbrush remained in the scummy chipped drinking glass we used as a holder. I went back into her room, the sight of her belongings making the churning of my stomach intensify. I could feel my heart thud in my chest, heard it pulsing in my ears.

Ellie kept her money in a Hello Kitty tin she'd had for years. It was part of an Easter egg set she got when she was still a child and, whether through practicality or sentimentality, she retained it and used it as a money bank. I prised off the lid and the sight of the tightly rolled notes of her savings conflicted me: relief that she had not planned to leave, and growing concern for exactly the same reason.

'No,' I said, a little out of breath from the exertion of running up the stairs. 'Her things are all here.'

'Is she on any medication?'

'Nothing,' I said. 'She gets headaches at times, but that's about it. Paracetamol,' I added, absurdly.

'She's not on any medication for mental-health concerns.'

'*She* isn't,' I said.

Another pause as he considered the implication of what I'd said.

'How was her mood before she left last night?'

'She was fine,' I said. 'She was heading out for the night. Asked when her stepdad was leaving today.'

'Her stepdad is leaving?'

I shook my head then realised the futility of the gesture. 'No, he's a long-distance driver. He's away to Rotterdam, for work.'

'When did he leave?'

'This morning.'

'Would she be with him?'

Again, I cursed myself for panicking without thinking to check. But then, would she have been with Eamon?

I had Ellie when I was eighteen. I was still at school, doing my A-levels, when I got caught. It hadn't been planned. Her father didn't hang around, but then I didn't particularly want him to, so we parted before she was even born, with an unspoken mutual consent and the odd birthday or Christmas card with a tenner in it until Ellie turned seven when all contact stopped. I learned afterwards that he'd moved to work in America.

Around that time, I met Eamon, on a rare night out with Brenda. He was a few years older than me and carried it with confidence, standing with Harry, our neighbour, at the bar, the pair of them dressed in matching jeans and checked shirts. Harry and Brenda had been married a few years by that stage. Eamon had come along for company; he'd separated from his wife, though never explained why beyond telling me she was a hateful bitch. I'd pushed him once or twice on the subject, usually when the two of us had drink in us, but had learned it was a subject best not broached. I still saw her in town, at times, working in the organic food market she'd set up after he left her. Part of me didn't want to admit it, but she looked better than ever the longer she was away from him.

Ellie liked Eamon, as far as I could tell. But he'd never been 'Daddy' to her; he was always Eamon. There hadn't been the same warmth in their relationship as we had, Ellie and me. She'd cuddle with me in the evenings, curled up beside me on the sofa as we watched some junk on TV. With Eamon, she was more guarded, self-aware. She leaned into any hug she gave him; with me, she wrapped herself into an embrace. But she was a teenaged girl with all that that entailed, so I never thought about it too deeply. Would she have gone away with him, without telling me? Without him telling me?

'Ma'am?'

The question hung unanswered between us. 'No. They're not like that, Ellie and Eamon.'

'Eamon's your partner.'

'Husband,' I said. A flash of the pair of us at the registry office, Harry and Brenda, Ellie and a few friends. Eamon had wanted to make a thing of it, take me away somewhere nice, but I saw no point in a big party. Money's tight enough without wasting it on nonsense, I'd said. He'd promised he'd take me away somewhere for our tenth anniversary instead. He'd meant it too. Back then. I saw Ellie, standing next to us, in a peach-coloured dress, a small bouquet in her hand, eyes wide at the novelty of a day off school and a new daddy. But she never called him daddy. 'He'd have told me if she was with him.'

'Maybe he doesn't realise. Could she have stowed away in his truck?'

'I'll call him and check,' I said, feeling a little guilt, and a little concern about what it suggested, that I hadn't contacted him first.

'Maybe put out feelers on social media and that, too,' the officer said. 'Someone will be out with you later, if she's still not home.'

I thanked him and hung up, then called Eamon, glancing at the clock.

Eleven thirty a.m.

The ferry would just have left the dock, his signal good for maybe another twenty minutes before it moved beyond reach. It rang eight times before he answered.

'I told you my Bluetooth was broken,' he said, by way of greeting.

'I thought you'd be on the boat,' I said. 'Sorry.'

I could hear a sudden burst of laughter in the background in response to a conversation I could not make out.

'I'm just in the lounge now,' he said. 'Sorry, lads,' he added, and I could hear the soft grunt he always made as he pushed himself to his feet. I guessed he'd been sitting with the other drivers and was moving away from them to take the call. Was I *that* wife, I wondered?

'Is Ellie with you?'

'Me? Why would she be with me?'

'She didn't come home last night.'

'Are you sure?'

'Her bed's not been slept in. Did you check on her this morning?'

'You know I don't like wakening her.'

That wasn't quite true. When she turned thirteen, they'd had a blazing row about his going into her room without knocking. She'd been getting changed, she'd said, and he'd just walked in, looking for something or other. I'd tried to explain to him; he'd never had a daughter before, didn't understand. She needed her privacy.

'She's a spoilt wee bitch,' he'd said, then seemed to see from my reaction that he'd gone too far. 'She's running this house and all in it,' he added as qualification.

'Knock on her door, please,' I'd said.

He didn't, choosing instead to avoid going into her room at all when the door was closed, perhaps through a refusal to yield to her demand that he knock rather than respecting her right to privacy.

It had made no difference to me how the battle was resolved, only that there was peace.

'She wouldn't have hidden in your truck?' I asked, echoing the police officer to whom I'd spoken.

'Sure I didn't have the trailer with me at home,' he said. 'I'd know if she was in the cab. She's probably at Amy's.'

'I've checked.'

'What made you think she'd be with me?'

'The police—'

'The police? You didn't call the police, did you?'

'I didn't know what else to do.'

'Do nothing. Have a cuppa, put on the radio, do whatever it is you do in the day. She'll rock in at some stage, hung over, like any normal teenager. She probably met some young lad.'

'She's seventeen.'

'Said the kettle of the pot.'

The comment stung more than he intended, for he quickly added, 'Look, I'm sure she's staying over with a friend somewhere. I wouldn't be worrying about her. She's a big girl.'

I nodded silently, telling myself that his failure to share my fears was an act, out of concern for me, to encourage me not to worry.

'Mind you, she needs a firm hand,' he added. 'I've told you that before. You let her get away with murder.'

Chapter Four

Amy phoned back a few minutes later to say she'd rung around, and no one had seen Ellie, but that she'd texted her and would let me know if she heard anything.

'Are you sure she wasn't with you?' I asked, aware even as I spoke of the absurdity of the question.

'I'm sorry,' Amy said. 'I saw her around eight. I went for a walk to the shop with her. I came on home then.'

'Where did she go?'

'I don't know.'

'Was she not going to a party with you?'

'I don't know, Mrs Condron.'

'You don't know?'

I could hear the catch in her breath on the other end of the line, her frustration palpable. But she was the last person to see Ellie as far as I knew. She must have told her something, I reasoned.

'I'm sorry,' she said. 'I'm sure she's okay.'

I sat in the silence of the kitchen. The sky outside had darkened, it seemed, the clouds gathering and heavy with impending rain. She'd no coat, I thought. I'd seen her go out, dressed in the waistcoat and top. She'd have not worn that just for going to the shop.

Keen for something to do, I pulled on my coat and walked the three streets round to the corner shop. I knew the owner, Madge; I'd worked there, once, a few years back. Madge was working at the till when I went in.

'All right, love? Eamon's off, I see. The usual?' she asked, winking conspiratorially as she reached behind her to the tobacco display. I'd not realised before the predictability of my routine.

'Have you seen my Ellie?'

Madge shook her head. 'Not today, love. She was in last night, before closing.'

'Did she say where she was going?'

Another shake of the head. 'She bought a quarter bottle of vodka though, for your Eamon.'

'Eamon didn't ask her to buy vodka,' I said, with more confidence than I felt.

Madge blanched. 'I'm sorry, love. I knew she was underage but she said Eamon had sent her. She's such a good lass, I just took her word for it. I thought maybe you and him were having a wee night of it before he headed off today.'

A night of it? Not in the way she'd imagined.

'Did you see which way she went when she left?'

'No. She was with the Logue girl. Amy. Is something wrong?'

I explained to her that Ellie hadn't come home, information which seemed to annoy her even more with the realisation she'd sold her vodka.

'Have you called her friends?'

'Of course,' I snapped.

'Stick something on Facebook. Ask has anyone seen her.'

I nodded, taking out my phone and fumbling to unlock it. I scolded myself: why was I not thinking of these things?

The truth was, I felt outside of myself, as if watching myself at a remove, in a movie or through a sheet of glass. I was aware of my movements but could not quite feel them. I needed to get home, to the safety of the kitchen. I felt myself sway, the aisles of goods next to me seeming to shift and heave on the periphery of my vision, the ground suddenly soft beneath my feet.

I made it out of the shop, my breathing ragged, my head spinning. The lamppost seemed to lean suddenly towards me, the pavement rippling as I walked. The sounds of the traffic distorted and stretched as the sweat popped on my forehead and I was sure I would be sick.

I made it back to the house, as if trudging through treacle, my body shaking with terror. I couldn't hold the key steady long enough to unlock the door, and when I did manage it, I jammed my finger in the jamb as I was trying to close it.

The house was eerily quiet. I was acutely aware of Eamon's absence and cursed his work. Usually, I could manage his trips away, so long as nothing too challenging or unexpected happened. I had come to rely on him; he'd become my crutch, willingly, preferring that I would count on him rather than my friends, most of whose visits to our home had become less frequent after our wedding. 'All we have is each other,' he'd told me one night, and I'd believed it with all my heart. In those early days, his love was almost suffocating in its passion: he'd a second chance at love, he told me, and he meant to make the very most of it. I believed him. I think he believed it too.

And through all that, Ellie was and had remained my safe space, her company provided the one place where I knew I was unwaveringly secure and where I could let such attacks pass without refuelling the flames of my panic.

But now I was alone.

I managed to post something on Facebook: 'Has anyone seen my Ellie?' I added a picture of her we'd taken together the previous summer when we'd been on holidays, sitting cheek to cheek outside a café. I cropped myself out of the image so that she seemed to lean into the edge of the picture, her smile gentle, her hair long and dark and gleaming in the sun. It had been taken in Venice. She wore a necklace I'd bought her on one of the other islands nearby: a silver chain with a glass heart, decorated with swirling blue lines inside the glass. We'd seen them being made there, had watched the glassblower at work.

With a pang, I realised that that was not how Ellie looked now. She'd started art college the previous September, in the campus downtown, and, in the weeks after, had cropped her hair shorter, into a pixie cut. She'd got a stud in her nose too, though small enough that its absence in the picture I posted wouldn't make any difference, I told myself.

Still, I was aware that the Ellie of our shared picture was already another person, the holiday a different time.

Chapter Five

My phone notifications began to ping almost instantly. Well-meaning neighbours and friends spread it to their friends and instantly *Shared in Glasgow, Shared in Derry, Shared in London* comments scrolled beneath it. Emojis of clasped hands, *God bring her home safely, Hope she's found* with a surplus of hearts posted at the end of the sentiment, lest its sincerity be in doubt. I'd done the same myself often; shared a missing-person post without even looking at the image, as if passing the whisper had been enough: acting on it would be someone else's problem. I found myself simultaneously grateful and furious at the growing comments. She's not in London, I wanted to reply. She's here somewhere, closer to me, just out of reach. Keep your pink heart and platitude: help me find Ellie. Do something.

But here was me, sitting at a phone in my kitchen, waiting for others to do something to find my child. I needed to do something myself.

I googled the number for the local hospital and called through, asking for the Emergency Department.

The nurse who answered sounded harried and a little breathless.

'I'm looking for my daughter,' I explained.

'What's her name?'

'Ellie Condron.'

'What time did she come in?'

'I'm not . . . she's not come home. I was worried she'd had an accident or something.'

I could hear the clatter of the keyboard. 'No. No one of that name was admitted last night. Wait a second.' A rustle of movement. 'Is Ellie Condron here?' the woman called. I imagined the packed waiting room of patients to whom she addressed the question. Imagined Ellie among them, nursing a broken arm, perhaps. That wouldn't be too bad. A broken arm. That would heal.

'I'm sorry. She's not been here.'

The doorbell rang and my stomach flipped. She'd forgotten her key. Or lost it and was late because she was looking for it.

'It's okay. I think that's her now,' I said, hanging up without even thanking the woman for her efforts.

Two figures stood beyond the glass pane in the door, one about the height of Ellie. Maybe it was the police, found her already, bringing her home, contrite and admonished.

Brenda must have seen my disappointment when I saw her and Amy on opening the door.

'Are you okay, Dora?' she asked, stepping in, already offering her embrace. She was taller than me by a few inches, well proportioned. More than once, I'd wondered if she'd been the object of Eamon's affections initially and not me.

Give me space, I wanted to say. *Don't force yourself on me.*

'I'm worried sick,' I managed, enveloped in her hug.

'Anything you need,' she said. 'Harry was saying Eamon's away.'

Harry, Brenda's husband, to whom Eamon had tooted farewell just a few hours earlier. It seemed like minutes ago and a lifetime past.

I nodded, felt tears gather, angry at my own powerlessness.

'Amy's phoned everyone she can think of,' Brenda said, holding me away from her with one hand, as if to examine me, while with the other she wiped her lower eyelid to stymie the tear that welled there.

'I need to get changed,' I said, acutely aware for the first time that I still wore my pyjama bottoms under my coat. I'd gone to Madge's shop like this, I realised.

'I'll stick on the kettle,' Brenda offered with a nod of agreement, her hand already moving towards her daughter, guiding her into the kitchen.

Amy, I realised, had not been able to look at me since she came into the house.

I dressed quickly. Amy knew more than she'd said. She must have known about the vodka. Must have known that Ellie was going on somewhere else. With someone else. Why wouldn't she say?

Brenda was standing by the open back door, one of my cigarettes in hand, blowing the smoke ineffectually into a draught that carried it back into the room.

'Sorry, love. You know how Harry is about smoking inside.'

Harry and Eamon: cut from the same cloth. Brenda though still smoked, albeit at open doors and windows, rather than pretending she didn't.

'You're in my house,' I said. 'Shut the door. It'll be fine.'

Brenda took a last drag, then nipped the butt before closing the door. She left the half end on the saucer I'd been using as an ashtray, the filter encircled with her lipstick.

Amy stood by the sink, her hands wrapped around a mug of coffee.

'I went to Madge's,' I said. 'She said Ellie bought vodka last night.'

Amy sipped at the coffee, her eyes lowered.

'Is that right?'

Brenda looked from me to her daughter, who nodded, blowing across the surface of her drink.

'Where was she going?'

'I don't know,' the girl said, quietly.

'Amy, where was she going?' I asked a second time, more urgently now, moving towards the girl.

'I don't—'

'You're lying,' I snapped, gripping her by the upper arms and shaking her harder than I intended, causing the drink to spill onto her hands.

'Ahh!' she cried as her mother rushed across to us and pulled me from her.

'Stop it, Dora! Jesus Christ, she said she doesn't know.'

'She knows,' I said, jabbing a finger towards the cowering girl.

'She said she doesn't.'

'I don't believe her. Please, Amy. Whatever you think you're doing to protect her, I'm going mad with worry. Please, where was she going?'

The girl raised her right shoulder in a vague shrug, but kept her gaze lowered to the floor, even as her mother fussed over her, leading her to the sink and running the cold water over her scalded hand.

'Please, Amy,' I pleaded.

The girl sighed, her shoulders slumping as she pulled her hand free of her mother's grasp.

'She asked me not to say,' she admitted, dropping heavily onto one of the kitchen chairs. 'She was meant to be meeting someone. A boy, I think.'

'Why didn't you say something?' Brenda snapped, and she and her daughter began bickering about the rights and wrongs of her breaking Ellie's confidence.

'What boy?' I asked, raising my voice to be heard.

'I don't know,' Amy said, glancing at me while Brenda continued scolding her.

'Brenda!'

She looked at me, almost as surprised as I was at the vigour of my rebuke. 'What boy?' I repeated.

Amy shrugged. 'He's called Nicky, I think,' she said. 'I don't know any of her— Look, we've not been as friendly since she fell in with that new crowd.'

Ellie and Amy had been inseparable, to my mind at least, the whole way through primary school and secondary, a friendship forged in the same fires as that of their mothers. Amy had stayed on at school to finish her exams; I knew, from Brenda's frequent reminders, that she hoped to go on to do social work. Ellie, by contrast, realised quite quickly into her senior years at the school that her interests lay in art college and had dropped out. I knew that the friendship had cooled; had explained it by virtue of the fact they weren't seeing one another every day.

'What new crowd?'

'Ellie has a whole new group of friends. The dyed-hair mob.'

I looked to Brenda who leaned now against the counter, her arms folded, but made no comment.

'A lot of them have their hair dyed blue or green or pink or something. Thank God Ellie didn't go that far,' Amy said.

That far, I thought. I remembered when she came home, having had her hair cropped. She'd always grown it long. As a child, she'd loved sitting while I brushed it out, over and over, chattering away about everything and nothing. While I'd been surprised by the change in style, and a little saddened that she'd done it – for it marked, for me, a movement away from her childhood – I'd assumed it was a statement of intent: a fresh start, a declaration of independence of sorts, not fitting in.

'What about them?'

'She was heading to a party with them last night. I don't think she was planning an all-nighter or anything, though. She was supposed to go with this boy, Nicky.'

'Where was the party?'

Amy shrugged again. 'I swear I don't know,' she said, offering the appeal of ignorance as much to her mother as to me. 'She was getting picked up at nine outside the art college.'

'By who?'

'I don't know,' Amy repeated, shaking her head. 'But that's where she must be. The party, wherever it was. Maybe someone in her class would know.'

'Who?'

'I don't know any of them. She talked a lot about Nicky. He'd know.'

Chapter Six

The art college was a modern building, all exposed steel and concrete and glass panels that caught the sun's glare at a hundred different angles.

Inside, an open-plan reception area ran onto a gallery space where a display of the students' work was being exhibited. A security man sat behind the main desk opposite the automatic doors. He looked up with annoyance when I came in, presumably because my entrance was accompanied by a gust of wind that carried through the reception and caused the sheets of artwork to flutter against the display boards to which they'd been attached.

'Can I help you?'

The space behind there unsettled me, stretching back into the building. The room seemed filled with white light and a constant knocking and chiming which, I found out, was part of an installation. The ceiling seemed to tilt, the lights glinting and winking at the edges of my vision.

'I'm looking for my daughter,' I said.

'There's no students in,' he said. 'It's the holidays.'

'No, I . . . She's not come home.'

He tried his best to look sympathetic, but I could tell what he was thinking.

'It's not like that,' I added. 'She wouldn't stay out all night, like that.'

'I've a boy of my own,' he said, as if that mattered to me. 'Sometimes things happen and they get stuck somewhere. Miss a lift or that. Did you phone around her friends?'

'Yes,' I said, gritting my teeth. The chiming had been replaced by the sounds of waves crashing on a shoreline somewhere, but I couldn't be sure if the sounds were inside my head or not. My skull felt packed with cotton wool or something, my eyes dry and sore. I wanted to cover my ears, escape the onslaught of sound and light and worry.

'I don't know her friends,' I said. 'She was to meet them outside last night.'

'She'll be okay, love,' he offered, kindly. He was a little older than me, I thought, though that may have been because he wore a beard, greyed already despite the fact his hair was still more pepper than salt. 'She's probably just staying over with a friend.'

'She's not like that,' I said, again.

He feigned sympathy, but I could tell he didn't believe me. The door behind me opened with a further gust of breeze as someone passed on the street beyond and I became aware of both the outside street and this inner space; light and greyness, traffic and waves, heat and cold, all competing, all pressing on me.

'She's not like that!' I said again and was shocked to hear the words echo back at me. The security man straightened, squaring his shoulders.

'It's okay, love,' he said, palm raised as if to calm a barking dog.

'It's not okay,' I said. 'Everyone tells me it's okay, but it's not okay. Ellie's missing and no one wants to help. I phoned the police, and they don't care; her friends don't care; my fucking husband doesn't care; you don't care!'

The man visibly took a breath and I realised he did so in the hopes that I might too. I noticed with some surprise that I was crying, the tears falling silently and without effort.

'Sit down, love,' he said, coming around from behind the desk and guiding me to where three low leather cube-shaped chairs squatted. 'Take a moment.'

He moved back behind the desk and appeared again with a flask and plastic cup. 'Do you want a cuppa?' he said. He held the cup in the crook of his arm while he unscrewed the flask, then poured out a cupful. It was sweet and milky and had that peculiar taste of flask tea that reminded me of childhood trips and Sunday picnics at the beach.

I sipped at it and felt myself well up once more, this time at the terrible cruelty of kindness.

'What can I do?'

I took a moment to gather my thoughts, trying to think beyond the waves and the light. 'She was meeting people outside. At nine. I hoped someone might have seen her.'

'I was on, but I don't remember anything unusual,' he said. 'Mind you, there's so many comes and goes past here in the evenings, you'd not notice anyone in particular.'

He considered a moment, hunkering down beside me, his hand worrying at the bristles of his beard. I noticed his name badge, hanging from the pocket of his shirt. His name was Philip.

'I can take a quick spin through the CCTV footage from last night,' he said. 'We've a camera over the door outside. See if I can spot her. What was she wearing?'

I told him and he promised me he'd not be long, heading into a room, the door to which had been recessed in the wall to the rear of the desk and which I had not noticed when first I came in.

I sipped my tea, suddenly aware of the expanse of the space and ashamed at my loss of control. With the mounting feelings that thought brought, I stood and drifted between the display boards of artwork in the exhibition space.

The work suggested varying degrees of skill and imagination. Some were self-portraits, traditional and obvious and a little nondescript. Others were more surreal in their versions of the artist, made up of fractured shapes and colours. There were a myriad of ceramic sculptures: bowls, vases, creatures of varied shapes and sizes and complexity.

As I rounded the corner, I saw, with a soft shock, Ellie's face staring at me from one of the boards. Her portrait caught my breath. She stared straight out from the page, but her face had been halved and was being torn in two opposing directions by her own hands. The left-hand side of her face was natural, her hair long, as it had been, her eye soft and bright. The right-hand side, however, had been flayed, the skin peeled back to reveal sinew and muscles, the eyeball large and round and unblinking. Something about it unnerved me, the exposed innards of her face and neck, around which hung the silver chain and glass heart, its blue lines spiralling inwards.

As I moved on, I noticed Ellie's face again on the next display board, one of a montage of pictures taken by another student. The images were arty, slightly blurred shots of a handful of girls, all in close proximity to one another, smiling, laughing, hugging, save for one girl, the same in each image, who remained unsmiling, staring straight into the camera. The project was clearly hers for in one of the shots, she held up a camera in front of a mirror, creating the effect of the image reflected continually in the curvature of the lens. Her face was thin, angular, with short, spiky hair.

'They're good, aren't they?'

I turned to where Philip stood, angling his head to look at the board while staying a little distance from me, perhaps not wishing to crowd me.

'I don't understand them,' I said.

'Nor I,' he admitted, a little conspiratorially. 'Good job I'm only security, eh? Is that your lass?' he added, gesturing to the photographer.

I shook my head and pointed to where Ellie was pictured. She was beaming in the image, her fingers lightly playing with the cropped ends of her fringe, her eyes looking towards the left-hand corner of the picture.

'I know her now,' Philip said. 'She's a great girl.'

'She is,' I said. 'That's her picture. I'm not sure what she was thinking.'

I moved back a few steps to allow him to see Ellie's split portrait.

He reserved comment on the image, simply saying, 'They had to draw a self-portrait of how they felt about themselves.'

'She must feel torn,' I said, for it might have seemed strange not to acknowledge it.

'She's a very good artist,' he said, diplomatically.

I nodded, unsure. 'I'm sorry about that earlier. I don't know what came . . .' The comment petered into silence, for it was not true. I knew exactly what had happened and why.

'Don't worry about it,' Philip said. 'I'd be the same in your situation. Kids, eh?'

He blushed, perhaps feeling the comment was too flippant for the circumstances and instead extended a sheet of glossy paper on which I could see an image of the street beyond.

'That's the best image I could pull,' he said.

The shot was taken from above the outer door. In it, I could see Ellie standing, a blue bag in one hand reaching out to open the door of a green car that had pulled up outside the college. She had her hand on the rear passenger-side door handle.

'Who owns this car?' I asked.

Philip shrugged. 'I don't know. It's a Volkswagen Golf, though. My own young lad is car mad. He's been looking for one for months,' he added, by way of explanation.

I took out my phone and took a snap of Ellie's portrait, then of the image of her and the unsmiling girl.

'What about her? Who's she?' I asked, pointing to the image.

Philip studied the display board until he located her name. 'Nicola Ward,' he said, pointing to her name. 'Though I know her friends all call her Nicki.'

Chapter Seven

I took the bus back home. Along the way, I studied the images I'd taken on my phone. I felt a mixture of shame and anger at Ellie's own picture. Why had she cause to feel conflicted? She'd wanted for nothing at home, had not had to work too hard to achieve what she wanted. I felt angry that she'd felt that way and not told me, not allowed me to help her. Yet I also felt ashamed that I had not noticed. She was my daughter. Strangers in the college had a better insight into her frame of mind than her own mother. It made me wonder whether she might, after all, have chosen to stay away for the night.

The unsmiling girl was another issue. Was she the same Nicki that Amy had mentioned, albeit she'd assumed Nicki was a boy? Did Ellie like this girl? Were they going out?

Ellie had never really shown much interest in boys, but then when I'd been her age, I'd been secretive about them too. I'd thought my own mother would kill me if she knew I was seeing boys. After I'd had sex for the first time, I could barely look her in the face for days afterwards in case she could tell just from looking at me. I dreaded the thought that she might find out, how disappointed she would be. Strangely, when I got pregnant with Ellie and had to tell her, her reaction was unremarkable, as if I had simply confirmed something she had always assumed. That reaction was almost worse than anger, as if she had expected it of me all along, expected me to let her down. But then, she'd had me at a similar age and in similar circumstances, so perhaps I had simply fulfilled my role, fitted into a predictable pattern.

My mother had died in her late forties. Breast cancer. It had hung over me since, like doom in my blood, if we were so alike, if I was so destined to repeat the patterns of the past. And to pass that on to Ellie.

I remember when Ellie was born, swearing that she would avoid that destiny. She would be the Condron girl who would challenge inevitability, who would achieve more than any of the rest of us had. I'd not got to college because of Ellie, but I was determined that she would not suffer the same fate. As a result, I'd not pushed her too much over boyfriends, not pried into who she was dating, content to let her focus on her work.

Now, though, I began to wonder if she'd never liked boys anyway. As I thought back, the only friends I could recall her mentioning were girls.

Had I driven her away somehow? Had she had to hide who she was from me?

The thought conflicted me. If she had lied, had stayed the night in Nicki's, then at least she was okay; she would be home. All I needed to do was track down Nicki Ward. That thought brought some comfort, at least.

While Philip had been as helpful as I could have hoped, he drew short at giving me the Ward girl's address. But he had suggested I might find her through social media. I opened Facebook on my phone. There were hundreds of replies to my post, most from people I did not know and would never meet, informing me that they had shared my call for my lost daughter to all corners of the world. Their kindness did not change the fact that I knew she wasn't in any of those places. She was here, somewhere; I was sure of that.

I checked Ellie's page first, in case she'd posted anything, but she hadn't. In fact, her last post had been sharing a competition from the local cinema almost ten months ago. She must have stopped using it and I wondered if it was because we were friends there and anything she did post, I would have seen. Had she felt unable to be herself because of me?

I wasn't wholly surprised either to see that Nicola Ward was not among her friends list, most of whom I recognised as school friends from years back. Whatever new group she had fallen in with at college, they did not feature here.

I searched 'Nicola Ward' next but could not find, among the list of profiles bearing that name, one who matched the unsmiling girl from the picture I'd seen.

The bus took the corner into our estate a little wide, causing me to slide across the seat. Straightening myself up, I glanced out to where I could see my house at the far end of the road and my stomach flipped. A police car sat on the street outside.

I rushed up the aisle, desperate to alight and see if they had brought Ellie home.

'Behind the line, love,' the driver said, apathetically.

'The police are at my house,' I explained.

He raised his chin lightly in acknowledgement of the comment but said nothing more, his attention shifting to the mirror as he prepared to pull in.

I ran towards my house as a heavyset man and a younger woman made their way back up the driveway towards their car.

'I'm Mrs Condron,' I shouted. 'Wait!'

The man looked to his colleague and then to me.

'Have you found her?' I managed, trying to catch my breath as I drew level with the car.

'Can we speak inside, Mrs Condron?' the man said.

'Have you found her or not?' I repeated.

The woman officer touched my elbow lightly, directing me towards my own house. 'Best we talk inside, love,' she said.

'Tell me,' I said, but neither of them spoke.

Chapter Eight

The man, who introduced himself as Detective Sergeant David Andrews, sat in the armchair opposite while the female officer, Detective Constable Anna Glenn, took a position on the other end of the sofa from me, perched on the edge of the seat, her body turned sideways towards me.

'We received a call from the art college that you'd been found in a distressed state,' Andrews began. 'How are you bearing up?'

'I wasn't *found*,' I said. 'I walked into the place that way. You make it sound like I was lying on the street, broken down.'

'My mistake,' he said, holding up his hands in a gesture of mollification, which I found strangely annoying. 'How are you doing?'

'I'm worried,' I admitted, feeling my lip trembling at the admission. 'It's not like her. I know everyone probably says that, but it's not like Ellie.'

'You know your own daughter,' Andrews said, a comment which gained a nod of approval from Glenn who had still not spoken beyond making grunts of agreement or sympathy as appropriate.

I bit my lip from questioning his assessment. Did I know the child whose self-portrait suggested someone being torn in two?

'Why did you go to the art college?' Andrews asked, sitting back in his seat in a manner that suggested he expected a lengthy response.

'Ellie goes there,' I said, contrarily, then aware of how self-defeating it was, continued, 'I was told she was picked up there last night at nine to go to a party. I wanted to know who had collected her.'

'Did you find out?'

I shook my head. 'A green VW Golf.'

'But you didn't know she was going to a party?'

Another shake of the head. 'Not there. I thought she was with another friend, Amy, but she wasn't.'

'Did she say anything that might suggest who she was meeting?'

'Nothing,' I said. 'Amy mentioned someone called Nicki that she thought Ellie had fallen in with, although Amy thought Nicki was a boy. In the college, there was a display of work from a girl called Nicola, which featured pictures of Ellie. I wondered whether that was the person she was meeting.'

'Nicola what?'

'Ward,' I said.

'Nicola Ward?' Glenn repeated, surprising me with her contribution.

I nodded.

Glenn glanced past me to where Andrews sat. I looked from one to the other, but he did not hold eye contact, his gaze slipping from mine.

'Why?' I asked, turning to Glenn again but she had resumed her silence.

'You offered our colleague this morning on the phone a description of the clothes your daughter was last seen wearing,' Andrews said, his tone soft and circumspect.

'That's right,' I said, though it had not been a question.

'You said that she had a bag with her. Could you describe that to us?'

I nodded and tried to speak, but the words seemed caught in my throat. I swallowed dryly and tried again. 'It's like an owl's face, with strips of leather hanging down, like feathers or something.' It struck me as suddenly absurd. Surely strips of leather would better represent fur than feathers?

'Is this it?' Andrews asked, pulling a sheet of paper from the inside pocket of his jacket and passing it to me.

The bag lay on a table, photographed inside a clear plastic bag.

I nodded, not trusting myself to speak for a moment.

'Where did you find it?'

Andrews glanced briefly at Glenn, then cleared his throat lightly. 'It was found in a layby off the A5. In a bin next to a picnic area, to be specific. Are you sure it's Ellie's?'

I shrugged. 'It looks like hers,' I said. 'She bought it in Italy when we were on holidays, at one of the markets. It's not something I've seen over here, but I suppose someone else could own one.'

'Would Ellie have had any identification on her? Anything in her bag that might prove this is hers?'

I shook my head. 'She'd no driving licence yet. Her stepfather kept promising to teach her to drive, but she didn't seem in much of a rush to learn. I can't drive,' I added, unnecessarily.

'Anything else?'

'Her purse would have her bank cards and that.'

'There was no purse in the bag,' Andrews said.

I thought of the holiday we'd had where she'd bought the bag. We'd been to Verona. Ellie had wanted to see the balcony from *Romeo and Juliet*; she'd been studying it in school. We'd written our names on the step outside afterwards.

We'd walked to the square the local market was on and that's where she'd bought the bag. We'd sat on the edge of one of the fountains afterwards, just enjoying the bustle. The two of us: Eamon had gone to the local bar for a beer and to watch a match. It had been one of my favourite moments of the whole week.

Ellie had dipped her hand into the fountain because she'd seen something shimmering beneath the water. She'd leaned in so far, I thought she'd fall and had grabbed her legs, which only served to make her jump and lose her balance even more. But she'd retrieved what she'd seen and when she opened her hand, a small heart-shaped pebble lay on her palm, already drying in the heat of the afternoon, a vein of quartz running through it. 'A heart,' Ellie had said, turning it over with her finger to examine the back. 'Just like my necklace. There are hearts everywhere, just like in *Romeo and Juliet*.'

She'd put it in the pocket of her bag, to christen it, she'd said. I'd had a €2 coin in my purse, which I took out and zipped into the small compartment in the lining.

'For luck,' I'd told her. 'You never give someone a bag without a good luck coin.'

I looked at Andrews, the memory so fresh I could almost feel once more that dry heat. 'There might be a €2 coin in the inside pocket. And a small grey pebble, heart shaped, with a strip of white running across it.'

Andrews looked again to Glenn, then nodded.

'It's Ellie's bag,' he said. 'Thank you, Mrs Condron.'

'Why would she have dumped her own bag?' I asked, my brain rushing to make sense of what they'd said.

'Well, the missing purse suggests she probably didn't dump it herself,' Andrews added. 'I'm sorry, ma'am.'

'What do you mean?'

'Something must have happened,' Glenn said. 'That's what we're investigating.'

'The last time you saw her was last night, then, around eight?' Andrews asked.

'Yes,' I said. 'She went to the shop.'

'And you went to bed before she came home. Was she often late?'

I shook my head. 'I wasn't feeling great last night so I went to bed early,' I explained.

That was not quite true. Eamon had gone over to see Harry for a drink or two before heading off today. I'd been annoyed that he'd chosen to spend the time with his friend instead of me. I told him that when he arrived back, and it had spiralled into a row.

'Thank fuck I'm away for a few days, away from this shit,' he'd shouted.

'You can leave anytime you want,' I said.

'Me leave? It's me pays for the house!' he shouted.

It had spiralled into accusation after accusation, one

remembered grievance after another unspooling as we fought. I couldn't remember just when things had soured for us. I'd once been his whole world, now I felt I was on the periphery. He'd been the centre of mine; slowly, and without my noticing it, he'd become more like its perimeter. Both of us seemed to sense that change, sensed the disappointment in the other at such a colossal misjudgement of love's potential.

I'd gone to bed early to be sure I was sleeping by the time he came up, for I knew what he'd be looking for once he'd more beer in him and was ready to make up before he left. Ordinarily, I'd have been awake when Ellie came home. But not that night. Not that one night.

'And you told our colleague that Ellie's dad – stepdad – left this morning without checking in on her.'

'No. He didn't want to wake her.'

Andrews nodded, but I felt judged by his comment.

'Ellie is very fond of Eamon,' I said. 'It's not like what you're suggesting.'

'I'm not suggesting anything, ma'am,' Andrews said.

'You're implying they aren't close because he's her stepfather.'

'Honestly, ma'am, I'm just trying to get a sense of how the land lies. Would Ellie have planned on leaving home for whatever reason?'

I must have frowned at the tone of the question, for he continued quickly, 'The fact that the bag was dumped in the layby of a busy main road and her purse, phone, cards and that are all gone suggests theft. But thefts generally don't include a missing person. The other possible avenue to explore is that she's run away and dumped the bag as a way to show she's leaving her past behind.'

'That's not Ellie,' I said. 'She was happy here.'

'I'm sure she was,' Andrews agreed.

Chapter Nine

'Can we see her room?' Andrews asked, seemingly apropos of nothing.

'I suppose,' I said, seeing no reason to refuse, though equally no reason for them to do so. Ellie wasn't there, clearly; the room wasn't big enough for her to be hiding or for me to have missed her, and the inference of the latter, even if unintended, annoyed me.

They followed me up the stairs, Andrews slowing as he passed each room, as if making a mental note of all that he saw and I wondered if this was part of his job or a side effect of it, a professional nosiness.

When I'd worked in Madge's shop for a while, years back, anytime the police came in for snacks or an ice lolly on a warm day, one of them stayed in the car with the engine running all the time, in preparation for a swift escape if it was needed. I remembered thinking how exhaustingly sad a life that must have been, spent constantly on edge. Seeing Andrews glance from one room to the next reminded me of that feeling.

Ellie's room remained as it had when first I'd checked it. It held the scent of her still and I found myself aching a little at the smell, longing to inhale it once more as I held her.

Andrews moved into the room while Glenn remained at the door. He cast an appraising eye over the pictures on her wall, art prints and postcards, the knick-knacks on her desk and bookshelf, then Leo, resting against the pillow.

'She'd had him since she was a baby,' I explained as Andrews reached out to touch the matted fur. 'I bought it for her in Galway.'

He nodded, his fingers hovering above the teddy, then seemed to think better of touching him, perhaps realising that to do so would be to somehow diminish the sanctity of the item.

Instead, he turned his attention to the drawers beside her bed, opening each and sifting through them.

'What are you doing?' I asked.

'Just getting a sense of her,' Andrews said, not looking back at me and continuing to rummage through the opened drawer.

'I'd like you to stop,' I said. 'Those are Ellie's things. Don't touch them.'

He continued as if he had not heard me.

'I said stop!' I said, more aggressively than I'd intended.

That got his attention and he raised his hands again in placation and closed the drawer.

I had the absurd idea that everyone was treating me with caution, this gesture a sign that I was being too emotional. I took a breath, tried to settle myself.

'Have you ever had any reason to think Ellie might have been involved with drugs in some way?'

'Drugs?' I said, incredulous. 'Is that what you're looking for?'

'Among other things,' Andrews said, turning to look at me. 'So, have you had reason to think she might be involved? Perhaps finding drugs paraphernalia in her laundry? Smells off her clothes, or that kind of thing?'

I shook my head. 'You don't know my Ellie,' I said. 'She's death on drugs.'

'Unfortunately, Mrs Condron,' the female officer, Glenn, said, 'frequently, parents don't know their children. What she tells you and what she tells her friends are often very different.'

I thought of what Amy said, about how Ellie had changed since she left school, the new friendship group she'd fallen in with. Nicola Ward. Maybe I hadn't known her quite as well as I'd thought, but I was still sure she wasn't involved with drugs. That I would have known, I told myself. That I'd have recognised.

'We have to ask these questions, ma'am,' Glenn continued, placing her hand on my forearm, bringing my attention back to her. 'We're not saying anything about Ellie, but it helps us work out how best to use our resources to look for her.'

'You will find her, won't you?'

Glenn's hold on my arm loosened. 'We'll do our very best,' she said.

'But she can't be far?' I said. 'She must be nearby somewhere.'

'I'm sure she possibly is,' Andrews admitted. 'But we will do our best to bring her home to you.'

'When is your husband back?' Glenn asked as we made our way back downstairs.

'He might be a few days,' I said. 'He's a long-distance driver. He's got a run to Rotterdam to collect freight.'

'What kind of freight?' she asked, her tone light, conversational, yet I still found myself wondering if I was being questioned. A lifetime of suspicion of authority taught to me growing up had left me guarded in any interaction with the police, even though I had nothing to hide. My sudden awareness of it meant I began oversharing to compensate, lest Glenn had been aware of it and that in itself had raised her suspicions.

'Different things. Flowers. Machinery. Clothing. Food stuff . . .' The sentence petered out as I realised I was just listing things. I didn't know what Eamon was carrying on this run. I realised that I'd stopped asking a long time ago. He went, he came back, life continued as normal.

When we were first married, we talked about our jobs, compared our days. At that stage I was a classroom assistant, working in a special school. I'd followed the same child, Terri, up through secondary school, helping with her physical needs. She was confined to a wheelchair and struggled with some of the more manual activities as well as keeping herself clean when toileted. Ellie was still a child herself at the time. Terri was bright as a button, staying on to do A-levels. Sitting in every class with her, helping her with her work, I'd had a second chance at an education myself, studying subjects I'd never have done in a million years when I was at school: Physics and Chemistry especially were the boys' subjects when I'd been young. Initially, Eamon had supported me in it, shared my sense of wonder at a world I was rediscovering, seemed to enjoy the vicarious thrill of learning as I told him about processes and procedures I'd learned. I thought of sitting exams myself, making up for what I'd failed to do during my own time at school. He'd even bought me some textbooks to use at home.

I remembered, though, one night I'd been out with Eamon and Harry and Brenda for dinner, when that all changed. We'd had a few drinks and were talking about work. Eamon and Harry were sharing horror stories about haulage: spoiled goods; leaks in the containers; breakdowns on the motorway; stowaways found clinging to the axles. I'd heard them before; we all had. Still, I laughed at the appropriate point and smiled in a pantomime of anticipation at the punchline of the tale, hanging on every word.

When they were done, I began to tell a story about one of the pupils in Terri's class. He'd fallen asleep during a lesson and the teacher, rather than being angry, had decided to play a trick on him by changing the time on the classroom clock until after 3.30 and getting the rest of the class to leave the room so that the child might think he'd slept beyond the end of the school day, whatever time he woke.

The kids all made their way out of the room as quickly as they could, but Terri's chair caught on the doorframe and the impact knocked her forward in her seat. Instead of being hurt, she'd howled with laughter and the other kids had joined in with her. We'd stood in the corridor, tears running down our cheeks, laughing at the harmlessness of the whole thing while inside the room, a seventeen-year-old boy lifted his head from the desk, smacking his lips as he looked around for the rest of his class. 'Go back to sleep,' Terri had called to him. 'We're not done yet. Go to sleep!'

As I told the tale, I knew it was one that had needed to be experienced rather than recited. But I'd had a few glasses of wine and had listened to Eamon's war stories, so I'd hoped he would reciprocate as Harry and Brenda were doing. But Eamon had had too many too.

Instead of joining in the good-natured laughter, he held out his hands and turned his two wrists inwards, flapping them together like a seal. 'Go to schleep!' he shouted slurring the words. 'Schleep!' he repeated, flapping his arms together.

Harry and Brenda roared with laughter now at the mockery as I sat, excluded from my own tale.

'Fucking spastics,' Eamon said, lifting his pint and draining it. 'I don't know how you deal with them,' he added, burping softly.

We'd rowed about it later, of course. Once home and in bed, when he reached for me and wondered why I wouldn't turn to face him.

'Is this about Terri?' he asked.

'You humiliated her,' I said. 'And me.'

'Dora, it must be humiliating anyway,' he said. 'Having to deal with someone else's kid like that? Do we really need to make money wiping shit off a seventeen year old's arse?'

'It's not like that,' I said.

'It's exactly like that. It's shameful.'

I glanced towards him, angrily. 'I'm sorry I'm such an embarrassment to you.'

'I'm ashamed *for* you, not *of* you,' he said, his hand resting on my rump. 'You're working hard and her family expect you to have to clean that up. Why don't they come in and do it, if they want her at school?'

'Her mum works in the bank,' I offered over my shoulder, as if this explained everything.

'So you have to wipe her daughter's hole? There's something not right there. That's beneath you.'

'I don't mind doing it. I enjoy—'

'You couldn't enjoy that,' he said. 'Be honest.'

'Well, I . . . I don't enjoy that—'

'See!' he said, tapping me lightly with his hand as if to emphasise the point.

'But I do enjoy other things.'

'Like what?'

What could I say? That I enjoyed the thrill of understanding? That I enjoyed the second chance that the job gave me, to study and think and explore in ways I hadn't when I was at school myself and Billy Bryce, Ellie's dad, was the only thing on my mind and the only focus of my attention in class. That I enjoyed the sense of independence that the job gave me, the sense of purpose, the sense of being more than just me. I expected him to *know* that, without my having to spell it out.

'But I love Terri,' I said. 'She's such a doll.'

'What did they give you for Christmas last year?' Eamon asked.

'A pack of soaps.'

'Soap? You spend your days doing the jobs they don't want to do themselves and they give you a packet of soap. Probably to wash the smell of their kid's shit off your hands.'

'But Terri—'

'You've your own daughter to look after,' Eamon said. 'Maybe you should be staying at home with her instead of sending her to a daycare just so you can go and babysit someone else's young 'un.'

'It's not like that,' I argued, turning towards him now, eager to convince him that he was wrong, that what I was doing had value. But what he'd said made sense of sorts. I was leaving Ellie so that Terri's mum could leave her daughter and I became her mother.

'You give the best of yourself to someone's kid that doesn't give a damn and your own child is . . .' He let the sentence drift, allowing me to complete it for myself in the worst possible ways.

'I'm not failing Ellie,' I snapped.

'I never said that. But I was ashamed for you tonight when you told that story. It *was* embarrassing.'

He turned away from me then, pulling the blankets in his wake and did not speak again, his breathing easing into sleep in moments while I worked through all that had been said, all that I could have said, should have said, might have said. I played through all the possible scenarios, all possible outcomes.

Two months later, I handed in my notice and, later that year, took up part-time hours in Madge's shop when we realised that, without my work, we were short on money after all.

I never heard what happened to Terri, did not reply to the Christmas card her parents sent me that first year.

'Have you told him about Ellie?' Glenn asked, and I realised I'd stopped on the stairs, caught in my reveries. I blinked against the light, unaware for how long I'd been lost in the memory.

'Mrs Condron?'

'Dora,' I said. 'Yes, I've told him.'

'I'm sure he's beside himself with worry, being away from home and everything,' she offered.

'Yes,' I agreed, thinking again of his earlier admonition that I'd let her get away with murder, as if her being missing was an indictment of me.

Chapter Ten

They left, but not before telling me that the best thing I could do now for Ellie was to stay at home in case she was lost or injured and tried to contact me. Or in case she arrived home herself and there was no one there. It made some sense, though I didn't want to point out to them that a mobile phone meant I would remain contactable no matter where I went.

Nor did I tell them that movement, busyness, was my coping strategy when things started to build and my anxiety peaked. Fight or flight, after all. Forcing myself to sit in the kitchen, waiting by a phone that stood silent sentinel next to me, took more effort than they knew.

But then, part of me suspected that the instruction was more to prevent me blundering into places. They'd known I'd been to the art college. The security man, Philip, had contacted them, concerned about me after I left. What did it say that a stranger had shown more concern for me than my own husband? I knew the ferry would have reached port by now, could guess that, by this time of day, he'd have been having lunch in one of the motorway services: a fried breakfast with extra toast and a mug of sweet tea.

I saw him sitting at a table by the window, watching those drifting in and out, all those travellers, all those journeys, all going somewhere, or having been somewhere. It was one of the things that had attracted me to him; that sense of a life lived, of crossings made. He'd talked about early mornings on the motorways of Europe, a foreign sun cresting the hills, unknown land stretching for miles like unbroken promises. I imagined the freedom of the job, imagined the three of us loading into his cab and heading off through Europe, just driving. Seeing flower fields at dawn, produce drawn from the earth as we passed, lines of rape seed plants waving in the wind. I imagined coffee at small terraced tables, wine by the canal, ice cream along promenades.

In the end, I realised, I had not managed to go on one long-distance journey with him. First Ellie was too young. Then he said his employers didn't allow passengers. Finally, I forgot that I'd ever wanted to even to begin with, or perhaps I didn't want to admit that I suspected too long together in such a confined space would surely end in an argument. Only now, as I sat in the chronic quiet of the house, did I recall, with almost physical yearning, that longing to be free. To see a road ahead and to be able to take it.

The phone's urgent ringing brought me back to the moment, to Ellie. It was Eamon and I privately nodded approval, as if he had passed a test he hadn't even known he was taking.

'I take it she's not back,' he said, without preamble.

'No,' I agreed. 'I'm at my wit's end, Eamon.'

'Did you call the bloody police again?' he asked, his anger palpable.

'They came here. I didn't ask them.'

'They were there. At the house?'

'They wanted to see her room. They found her bag in a bin off the A5,' I managed before I began to cry again, harder now that I was in my own house and had Eamon on the phone. 'They think something has happened to her.'

'Jesus, Dora,' he offered, softer now. 'Look, I'm sorry about earlier. I didn't mean it. I'm sure she's okay. Maybe she had an accident or something. Nothing bad, like.'

His apology mollified me. 'I've phoned the hospitals,' I said. 'The police would know if there'd been a road accident or something.'

'That's true. Look, I'll phone through and see if I can get someone to take the run for me,' Eamon said. 'And get back home.'

'It's okay,' I said, sniffing back my tears. 'I'm managing okay.'

'I should be there,' he said.

'Thank you,' I said, regretting my earlier doubts about him.

'Even to help manage things,' he added.

He did not explain what 'things' he imagined would need managing, nor did I ask. Of course I wanted him home, but I would not have put him in a position where he might feel I expected it; partly, I admitted to myself, because I could not be sure that to do so might not make him less amenable rather than more.

'How did you know? About the police?' I asked, wondering if Harry or one of the neighbours had seen them at the door and called Eamon to see if everything was okay.

'They've it all over Facebook,' he said. 'They're appealing for information about her movements, where she was and that.'

Something niggled in my memory, something I was sure Eamon had said, something about Ellie. I fought to retrieve it, could almost feel my thoughts tumbling backwards, folding one on the other until I had it. I wondered if, perhaps, I'd misremembered.

'Last night,' I said. 'When you came back from Harry's, I asked you if Ellie was okay and you said yeah.'

'Wait a second.'

I could hear his breath rasping against the receiver. 'Thanks, love,' he said, and for a second I was confused about to whom he addressed it.

'I'm just leaving the services here,' he said. 'Stopped for a bite to eat. What were you asking?'

'Last night,' I repeated, stressing each word so he could not miss them. 'When you came back from Harry's, I asked if Ellie was okay. You said she was.'

'She was,' Eamon said. 'She was fine.'

'She wasn't there,' I said.

There was a moment's pause, the line fuzzing with static between us. 'Wait a second, love, till I put you on speaker,' he said.

'You said your Bluetooth wasn't working.'

There was a moment's silence, as if the line had gone dead, then I heard the shudder of the ignition as it sparked to life.

'What?'

'You said your Bluetooth was broken,' I said.

'Jesus, Dora, it is. I've you on the phone speaker so I can drive. What's with all the questions?'

What could I say? That the foundations of my world had shifted and I needed something stable to hold on to. Something I could trust.

'Was she at Harry's or not?'

'I assumed she was,' he said. 'But if you say she wasn't, she wasn't. I thought you were worrying about her, so it was an off the cuff answer, to put your mind at ease, you know. That's all. You know how you get when you've a worry in your head,' he said. 'Sometimes, it's better to tell you what you want to hear, just to let you rest easy. You know?'

He said nothing more until I grunted agreement.

'So where was she then?'

'She was meeting a girl she's become friends with at college. Nicola Ward.'

'Never heard of her,' Eamon said. 'Look, I'll try my best to get cover for the run and get myself back home. Okay?'

'Thanks, Eamon,' I said.

The line went dead and I was left alone again in the kitchen. I opened Facebook, noting the huge number of notifications on my own post about Ellie. I scrolled through them, but none of them offered any information beyond wishes and prayers and expressions of concern.

I searched the local police page and was a little shocked to see the picture I'd shared of Ellie smiling at me from that page too, though part now of a longer post.

We are concerned for the welfare of seventeen-year-old Ellie Condron who was last seen yesterday evening around nine p.m. near the art college on George Road. Ellie is described as five foot five inches tall, of slim build with cropped brown hair. She was last seen wearing a tan leather skirt, a cream fur waistcoat and brown top and carrying a distinctive owl handbag. She may have been injured or involved in an accident. Anyone with information on Ellie's whereabouts is urged to contact police on 101. We would also encourage Ellie to contact us or to call home immediately if she sees this appeal.

Seeing it put into words, formalised by authority, made her disappearance all the more real for me and all the more distressing.

'Please come home,' I whispered, stroking the image of her smiling face.

Chapter Eleven

The day bled into evening with constant messages and phone calls from old friends and colleagues, calling to offer their best wishes, their prayers, or to satisfy their grim curiosity. Sometimes all three at the same time. What had happened? Did they think she was injured? Where was she?

The first few calls I answered as best I could, grateful for the distraction of company, even at a remove on the telephone, explaining what I'd been told and all that I'd learned. My worry was raw, the consolation of a compassionate audience so appealing. But the consolation did not last, the emptiness and the jagged edges of my thoughts flooding back in to fill the space when the call ended and the silence returned.

As the day wore on though, I noticed the pattern of the calls, the feigned concern segueing into, 'What do you think happened?' or, 'Was there blood?' One old friend from school even asked if the police thought 'there's a sexual element to it all?' I knew the tuts of shared sympathy were marking time while the listener waited for a gap to direct me to the next prurient detail.

I worked out very quickly the difference between those asking 'How are you?' and those asking 'What happened?'

The former call only required a moment or two of conversation. By day's end, the latter got even less.

And yet, with each ring, each unrecognised call, I felt I had to answer, in case Ellie was at the end of one such number, found somewhere, or stumbling into some remote bar or house to call back home and ask to be collected.

At five p.m., a woman reporter from one of the national papers called. Initially, I thought they knew something. Why else would they take an interest in Ellie? In me? 'Has she been found?' I asked, my voice cracking, stomach churning in the expectation of their response.

'Has she been found?' echoed back at me. 'Have the police said?'

'Said what?'

'Sorry, Mrs Condron. Has your daughter been found?'

'No!' I said, 'I thought maybe you knew.'

'I'm afraid not. I was just looking for some details of what happened?'

'Are you doing a story on my Ellie?' The thought lifted me. A national paper, appeals in the press, on TV. Someone was bound to see, someone who knew her. Knew where she was. I imagined her in some distant hospital, spotting herself on the news, or on the front page. Perhaps she'd lost her memory, lost her way home. This would bring her back to me.

'Perhaps,' the voice said. She'd told me her name when she called but its unfamiliarity and her accent combined meant if I'd caught it at all, I didn't remember it now.

And so, despite the lack of assurance in her response, I went through every detail of the day, each moment of Ellie's movements, each word the police spoke, the bag, the vodka, the party. Nicola Ward.

I could tell the reporter was frustrated by my answers, seeking more in each thing I said. 'Did the police say where exactly?' 'Did they mention which layby?' 'Who found the bag?'

And, clinging to the hope that national coverage might help, I answered each question gratefully.

'When will this run?' I asked when she'd finished her own questions and thanked me for my help.

'I'm not sure,' she said.

'Will it be tomorrow? It would be so helpful.'

'It depends on my editor, whether he thinks it's a story,' she said, then corrected herself. 'Of course, it *is* a story. That's not what I mean. But whether he thinks there's enough to really push it.'

'When will you know?'

'I'm not sure, Mrs Condron. Look, I've another call coming in now. Thanks for your time.' She hung up without even expressing hope that Ellie might be found.

I could not shake the feeling that the whole thing had been a fishing trip, a reporter bored, scanning the police pages in the hope of finding something that would generate a story for her. Somewhere now, in my imagination, Ellie lay in an unfamiliar hospital bed, watching the news, unaware that I was looking for her.

I should have tried harder, made the details more newsworthy, given the reporter what she needed.

I felt like I had failed.

* * *

Before the police had left earlier, Glenn had given me her number and told me she was my Family Liaison and that I could contact her if I needed anything. I was struck by how many people had ended their calls like that: if you need anything, just ask. But I wouldn't ask. Who would? I found myself longing for someone to ask me, 'What do you need?' Taking responsibility for kindness, not leaving it to me to have to ask for it, to impose myself.

When such a call came, it was not from a source I was expecting.

Just after eight, the phone rang.

'Mrs Condron?' the voice asked; male, hesitant.

I didn't speak, waiting for him to continue, wary now of strangers on the line.

'Mrs Condron, this is Philip from the art college,' he said. 'I'm sorry for calling.'

'Is she there?' I asked, seeing no other reason for his call.

'No,' he said quickly. 'God, I'm sorry. I should have thought. No. I just wanted to check to see how you were.'

'I'm fine,' I said, waiting for the inevitable next question, looking for details.

'Okay. I was a bit worried about you this afternoon. After you left. I felt bad letting you go home like that. My wife said I should have ordered you a taxi or something, so I just wanted to say I was sorry.'

'It's fine,' I said. 'There's no need for sorry. You were very helpful.'

'Look, I've printed off some flyers with your wee girl's picture on them. We'll distribute them on Monday if she's not come home by then, see if any of the post-grad students or staff have seen her or know where she is.'

I felt tears well at such unsolicited kindness but struggled to contain them. He had already seen me break down once today; a second display would surely have him contacting the police again.

'Thank you,' I said. 'That's . . . that's lovely of you.'

'We've one of our own,' he said. 'I can only imagine what you're going through. It'll be okay, God willing.'

I nodded, despite the futility of the gesture, freeing the tears which had built and which now fell soundlessly on the receiver.

Chapter Twelve

Brenda arrived back around nine p.m. that evening, with a bottle of white wine.

'I thought you could use company,' she said.

Having spent the day in the silence of the house, my only companions my worst imaginings, I was grateful to see her, grateful for the cold relief a glass of wine offered, just to take the edge off my feelings.

Yet, as she sat, talking about Amy, about Harry, about Ellie, retelling stories to which I had myself been party, I found the noise suddenly oppressive. Each word she spoke seemed to be pulling my attention from my own thoughts, as if there was something, some thought, just beyond my grasp which, as I reached for it, as I brushed my fingers against its insubstantial edges, was drawn further from me at the distraction of her voice.

At first I smiled, nodded, murmured agreement with her comments, but even that I found exhausting. I wanted to be alone, to be by myself. I felt as if my space had been violated by her arrival.

She seemed to sense my mood, for she poured me a second glass of wine and then, gathering her legs beneath her on the sofa, her shoes lying on the floor, she nodded towards me.

'Are you okay? You're somewhere else completely tonight.'

'I am,' I admitted. 'I don't even know where I am or what I'm thinking.'

'No wonder,' she said. 'You've had such a hard day. And dealing with it on your own. Do you want me to stay over?'

She tilted her head to the side, in a show of empathy, I guessed. She'd cut her hair about a year ago; it had been long and blond, hanging past her shoulders. Then, one day, she'd had it cut and dyed into a boyish cut; gamine, my mother would have said. It had served only to accentuate the sharpness of her features, but she carried it with such confidence. Even now, sitting with her shoes off, feet up on my sofa while I fidgeted with my glass, my own legs skittish with adrenaline.

'Is Eamon home soon?'

'He's trying to find someone to take over the run,' I said. 'Hopefully he'll be on his way back then.'

'That's good,' she offered, taking a sip. 'You'll be glad to have him back to take over. Do the heavy lifting for a bit and give you a break.'

I managed a brief, brittle smile at the comment. I knew it was well intended, but the idea rankled me, that I would need Eamon to take over my concern for Ellie.

'She's not his daughter,' I said, unnecessarily, then winced at what I had said. I set the wine glass to one side, afraid that it had relaxed me more than I wanted. I did not want to be oblivious to my feelings, did not want to forget what had happened; I wanted to know everything, to be aware of everything.

'I know,' Brenda said. 'But he's her daddy in every way that counts.'

I said nothing, though privately wondered if this was the case. The fact that he still wasn't home, despite her being missing now over twenty-four hours, suggested something about the nature of their relationship. I was furious at him for not being home, yet was simultaneously grateful that he was not. His 'firm hand' comment remained with me. I knew he meant nothing by it – or at least told myself that he didn't rather than countenance the alternative – yet this was still the first thing he thought of when he heard she was missing, assuming that she was somehow to blame. Or that I was.

I'd had a sense, even when she was still young, that he'd resented the competition he perceived to exist between them for my affections. For my part, I'd been flattered to have two people both vying for my love, for my time. I'd not realised that by the time my daughter would, naturally, begin to drift from me into independence, my husband would already have done so.

Despite his comment, I could not imagine a situation in which Ellie would deliberately have done this to me.

Brenda was staring at me now, her head tilted, and I realised I had blanked once more, disappearing into my own thoughts.

'Was Eamon over with Harry last night?' I asked. 'He told me when he got back that Ellie was at yours, but she wasn't.'

Brenda shrugged, looking into her glass, then drained the last mouthful before reaching for the bottle, which sat on the floor beneath her, and pouring herself another. 'I think so,' she said. 'I was out, meeting a new client in the City Hotel.'

'Who was it?'

'A software company that have opened up. They want me to run a few coaching sessions with their staff.'

'Very good,' I said, not fully aware what that entailed. Brenda had walked out of a job in an insurance firm one day and enrolled on a course in life-skills coaching or something. Now businesses brought her in to speak to their staff about how to balance their lives and look after their mental health.

This had happened around the time of the haircut and had marked a new direction in Brenda's life. For a while, she had encouraged me to follow her example, in terms of the retraining more than the hair styling, but Eamon had been resistant to the idea.

'Could you be bothered, love?' he'd asked. 'You want to be winding down at this stage, not starting all over again.'

'Brenda's my age,' I'd protested, punching him softly on the forearm in a good-natured show of my displeasure. 'She's done it.'

'Brenda's younger than you in spirit though,' he'd said. 'She's got that energy to get up and do that type of thing. Would you want to be standing in some company, all those men staring up at you?'

I'd found his jealousy, if not endearing, then at least well intentioned, comforting in that he still felt for me in that way. That he still cared.

And so, I had demurred when Brenda offered to involve me in her business, offering excuses as to why the time wasn't right, that sometime I would surely do it, that I would be delighted to work for her.

Brenda offered for me to stay in their house that evening, though I told her the police had advised me to remain at home, lest Ellie returned. Then she offered to stay with me. Again, I found myself longing for the solitude of my thoughts of Ellie.

'Amy will want you home,' I said. 'What with what's happened to Ellie, she'll want her mummy more than ever.'

'Amy's a daddy's girl,' Brenda said. 'But, if you're sure you're okay?'

I nodded.

'I'll be back in the morning. Phone me straight away if you hear anything about—' She corrected herself. 'From Ellie.'

She leaned in and kissed the air next to me, her cheek pressed against mine, the space between us cloyingly sweet and resinous with her perfume.

I went to bed just after eleven, believing that to do so would speed up the arrival of the next day and might herald Ellie's return, or at least some news of her whereabouts. I imagined that the police would be actively searching for her now, following up on Nicola Ward, searching through CCTV footage for signs of her. I lay for an hour, my eyes closed, my mind racing.

I remembered Ellie's first pair of proper shoes. Brown sandals, with a silver clasp. She'd been wearing Velcro-strapped shoes and wanted to prove that she was a big girl.

We'd gone to Clarks in town; the shoes were dear but hard wearing.

Ellie had worn white socks with swirling lace. I think she wore a red dress, but I couldn't be sure. It might just as easily have been blue shorts and a white blouse; both blossomed in my mind's eye. I do remember marvelling at her feet though, at their shape and size, their perfection, as she placed them in the Brannock device. Why did I know it was called that? Had I read it somewhere? Heard it in a quiz? Why had I retained that piece of information but not the colour of the dress she wore? It was a dress, I was sure now. I could see the hem as I leaned down to look at the sizing, at her perfect foot held in the metal grip of the Brannock.

I opened my eyes. It was past midnight. I'd gone a full day without seeing her, I realised, my heart seeming to drop in my chest at the thought. I'd gone a full day without hearing her voice, without the casual intimacy of her touch, the light peck of her kiss as she left the house, the welcome trill of her greeting when she returned.

Why had I not checked on her last night? Why had I not waited up? Because of Eamon? But it wasn't him: I'd made that choice. I'd failed her. If I'd known last night that she was not home, things would have moved faster. Time was key. I'd heard somewhere that the first seventy-two hours are the golden hours when someone is missing. Three days. Seventy-two hours, and I had wasted how many of them because I couldn't help myself but be petulant with Eamon? I'd let down my daughter over a stranger.

I had failed her.

I went into her room for the comfort of her smell, but it engendered a hunger in me for something more than the insubstantial air of that space. I wanted to touch my daughter, to feel her warmth.

I lifted her pillow, reverently, pressed my face against its coolness and breathed in her scent. My thoughts, loose as butterflies in flight, struggled to grasp it, to create a fully realised version of her in my mind, constructed from all that the smell brought to life.

I considered sleeping in her bed, just to feel closer to her, to feel some warmth, to breath her in so that each particle might create some form of communion between us, so she might know, wherever she was, that I was both here and yet with her in some form. Or she with me at least.

I hungered for her touch with a ferocity that surprised me, that registered physically at my core with a pain that could not be satisfied or allayed.

In the end, wary of disturbing the sanctity of her bed, aware that only she should lie there and that the next person to sleep in it should be her, I took in my duvet and, wrapping it around me, lay on the floor, her pillow cushioning my head so that I might sleep with her alive to my senses.

And there I lay all night, as sleep fitfully fell.

Chapter Thirteen

If I dreamed, I don't remember it. The night passed in fragments. By dawn, I was awake, stiff from lying on that floor, taking in each piece of Ellie's room, as if the place itself would soon be taken from me too and I had to commit it, each crack and paint stain and rough plaster spot, to memory.

I studied each picture on the wall: a woman lying on her back in water, surrounded by flowers; another sitting at the front of a rowing boat; a child's face appearing from a red background, one half of her face a crisscross of paint strokes. They were part of a project she was doing about women in stories. She'd talked about them to me – all those tragic women.

I scanned the titles of the books on her shelf, reorganising them in my head, first by size, then by colour and finally alphabetically.

I got up around six and stood before her make-up set, which was scattered on her desk. I picked up her blusher brush and lightly touched it to my cheek, another form of connection. I touched each piece, carefully, putting it back exactly where it had been, each location mapped by the light dusting of foundation that lay there.

By six thirty I was breakfasted and dressed. The streets beyond were quiet, a light summer haze having wrapped itself around the estate. I could hear no traffic, no slamming of doors, no rattle of dishes from my own kitchen. The world felt abandoned to such an extent I wondered if I might not still be dreaming.

I needed to contact someone, to hear a voice, to reassure myself that *I* had not disappeared. I phoned Eamon.

I could tell as he spoke that he'd been fast asleep and I resented him its depth and solace. His first few sentences struggled into life, merging into gibberish and repetition until he roused himself.

'Is she home?' he managed.

'No,' I said. 'I've heard nothing. I'm phoning the police again.'

There was a moment's silence and I could hear the rising crescendo of traffic passing wherever it was he sat.

'Aye. Probably best,' he agreed. 'I've got someone to take the run on from here and I'm on my way back.'

'Where are you?' I asked, my heart lightening a little at the prospect of having him home, having someone with whom to share this.

'Parked up on a layby near Sandhurst. I drove till two but I was starting to drift and needed a break. The lad taking it on wanted me to bring it to him.'

'When will you be home?'

'Later tonight,' he said, then audibly yawned. 'Jesus, I'm knackered. How are you?'

'I'm okay,' I said, misunderstanding the question by the juxtaposition of his two statements. 'I slept a bit.'

'No. How are you doing? Are you holding up okay?'

'I'm okay,' I said. 'What else can I do?'

'Look, I'll get home and get out looking for her. She's bound to be somewhere near by. People don't just vanish into thin air. Someone will know where she is.'

'I hope so,' I said. 'She's gone thirty-six hours now. That's half.'

'Half what?'

'They say seventy-two hours. If they don't find someone missing in seventy-two hours, they won't find them.'

'Who said that? Who's they?'

'Everybody,' I said. 'I read it somewhere. The police.'

'The police told you that? What the hell?'

'No. But I know it's true. And she's already gone half that.'

'She'll turn up,' Eamon said. 'Look, I'm going to grab a quick bite and a wash and then get on the way again. I'll be home soon, okay, love?'

'Thanks, Eamon,' I said, grateful that it was this version of him that had taken my call and guilty that I had doubted him at all before now.

Chapter Fourteen

I'd planned on waiting until nine a.m. and then calling Glenn for an update on the search for Ellie. Instead, her car pulled up outside the house at 8.45 a.m. I was standing at the window, angling my face towards the opening as I smoked my fourth cigarette of the morning. Hope fleeted from my chest as a wave of dread flowed in its wake. I watched her as she stepped onto the pavement, came up the driveway, reading each movement, studying the set of her face lest it presage the news I did not wish to hear.

I went out to meet her, opening the door before she had a chance to knock.

'Mrs Condron,' she said. 'Good morning.'

'Is there news?' I asked, blocking her entrance until she answered me.

'Not much, I'm afraid,' she said. 'Can I come in?'

I stepped back, allowing her to pass me, then closed the door, glancing out to the street beyond where faces peered from various windows, watching to see what news the arrival of the police car might bring.

'How did you sleep?' she asked.

'I didn't, much,' I said. 'What news is there? You said not much. That means something, right?'

Glenn moved through into the kitchen. 'Shall I make tea?' she asked, already taking the lid from the kettle and moving across to the sink. 'Have you had breakfast? It's important that you eat.'

'I ate,' I lied. The saucer serving as an ashtray and my empty tea cup were the only evidence of used dishes in the kitchen.

'Would you like toast?' Glenn asked.

'If I want toast, I'll go to the bloody café,' I snapped. 'What about Ellie?'

'There's very little, Mrs Condron,' Glenn said. 'But it is important that you eat, keep your strength up. However the next few days play out, you'll need to be at your strongest.'

'What do you mean "however"? You don't think she's coming home?'

'Sit down, love,' Glenn said.

'I'll stand,' I said, folding my arms and leaning against the doorframe.

'I'll sit, then,' she said, taking a seat on one side of the table very deliberately. Grudgingly, I followed suit and sat down opposite her.

'We've no sightings since the night before last,' she began. 'We do think she ended up going to a rave in the woods out past the river.'

'A rave?'

Glenn nodded. 'They've become a bit of a thing again.'

'Why do you think she was there?'

'You mentioned Nicola Ward,' Glenn said. 'We've reason to think that she was there along with a group of friends. We were able to trace her phone location up until the point it either was turned off or ran out of charge or network, which was around 1.45 a.m. on Saturday morning. We know she phoned a friend at around 11.05 p.m. on Friday night. We've spoken to that friend who confirmed that Ellie was at the rave and who was able to hear the music playing in the background. She was still there – or her phone was still there – when it ran out of charge a few hours later.'

'And did no one see her leave?'

Glenn feigned a grimace. 'It's tricky to get anyone who was there to talk to us. Most people are afraid they'll get into trouble.'

'Why?'

'Raves tend to be pretty drug-fuelled events.'

'I told you: Ellie doesn't do drugs,' I said. 'I'd know if my daughter was a druggie.'

Glenn reached across the table, laying her hand on top of mine in a manner that was meant to be comforting but which struck me as simply patronising. 'Mrs Condron—' she began, until I pulled my hand from beneath hers. She sat back in the seat then, her hands clasped together in front of her and regarded me more coolly.

I returned her stare, taking in each feature of her face, which was long and narrow, as if stretched slightly. Her hair was short and spiky, with a dye that had left it magenta rather than red. Her eyebrows were high, her nose thin, her lips tight, giving her a haughtiness I found hard to like.

'I know my own child,' I said.

'I don't doubt that,' she agreed. 'But you'd be surprised how many times I've been sat in just this situation, having just this discussion with other parents who knew their child. I'm not saying Ellie was doing drugs . . .'

She left the sentence dangling. I nodded, encouraging her to complete it.

'But she was undoubtedly in the company of those who were doing drugs. I have to ask, was there anything that might suggest she was . . . Anything that might suggest she needed money? Changes in mood? Clothes smelling funny? Anything like that?'

I shook my head, seeing little point in restating my view of Ellie.

'Anything happen with regards to friendships? Any issues at home? With you? With your husband? They weren't close, you said.'

'I didn't say they weren't close.'

'He didn't check in on her to say goodbye before heading across Europe for several days,' Glenn said. 'Ellie's friend also suggested Ellie might have felt a little uncomfortable around him.'

'Which friend said this?'

'I can't say,' Glenn replied. 'Was that true?'

'Why are you asking her friends about us?' I snapped. 'We're not being investigated.' But even as I said it, I guessed that, perhaps, we were.

'Any teenager who goes missing, we look for pushes and pulls. Pushes are things happening in their lives that might push them from home. Violence, abuse, domestic disagreements, sibling problems and the like.'

'None of those apply to Ellie,' I said. 'She's happy here. We're happy.'

'Then pulls are forces that might draw a teen away from home. A boyfriend or girlfriend, work, money, independence.

If, as you say, nothing was pushing Ellie away from home, we have to consider that something or someone was pulling her away from home instead.'

I felt myself slump a little in my seat, my ire at Glenn punctured by the logical manner in which she had explained to me something I had known already, at heart, but been unable to articulate. The only thing that could feasibly have been pushing her from home, I reasoned, was Eamon, but he'd not been that bad, surely. I couldn't have been the one pushing her away. As for something or someone pulling her from me? I had to admit that I didn't know her well enough to be able to say with complete certainty.

'I . . . I can't be sure,' I said.

'That's okay,' Glenn said, and I couldn't work out whether she was reassuring me that it did not hinder her work or if it meant more than that and she was absolving me of the guilt I felt at not knowing everything I should about my own daughter. 'It's our job to work out what the pushes and pulls might be. That's why we ask those questions. We're not prying; we're aiming to find Ellie as quickly as possible and bring her home safely.'

'Thank you,' I said and I saw Glenn seem to relax a little where she sat. I realised I'd been unduly harsh with one of the few people actually actively looking for Ellie. 'I'm sorry.'

She waved away the apology. 'But I do think tea and toast would be a good idea,' she said.

I nodded, accepting the offer of breakfast as a way to show I appreciated her efforts.

She moved across and flicked on the switch of the kettle. 'Meantime,' she said, turning and leaning her rump against the worktop, 'it would be great if we could take a look at any devices Ellie might have used; laptops, tablets, things like that. I know she has her phone with her, but anything else.'

'What good would they do?'

'Often we can work out the pull factors I mentioned, looking at communications, DMs, Snaps and so on. If she logged on through a device at home, we should be able to access her account and see what she's written or who has contacted her. It's just one more way you can help us create a full picture of Ellie, who she was and what was happening in her life beyond her family.'

'Do you need a warrant or something?'

'Only if you've something you'd rather we didn't see,' Glenn said, smiling lightly at the absurdity of such a suggestion.

'Of course not,' I said, mindful again of that wariness of authority that I'd carried all my life and which was instinctual in everyone I knew. 'I'll get it for you,' I said, while Glenn turned from me and began hunting through the kitchen cupboards, looking for bread.

Chapter Fifteen

After Glenn had left, I began to wonder if I should have agreed to give over our laptops and Ellie's tablet. I could see no reason not to do so, though wondered at what they would hope to find that might help bring her home. I worried that they would try to create a different version of Ellie, to discredit her in some way or suggest that she was to blame for her own disappearance. Glenn had already talked about drugs. Ellie was already physically missing: I did not need the police taking the idea of her from me too.

When I heard the knock at the door half an hour later, I assumed it was Glenn returning with the devices. Instead, a heavyset woman stood on the step, a little breathless with the exertion of her walk to get here, it seemed.

'Yes?'

'Mrs Condron,' she began, offering me her hand. Her skin was warm and hard, callouses on her palm. 'I'm Ann McBride. I work for the *Herald*.'

I knew the name of the paper, if not the reporter. It was a local paper, its pages filled primarily with photographs of people on nights out and advertising that allowed it just enough budget to cover news from the district.

'I've nothing to say,' I said, motioning to close the door, but she stuck out her hand, holding it open against me.

'Please, Mrs Condron. We want to help find Ellie. You know we're local – we'll make sure her face is in every shop.'

'I already had someone on from the *Mail*,' I said.

'We're local,' she said a second time. 'Please.'

I realised that refusing to speak would not prevent them writing a story anyway and said as much.

'People will want to hear your story,' she said. 'I'm not being cruel, but that's the type of thing readers respond to.'

'Why?'

She shrugged. 'People are nosey,' she offered.

Something about the frankness of the answer, the lack of affectation of the woman made me more inclined to trust her and I held the door open a little further.

'We want to help,' she said.

'You want to sell papers.'

'The two go hand in hand,' she admitted.

I opened the door wide, allowing her to come in. She stood and waited for me, then followed me into the kitchen.

'You don't have journalist's hands,' I said.

'That's a new one,' she said, laughing lightly at the comment. She was squat, her red hair frizzing beyond control of the barrette she wore. Her face was open and ruddy, bust blood vessels snaking her cheeks.

I shrugged and stood, waiting for a response.

'My husband's a farmer,' she said. 'I do this gig part time.'

I nodded, admiring the fact she was, in effect, managing two jobs.

'Can we sit?'

I took a seat opposite her.

'I've spoken with the police and got the basics,' she said.

'But there's some things they can't tell us. What type of a girl is Ellie?'

'She's the light of my life,' I said simply and, in that moment, knew it to be true. She was the one constant in my days, the one person I could rely on, the one person who could make me smile no matter how bad things got. 'My life would be over without her.'

I found myself hoping that she would read this, that she would come home so I could tell her this. I'd told her I loved her numerous times, of course, when she was heading out for the night or at bedtime. When she was younger, I'd done it more often, partly because I could rely on the reciprocity of her reply. When she'd become a teenager, we'd not told one another quite so often, though still enough to know it to be true, the occasional row or huffing match notwithstanding.

But I had said it so often, it had lost meaning, delivered with the same ease with which I told Eamon I loved him, or said I loved a meal, or a book or a movie. It had become devalued through overuse. Now, I realised, it had not for some time encompassed the sheer depth of feeling I had for her, the urge to envelop her in my arms, a physical hunger at the centre of my being. My arms felt empty without her there, like a limb had been amputated, a phantom feeling.

I became aware of the silence and looked across at where McBride sat, quietly, waiting for me.

'Sorry,' I said.

She shook her head. 'No need to apologise,' she said. 'I totally understand. What kind of girl is she? Is she sporty? Good in school?'

'A little,' I said. 'Sporty, that is. She goes to the gym sometimes with her friends. Went with Amy, her old friend. She doesn't go so much now since she started college.'

'She's at the art college, is that right?'

I nodded.

'She's very talented, I'm sure.' McBride offered the brief warmth of a smile.

I thought again of the self-portrait, of Ellie tearing herself in two. 'She loves it,' I said, claiming her talented seeming a little boastful. I'd been raised never to boast, though I immediately realised how ridiculous the thought was, in the current situation.

'She was last seen on Friday night, is that right?'

I nodded.

'Getting into a car at the art college?'

Another nod.

'Do you know where she might have been going?'

I assumed, from the nature of the question, that the police had not divulged this information to the press just yet.

'No,' I said.

'There are rumours that she was spotted at one of Leo Ward's raves,' she said, studying me, I felt, to gauge my reaction.

'Who is Leo Ward?'

'That depends on who you ask,' McBride said.

'I'm asking you.'

She nodded. 'That's not a no in terms of the rave, then?'

'I don't know where she went,' I said. 'If I knew, I'd have gone there myself to find her.'

'Ward is a businessman,' McBride said. 'Or a drug dealer and thug, depending on how you view his business.'

Ward, I thought. Nicola Ward.

'Does he have children?'

McBride angled her head a little and I knew the personal nature of the question had piqued her interest.

'Two. He has a boy and a girl,' McBride said. 'The girl's around the same age as Ellie. Now you mention her, I think she's at art college, too.'

I tried my best not to reveal my thoughts, but I could feel the scrutiny of her stare. I suspected she'd known this all along and was only pretending to have been struck by the thought in that moment,

'Is she a friend of Ellie's?'

I shrugged, not trusting myself to lie convincingly.

'Off the record,' McBride said. 'Is she a friend?'

'I've heard her name.'

She winced lightly. 'Ward is bad news. The only thing is, he's got his fingers in every business in town. If he wanted to find Ellie, he could do it.'

'What are the woodland raves?' I asked, a question I'd been afraid to ask Glenn lest I seem stupid. I knew what a rave was, obviously, and a woodland, though was not clear on the precise nature of the two combined.

'They run every weekend, around the county,' McBride explained. 'In woodlands or areas that are that bit less accessible to the police. The locations tend to be a well-guarded secret, unless you know someone connected with Leo and his crowd. The kind view of that is that it maintains the exclusivity of the event. The less generous view is that it means all kinds of substances can be bought and sold, safe in the knowledge that the police are unlikely to arrive. There's no overheads beyond the cost of the equipment and a lot of profit in having several hundred people all cramming into a woodland clearing at twenty quid a pop.'

'And where was the rave on Friday?'

'Out at the county line, along the river.'

'Who told you Ellie was there?'

'A few people,' she said. 'I heard it as a rumour, then double-checked with a few kids who attend these things. They said they'd heard she was there too. The problem is, it's so dark that with the lights and the shadows of the branches and that, it's going to be hard to find anyone who will know for definite, unless they were actually with her. In which case, they should know where she is.'

I nodded.

'But if the police haven't told you that, they should have,' she added. 'They've search teams out looking there this morning.'

She must have guessed from my response that Glenn had not shared that detail with me, for she took out her phone and, opening it, brought up an image on the screen, which she held across the table for me to see.

It was of a woodland, where I could see, among the trees, a line of police officers, sticks in hand, searching the undergrowth.

'It's good that they're taking it seriously,' she said. 'It's early days yet. She could still turn up, love, eh?'

I nodded, though I had not registered what she said until after she had left.

Chapter Sixteen

The day passed much as the previous one had, like an ache, increasingly gnawing at me. I couldn't sit for any extended period, made cups of tea I did not drink, lit cigarettes I forgot to smoke, finding them lying across the tar-stained saucer, a perfect cylinder of ash, which crumbled to dust when I tried to touch it.

Brenda called over again in the mid morning with a pot of curry she'd made for me. Other neighbours passed the house, their step slowing, glancing in through the front windows as if to catch a glimpse of the pain, as if looking for some physical sign of Ellie's absence, my grief a sideshow spectacle.

'How are you holding up?' Brenda asked, taking her usual spot in the kitchen, leaning against the counter.

I considered the question. The panic that I'd felt the day before, the sheer terror of what might have happened to Ellie seemed to have given way, through the night, to a sense of complete dislocation. I knew that my child was missing, knew that Ellie was somewhere beyond me, but I could not *feel* it. Not in that visceral way I thought I should, as if one of my own organs had been torn from me.

'I feel like this is happening to someone else,' I said. 'And I'm watching it, at a remove.'

'Your brain's trying to cope,' Brenda said. 'It's too big to be able to face all in one go.'

'But I should *feel* something,' I said, urgent now, having articulated and so recognised fully the numbness I'd carried all morning and tried to put from my mind. I should feel something, I told myself; this was my daughter. What did it say about me as a mother that at my core, I felt an absence, not of my daughter, but of everything?

'It'll come,' Brenda said. 'For now, we have to keep hoping and praying.'

After she left, I thought on what she had said. It was Sunday. I should have gone to church.

I'd stopped going when I was a little older than Ellie was. In fact, it was after I had Ellie, I couldn't go on Sunday because I had to look after her, and it became my new habit, just as going had been an old one, developed through a childhood of being told I must. I'd been a handful of times since, to bury my parents, some friends, but I'd not known what to do. I remembered my last time, watching those around me to know when to stand and kneel and sit, always a moment or two behind the habitual attenders, like a poor waltz, up and down and round and round.

I'd felt nothing then either, had no sense of God in that building, or in the phrases learned by rote and repeated without any sense of engagement. If God existed, did he find comfort in such performances?

But I felt a hunger now to pray, to offer this situation into someone else's hands, to rely on someone else to bring my

Ellie home. It had been so long since last I'd prayed, I didn't know where to start.

There should be candles, I knew, so I hunted through the drawers and cupboards, finding only the brittle sticks of birthday-cake candles and a larger scented one, encased in a glass jar, fragranced with cinnamon and Christmas spices.

I reasoned that God would not mind and, lighting it, stared at the flame, guttering and hissing as it took on the wick. I should kneel, I thought, as I slid to my knees on the kitchen floor, my hands clasped. I squeezed my eyes shut, hoping that the act of concentrating would help me feel this prayer, would make it more effective, would allow God to hear it over the chatter of pleas chanted at him hourly.

'Dear Lord,' I began. 'I sit here – kneel here, before your greatness. I implore that you bring my daughter . . .' The prayer died on my lips. This was not a prayer. This was not me. This was not how I would speak to anyone.

I sat up again on the seat, my knees raw and sore from the hard linoleum floor. 'Please bring Ellie home, God,' I muttered. 'Please. I'm begging you. Not for me, but for her. She's such a good person. A good, good person. Please. Take me instead. Let me die in my sleep or drop dead with a stroke. Something. But please, let Ellie come home. If she does, I promise, I'll go to church. Every week, I'll go to church. I'll help people. Just give me a chance. Just bring her home to me.'

I stared at the candle flame, which seemed to flare and sizzle under my gaze. 'Please,' I muttered. 'Please, please, please.'

I waited for something, some sign, some change in the light, something that would let me know I had been heard. The silence in the room settled like dust.

'There must be a reason for you doing this,' I said. That, I realised, was one of the things I found hardest to grasp: that Ellie vanished without reason. Glenn had talked about pushes and pulls: those, I could understand. At least it would be a reason, would give it meaning. Otherwise, her being missing was senseless.

I sat like that for over an hour, speaking to God while, all the time, I seemed to watch myself from above, looking down on myself as He might.

Chapter Seventeen

The *Herald* ran the piece just after lunchtime. I'd put on the radio to hear the local news, in case there was some mention of Ellie, but nothing was said. Frustrated, I opened Facebook and checked the *Herald* site, refreshing the feed every few minutes, hoping that something would be published, that the word about Ellie would spread. Around 2.25 p.m., the story appeared.

There was nothing much in the story more than we had discussed: I wondered if she would mention the rave, or Ward, but there was nothing beyond that the last confirmed sighting of Ellie had been at nine p.m. on Friday evening at the art college, though there was the possibility she may have been in the Rowan Woods area later that evening. She quoted me a few times in the piece, sometimes reporting that I'd confirmed details released by the police, but also including my comment that Ellie was the light of my life, that my life would be over without her.

Around four p.m., someone knocked at the door. I moved into the living room first to see who it was and was surprised to see a gaggle of the neighbours standing on the street. One of them spotted me and called something, and a second later, Harry stepped back from the alcove of the front door and waved to me briefly.

'We saw in the *Herald* that wee Ellie was seen out at

Rowan,' he said. 'Some of us are going to head out to help look for her. Do you know whereabouts it was?'

'She was seen by the river,' I said. 'At the county line, apparently. But you don't have to do that.'

'You're one of us,' Harry said, patting my upper arm lightly in a show of camaraderie. 'Ellie's one of us. We look after our own, eh?'

He offered me a wink of reassurance, then headed back out to where several of the neighbourhood men moved to meet him and I watched him offer instructions.

A few of them glanced over at me; their expressions ones of sympathy. Pity.

'Thank you,' I called, then felt the billowing of tears once more at the kindness. I closed the door and the tears stopped just as abruptly, like a reservoir drained.

At five p.m., or just after, Glenn arrived at the house once more. She was curter than before.

'You shouldn't talk to the press without me there,' she said. 'We can coordinate it. Manage it to make every appeal more effective.'

'She landed at my door,' I said. 'What was I to do?'

'Not answer it,' Glenn said, matter-of-factly. 'Dora, you have to trust me. We know what we're doing. There's a procedure we follow for a reason.'

'I don't know what your procedures are,' I snapped. 'I'm sitting here all day on my own. She came and offered to help. What difference does it make if it's your press conference or some reporter calling at the house?'

'Your story sent a squad of your neighbours down to Rowan woods.'

'Is that not a good thing? More people looking?'

'We need to be careful that we preserve the scene while we search,' Glenn said, and I got the sense she was picking her way through her words with care. 'It's great that your neighbours want to help, but we can better direct them where that help would be most useful. If we decide the timing of press releases and that, it means we can control things better.'

'Things don't seem controlled,' I said. 'I don't feel in control. None of this feels controlled!'

I felt my lip give and quiver and stopped myself from speaking. I felt like I had ceded enough already to them all, without giving away the last shred of myself.

'We are following a definite line of inquiry,' Glenn said, sitting. 'I know this is difficult, Dora, but you need to be patient.'

'Patient?' I asked, the dam I've managed to build shaking once more. 'What line of inquiry?'

'I'm afraid I can't say.'

'Why not? This is my daughter. Ellie's mine. Mine. I deserve to know.'

'I understand. But for operational reasons—'

'Operational reasons. Lines of inquiry. Speak like a person. Where's my daughter?'

Glenn inhaled slowly, as if mentally resetting. She straightened in her seat, then slowly released the breath she'd been holding.

'We are following a certain line of . . . investigation,' she said.

'These are just words,' I said. 'Words to hide behind. Ellie's not an investigation, an inquiry. She's my girl.'

'Dora. We think we might have some ideas and we're looking into them. In most cases, we follow dozens of ideas before we find the right one, and sometimes we never even do that. If we told you every one we're following, we'd be getting your hopes up, or maybe worrying you, unnecessarily. That wouldn't do you or us any good. So, please, be patient. Trust me: we're doing everything we can to find Ellie and bring her home.'

'Do you think . . . ?' I faltered, having to take a breath before I could complete the question. 'Is she dead?'

I braced myself for her response, studying every movement of her face for a show of her thoughts, one way or the other, but she remained impassive.

'We don't know. We're still looking. We have to hope.'

'You said preserve the scene,' I said, finally understanding the delicacy with which she had stepped through my questions. 'You think it's a crime scene.'

Glenn shook her head, but did not look at me.

'You do. You think it's a crime scene. You think something's happened to her there.'

'No, Dora. But we can't rule it out. It's one of those ideas I mentioned. But we have others, and we've teams within teams following up on each of those.'

'What can I do?'

'Wait and be patient,' she said. 'We would like to run a press conference in the morning, if she's not home by then. If we run it after eleven, it'll hit the lunchtime bulletins and get traction through the day. Does that sound reasonable?'

I nodded, and she smiled sympathetically, though without warmth.

'When is Eamon home?' she asked.

'Tonight, hopefully,' I said. 'Do you want him there too?'

'Absolutely,' she said. 'We'd be keen to have a chat with him too.'

She smiled again, but this time it was brittle and left me with an uneasiness I could not dispel.

Chapter Eighteen

Brenda called again later that evening and sat with me while the TV played in the background. I do not remember which programme, only that the constant soundtrack helped hold at bay the quiet of the house.

'Eamon will be home soon,' Brenda said.

'Mmm,' I agreed.

'You'll be glad to see him.'

'Mmm.'

She looked about, casting for some topic of conversation that would hold me, then, deciding rightly that there was none, sat back and watched the show flickering in front of us.

That sounds ungrateful of me, and I don't mean it to be. But I had run through every possible scenario, every possible outcome, in my mind: had pictured Ellie walking in unharmed; struggling in injured; lying in a hospital bed with a bandage wrapped round her head and amnesia, like so many films I'd seen; lost in a different city, wandering the streets, longing to find home; lying in a morgue while someone pulled back a sheet to reveal her to me and my heart shattered.

I'd run through every permutation of every ending. But the longer this went on, her not being found, the more likely it was that she was not going to be at all. Forty-eight hours of the seventy-two had gone now and she was no nearer home. And I no nearer her.

Some time later, maybe minutes, maybe hours, the front door clicked open and Eamon appeared in the doorway of the living room, his travelling bag in his hand.

'Eamon!' Brenda said, jumping to her feet with relief that someone had come to share the burden of her watch with me. 'It's Eamon, Dora.'

I stood and looked at him, searching myself to see how I felt. Though I was glad to see him, I did not share Brenda's relief. It was merely as if one missing piece had been slotted back into place; the remainder of the picture, the key part, was still gone.

He moved across and kissed me roughly, his jaw bristles sandpapering the side of the cheek. Then he turned to Brenda and hugged her tightly. I watched her hands rub his back, felt the familiarity between them.

'All right, Bren?' Eamon said. 'Thanks for . . . you know.'

The comment angered me, as if they had all been speaking about me, doubting my ability to cope. Had Brenda been sent to keep watch on me? Was Eamon now taking over the shift?

'I'm not a child,' I said, articulating thoughts that the others had not shared and gaining, as a consequence, their bewildered looks in reply.

'I know you think I need to be watched. I'm an adult.'

'That's not what I meant,' Eamon said. 'Jesus, I'm only in the door—'

He stopped himself, or the pressure of Brenda's hand on his arm stopped him. Either way, his comment lay unfinished, his frustration unmistakable.

'Any word?' he asked, instead, as the three of us stood regarding one another.

'Nothing,' Brenda said. 'Look, I'll go on. Ring if you need anything.' She moved across and gave me a quick hug, then stepped back and looked me full in the face. 'Anything, Dora. Just ring.'

Then she was gone, the air sweet and perfumed in her wake.

Eamon went out to the kitchen where I could hear him clattering through his routine of making tea. There was some comfort in the familiarity of it, the order of sounds, the disorder I knew he'd leave behind which would annoy me later but at least would give me something to do, a distraction in the cleaning of it.

A few moments later he came back in, handing me a cup. He pulled two Breakaway biscuits from his back pocket and handed me one. The chocolate had melted and was smeared across the inside of the wrapper from the heat of his carrying it. Its sweetness was at once cloying and welcome.

'What's the latest?' he asked, taking his seat in the chair opposite with a mild grunt of exertion as he did so.

'They're searching in Rowan Woods, by the county line,' I said, as if the precision of Glenn's description was meaningful. I didn't know where the county line was, did not know how anyone would tell in the middle of a woodland.

'Why there?'

'She was at a rave.'

'Ellie? A rave?' he said, incredulous.

Finally, I felt the relief missing on his arrival. Someone else who knew Ellie, knew her personally, could validate my version of her. I realised that the loneliness of the day had resulted in my doubting my own memories of my daughter. What if she wasn't who I believed? Here, now, in Eamon, I had someone to reassure me that I knew my daughter best, whatever the police said. For that alone, I was so grateful to have him home.

'That's what they're saying,' I said. 'It sounds stupid, I know.' I took a sip of the warm tea, felt myself slump a little, as if the burden I had carried alone all day was alleviated, just a little. Just enough for me to take a breath.

'Thanks for coming home early,' I said. 'I'm glad to see you.' And I meant it now.

'She's my daughter, too,' he said. 'What I said on the phone, about her getting away with murder. I didn't mean it. I was kicking myself the moment I said it. I was annoyed that you were upset and I couldn't do anything, so far away. But I know it's not her fault.'

'She could never upset me,' I said. 'I remember the day she was born. I'd been in labour all morning. She didn't appear until almost gone seven that evening. I was exhausted, my arms were shaking from the epidural they gave me, like uncontrollably. They handed her to me for a moment, but I think they were afraid I'd drop her. But for that moment, I looked at her face, looked at her looking at me and I just knew. It was like I had arrived home. I'd not known what to expect, but she was exactly it. I never felt happier, more right, than in that moment.'

'I know. It was hard to compete with that,' Eamon said. 'Coming into the family. Always being second best.'

'It wasn't a competition,' I said. Because Ellie would win every time, I thought. She was part of me and I was part of her. Nothing would change that. Certainly not someone outside of us.

'That's not what I meant,' he said, but I knew it was. He sipped at his tea. 'You've started smoking again.'

I nodded, not ready to tell him that I had never stopped.

'I suppose it's extreme circumstances. Can you open the back door when you do, though? It catches my chest.'

I said nothing and he seemed to regret the comment.

'What are the police saying?'

'I don't know. Not much. Lines of inquiry.'

'Lines?'

I nodded, having not thought of the significance of that before.

'That means they're thrashing about, looking in all kinds of directions. Surely if they're searching the woods, that must mean they've some definite idea.'

'The Family Liaison Officer was here earlier and said they're looking at various things. She even took Ellie's computer and stuff to see if that throws up anything.'

'What stuff?' Eamon asked.

'The devices. Ellie's laptop and iPad, and the old laptop in the junk room.'

Ellie had used an old machine Eamon had bought, repurposed, a few years back on one of his trips. The previous Christmas, she'd complained that it was too slow and that she couldn't use it anymore. She had begged for a new one of her own for Christmas. The old one sat now in the spare room, rarely used, as far as I knew, but Glenn had asked for all our devices.

'Did they have a warrant?'

'I don't know,' I said. 'She just asked for them.'

'And you gave them to her. Just like that?'

'It'll help find Ellie.'

'How will the old laptop help find Ellie, Dora? For Christ's sakes, use your brain. They just want to snoop around our family. You know what the cops are like.'

'They said they would just be looking at any messages Ellie sent, anything that might explain where she went or who she was with.'

'You should have checked with me first,' Eamon said. 'You shouldn't have just trusted them.'

'They're looking for Ellie. They're out there, in the woods, looking for her. So was Harry. And the neighbours. All out looking.'

'And what were you doing? Sitting here?'

'They told me I had to stay here, in case she phoned.'

He scoffed at the excuse. 'You'd probably have been in the way.'

'What's that supposed to mean?'

'Nothing,' he said. 'You know how you get. Hysterical and that.'

'At least I was here!' I snapped.

'So am I.'

'Eventually,' I sniped.

'And there we go. It's my job. My job!' he repeated a second time, drawling out the words as if explaining them to a child. 'To pay for all this,' he added, indicating the house with the wave of his hand. 'I should have just stayed away, instead of coming home to this.'

'Maybe you should have,' I said. 'For all the good it's doing having you back.'

He stared at me a moment.

'What the fuck is wrong with you?' he said.

Chapter Nineteen

We slept that night in different worlds, albeit in the same bed. I'd wanted to lie again on Ellie's floor, but I was so tired, so drained by the day, and the argument with Eamon, that I was grateful to get into bed.

I wouldn't think about myself and Eamon, couldn't allow myself to wonder what had become of our marriage: when had our love become resentment? It was something for later, for after Ellie came home, when I would have the time to think about it.

I woke at three thirty. Eamon lay with his back to me, the duvet bunched up in his hands beneath his chin. His face, in sleep, was free of the anger and judgement and harshness that I so often witnessed there and instead I saw the man I first met. Despite myself, I wondered when that had changed. Had it changed? Or had I changed? He'd been funny, charming in a rough way, when we first met, that first date.

He and Harry had clearly already discussed the evening's events. We met at the bar for a few drinks, then they suggested we go bowling. Brenda and I weren't dressed for it; both of us had worn heels, thinking we'd go dancing. 'Later,' Eamon had said. 'It's early yet.'

So, we'd gone to the bowling alley, the building alive with kids using it as a meeting place on a Saturday night, the air filled with the chatter of amusement machines, and money, and the clatter of bowling pins.

Eamon had gone to the bar and brought back vodka and Cokes in paper cups, heavy with crushed ice. It became clear we couldn't play in our shoes, so I ran barefooted with the bowling ball, my own lack of coordination compounded with the ice-cold drink, meaning each bowl went straight into the gutter. Eamon walked me up for my following throw, his arm around my waist, his face so close to mine, his breath warm and sweet against my cheek. His solidity, his balance, his touch surrounded me and I felt myself relax into his arms.

We threw together, his fingers laced over mine as we let the ball go and watched it edge the lane and knock down a couple of pins, his hand on mine, his body pressed against me.

When we danced together later, at the club, he leaned to kiss me and I stopped him, my hand on his chest, my breath broken fragments of excitement and fear.

'I have a daughter,' I said, looking up at him, his face unreadable beneath the shifting colours of the lights.

'That's cool,' he said, then leaned in a second time for a kiss.

And that was us. He met Ellie a week or two later, made an effort to play with her, sitting on the floor with her dolls, drinking imaginary tea from a tea set absurdly small in his thick hands, his pinkie finger jutting out in a parody of politeness which had her in kinks of laughter. He beamed up at me, as if amazed at how easily she was entertained. I'd made my decision then: here was someone with whom I could share my life, my family, my child. She'd seemed happy in his company. Safe.

Her room was silent now, Leo the teddy bear maintaining his watch. But it seemed colder, somehow, that space, the air chilled, as if something had changed that I could not quite grasp.

I went down to the kitchen, made tea, had a smoke. Facebook offered me no distraction, the notifications and posts or comments in which I'd been tagged overwhelming. I scrolled through some of them, hoping I might find something of use, someone who'd seen something. The early ones were manageable – pleas for prayers and information and God love her poor mother. Then I found darker ones. A few mentions of the rave. Some of the comments suggested she was off her head, that she'd fallen in the river, that she'd overdosed.

Then I found one in which someone had shared a screenshot from Twitter. The account posting was a jumble of numbers and letters. The post, however, read: *Heard that girl in Rowan was raped before she was done for. Anyone else hear that?* Someone replied under it: *She was a slapper so aye, sounds likely.*

The cry escaped from me before I could control it. I felt sick, my stomach roiling, sweat breaking on the back of my neck. The room began to shift and spin and my head felt light from the cigarette smoke.

I imagined Ellie in the woods, imagined someone after her, taking her. I wanted to reach out to her, call for her. I could not get the image of her being raped from my head. I longed to sleep, to forget, but each time I closed my eyes, I saw it once more.

I phoned Glenn, wanting to know if there was any truth in it, but she did not answer. I hung up without leaving a message, unsure how to articulate one without losing whatever reserve I had left.

They couldn't be right, I reasoned with myself. I knew Ellie wasn't a slapper. That wasn't her. If that part was false, so too must be the first part. It had to be wrong. It must be.

The room began to spin again and I just made it to the sink before vomiting.

Eamon woke around dawn. I heard the creak of the bed, the soft footfalls across the carpeted floor and into the bathroom. The steady flow of his piss, the hiss of the taps. When he came down, ten minutes later, he was dressed.

'I'm heading down to the woods with Harry and a few of them,' he said. 'To help look.'

'Glenn said we shouldn't in case we damage the scene.'

'They can try to stop me,' he said. 'We have a right to be there. Ellie's *our* girl.'

I nodded, grateful. Here was the man who'd played at tea parties with her, the man I'd brought into our lives, a provider, a protector.

Sure enough, while he spooned breakfast cereal into himself, a group of men gathered on the street beyond, the flickering of their torches revealing expressions of grim determination and moments of guilty levity as they waited for Eamon, as if to set off on an adventure together.

'I'll be back for the press thing at eleven,' Eamon said, gathering his coat and a walking stick, which had once been his uncle's and which had been left to him for some reason too complicated and insignificant to remember.

He looked past me to where the group outside were suddenly illuminated with the intermittent flashing of blue lights. 'That's the cops,' he said, unnecessarily. 'Maybe they've found something.'

'Maybe it's Ellie,' I said, rushing to the door and opening it, the expectation that I might see my daughter's face almost more than I could bear.

Instead, Glenn and Andrews, the detective from the first day, got out of the car and made their way up the drive. Two uniformed officers in a second car got out and stood at the bottom of the driveway.

'Have you found her?' I asked, moving down to meet Glenn who took me by the arm.

'We need to go inside,' she said.

'Please, no,' I said, feeling my stomach lurch. 'Please don't. Please.'

'We've not found her,' she said, urgently. 'But we need to get you inside.'

I allowed myself to be directed back inside my own home. Andrews closed the door behind him, leaving the other officers standing outside.

'You're Eamon Condron,' Andrews asked, turning to Eamon, who straightened at the question, seeming to square himself a little on the balls of his feet.

'That's right.'

'Can I have a word, sir?'

Eamon looked to me, confused as to what Andrews was doing, even as Glenn directed me towards the kitchen.

'Let's me and you have a chat, love. Sorry I missed your call earlier. What's happened?'

I looked back to where Andrews was leading Eamon into our living room, as if the house were his and Eamon the guest.

'Dora?' Glenn repeated. 'Forget about them for now. What happened?'

I turned and tried to focus on her, but my vision blurred. 'I read . . . I read something that upset me. Someone posted something from Twitter: someone said Ellie was . . . raped.' The word died on my lips and I had to sit. I took out my phone and found the post again, showing it to Glenn.

'I'm so sorry, Dora,' she said. 'There are people who post these types of thing, don't think about the family. We'll have it taken down and we'll charge whoever posted it. Try not to get upset by it.'

'Is it true?' I asked, dreading to hear the answer. 'Was she?'

Glenn shook her head. 'We don't know,' she said.

It was not the flat denial that I'd expected and I felt my stomach churn again.

'What do you mean?'

'Maybe best to take a seat, Dora?'

'Have you found her? You said you'd not.'

'Maybe sit.'

'I'll stand,' I snapped. 'Would people stop telling me what to do! Have you found her?'

'No,' she said. 'But we did find something on the devices you gave us. Things that have changed the nature of our investigation.'

My thoughts swirled. Had Ellie been in contact with someone? Had she arranged something? Flights? A ferry? Was she planning on running away and they'd found evidence of it?

'What?'

The living room door opened just then, and Andrews appeared in the doorway. 'We're heading on here,' he said to Glenn. 'Did you tell her?'

'We?'

I pushed out of my chair and into the hallway to see Eamon standing, his hands cuffed before him.

'What are you doing?' I screamed.

'It's not . . . it's not how it looks, Dora,' Eamon said as Andrews drew him by the arm and out the front door.

I followed them until Glenn gripped my arm and held me back at the door. 'Don't, Dora,' she said. 'Don't let them see you. It'll be on social media in seconds. We'll leave in a bit.'

And so I stood, watching as Eamon was placed in one of the cars, the neighbourhood men watching him being driven away in cuffs. Then they looked up to where I stood and stared at me, not in sympathy, or neighbourly concern, but in judgement.

As if it were my fault.

Chapter Twenty

We left the house about twenty minutes later, once the last of the neighbours had drifted away. They'd stood outside the house after Eamon's departure, some on phones, some in animated discussion about what it meant. None came near the house and none went to Rowan Woods to continue the search for my daughter.

Glenn had made tea only she drank as she explained what had happened.

'You gave me your devices, as you know,' she said. 'When we examined them for evidence of communication with Ellie, we found some rather disturbing images and a history of web searches that are consistent with the dates that Eamon was at home.'

'What kind of sites?'

'Porn,' she said, holding my stare. I sensed I was being questioned too, rather than informed. 'Did you know he used porn?'

'I assumed he must look at it sometimes,' I said. 'We didn't *use* it, if that's what you're saying.'

'I'm not saying anything, Dora. Some of the content is illegal. Underage.'

I felt the groan break from me, as if I had no longer the strength to contain it. 'Please stop.'

'What's wrong?'

'I can't take any more,' I said. 'I can't deal with any more. Ellie, now this. Please.'

Glenn nodded, extending her hand, cautiously, and laying it on mine, as if she realised that my prayer was not directed at her. I allowed the gesture this time, grateful for some human contact.

'You'll get through this, Dora,' she said. 'I promise.'

'I'm not a bad person,' I said, tears slipping down my cheeks, surprising me. 'I do my best. Why me?'

'It's not fair,' Glenn said. 'You're right. But you *will* get through it.'

'Promise me you'll bring Ellie home,' I said. 'Just promise that.'

'We're doing our best,' Glenn said, straightening a little, her gaze slipping from mine. 'We'll do all we can.'

We left soon after and drove straight to the police station while a team took my keys in order to search our house. I knew the neighbours would be watching, so I sat in the front, next to Glenn, the car unmarked, as if to make it clear that I was not a suspect, that I was travelling with her by choice.

The station was busier than I expected considering it was still early. 'Shift change,' Glenn had explained as she led me through the reception area and across to the main door into the body of the station, where she entered a pin code to open it.

'I thought you'd have swipe cards,' I said.

'We do for most doors. But they can be stolen, so the main doors are pin-code operated.'

The incident room was open plan, carpeted, with low ceilings of polystyrene tiles and long fluorescent tubes that buzzed. I couldn't imagine working here every day. Despite the busyness, it felt stagnant.

Against one wall stood a series of display boards on which were pinned various images. My throat caught when I saw the smiling picture of Ellie that I had first shared two days ago. Below it were various other images, of woodland, close-ups of branches, tracks in mud, the river. Maps with circles drawn and different coloured pins marking different areas sat alongside these pictures, with markers running from each image to what I assumed to be their actual location on the map.

I wanted to go across, to read through it, understand the story that they were telling of my daughter's disappearance. For that is what they were doing: creating a story to fill in the missing part of Ellie's life, the previous three days.

Glenn encouraged me along to a small interview room and, after gesturing to the seat she wanted me to take, offered me tea or coffee. I wanted neither. She left for a moment, to get her file, and returned with a bottle of water for us both anyway, as well as a folder of documents.

She sat and nodded towards the red camera light that shone from the corner of the room. 'Just so you know, this is being recorded,' she said. 'You're not under caution or anything. It's always running when we have people in here. Don't be worrying about it.'

I nodded, swallowed dryly, tried not to look up at the camera and immediately found myself compelled to do so. Was someone watching me? Gauging my reactions? Did they somehow think I was connected to Ellie going missing?

'As I told you, Mrs Condron,' Glenn began. 'During the analysis of the devices you gave us permission to study, we found a range of images which cause us some concern. These include images of children being forced to engage in sexual activity.'

I felt the sweat pop again on my forehead and became acutely aware of the glare of the red light, unblinking and constant.

'We also spoke to your husband's employer and identified dates when he was not at home. Looking at the activity on the silver device you said was stored in a spare room, it's clear he was accessing pornography from that device, with no activity on the device detected at all during the dates he was away from home. Thus, we can conclude that the sites were being accessed by Eamon.'

'I wouldn't . . .' I said, but my mouth was too dry. I opened the bottle and sipped some of the water, dripping it onto my top and the table, my hand shaking more than I'd realised. 'I didn't . . . That wasn't me,' I finally managed, unsure quite what I was trying to say, but certain I had to say something.

'We know. Some of the videos accessed included "Slutty stepdaughter", "Stepdaughter begs for it", and "Daughter needs taught a lesson". As you can imagine, they all have something in common.'

I felt sick. How had I brought this man into my home, into the home where Ellie lived? A protector? How had I done that? Put her at risk like that?

'There's something else,' Glenn added.

'Please,' I said, feeling the heat in the room suddenly oppressive. The walls seemed to tilt towards me and I had to grip the sides of the seat to stop myself from slipping from it.

Glenn handed me a series of images of Ellie, undressed, taken in her room. She did not seem to be aware of the camera, based on the direction she was facing. The final image was of a male hand reaching across the screen and, in the far corner, the side of Eamon's face.

'These are taken from several videos of your daughter getting undressed,' Glenn said. 'Based on the series of images, we think that the camera was turned on and left running on the laptop, without Ellie being aware. In each video, we can see Eamon set the camera to record and, at the end, recover the laptop. We think he must have been filming her in her room, without her knowledge. The videos were deleted but kept in the wastebasket. They were last accessed a few weeks back.'

I looked at the image, the vulnerability of my daughter. 'I want to kill him,' I said.

Glenn blanched. 'I understand your feelings, Mrs Condron,' she said, nodding lightly towards the camera, as if to remind me of its presence. 'Best not though, eh?'

'I don't care,' I said. 'Did he hurt her? Is he the one who took her?'

'We don't know. Probably not, based on what you've told us.'

I frowned in bewilderment.

'You said he was home around ten thirtyish on the night Ellie went missing?'

I nodded. 'He said he was over with our neighbour, Harry.'

Glenn shook her head. 'He wasn't. We picked up his car on CCTV heading out towards Rowan Woods around seven thirty p.m., before Ellie had headed that way. We have him parked at the Airport Hotel car park, which is a thirty-minute walk approximately to the site of the rave and his car left around 9.55 p.m. so he could certainly have been there while Ellie was there. But we know Ellie used her phone to call a friend after eleven p.m. and was at the rave at that stage. Are you sure he was in by ten thirty?'

I thought back, trying to remember the detail of that night. 'I'd done the ironing and watched a thing about puppy farms. It ended and the ten o'clock news began. I was just watching the end of it when he came in. I remember because the weather started and he said something about having a smooth ferry crossing if the forecast was right.'

'Then, thankfully, we don't think he was involved directly in her disappearance. But this could be one of those push and pull factors I mentioned. This would very much be a push, if Ellie knew what he had done. Did she give any indication that she was uncomfortable around him? Or that she didn't want the laptop in her room, perhaps?'

'She asked for a new laptop of her own,' I said. 'Last Christmas. But I thought it was just that she wanted something new that she could keep herself without us using it. To give her a bit of privacy.'

I couldn't stop looking at Ellie in the images in front of me. It was like seeing her anew, the first pictures of her I'd looked at since Friday with fresh eyes. And they simply reinforced that I had failed her. I had brought Eamon into our family and, in so doing, had put her at risk. This was my fault as much as his.

I noticed then the duvet cover on which she sat. 'We changed the room a few years back,' I said. 'She'd outgrown it, she told me. So that must have been taken before we redecorated. She must have been fifteen at most.'

'That would match the dates of the recordings,' Glenn said.

'What are you going to do with him?'

'He'll be charged under Child Sex Offences legislation,' she said. 'Once we've questioned him about the current issue. He may not have taken Ellie himself, but we can't discount the possibility that he passed on these images to others: that someone else might have taken her, prompted by these images. We're checking his phone at the moment.'

'And then?'

'That'll be up to the courts,' she said. 'But he will be looking at a custodial sentence.'

I could feel the heat building, my head aching with the pressure of the walls pushing in towards me. The ceiling seemed concave, the lights' glare hurting my eyes, but when I closed them, I could still see it, as if it had burned its image onto my very eyeballs. What had I done? My poor girl. 'My poor girl,' I said, out loud, then my words dissolved into tears as everything I had felt, thought, imagined, all seemed to coalesce into a physical force that caught my throat and tore the grief from me.

Glenn sat opposite, gathering in the pictures and waiting with me.

'I know this is hard, Dora,' she said. 'I can only imagine.'

'No,' I said. 'You can't.'

She nodded, as if accepting the comment. 'Are you still able for the press conference? We're starting at eleven.'

'I . . . I can't,' I said, trying to steady my breathing, to bring my own emotions under control again. 'I can't go out like this.'

'It's actually better if you do,' she said. 'Let people see what this has done to you. What it means to you to not have Ellie home. Perhaps whoever knows something and is staying quiet will realise and speak up.'

'What has Eamon said about this?' I asked, gesturing towards the now closed folder.

'I'm not sure,' Glenn said. 'But DS Andrews will lean on him. If he was involved, we'll find out eventually.'

'And if he wasn't?'

Glenn shrugged, slowly. 'Then we're back to square one.'

Chapter Twenty-One

I do not clearly remember the press conference, but rather fragments of it, like flashbacks. I was led in through a side door to a room where a group of reporters had already gathered. One long table was set at the head of the room on which already sat a range of microphones. At our entrance, a number of the reporters rose to their feet and, moving forward, placed their phones on the table to record what would be said. Bright lights on stands glared from each corner of the room.

I was directed to the middle of three seats positioned behind the table, with Glenn to my left and Andrews to my right. Glenn had encouraged me to write a short statement that I might read out and I had done so. I gripped it now in my fist, the paper already damp with my nerves. By the time I unfolded it, the writing was smeared, the page frayed at the folds so that I struggled over the words, despite having written them.

Andrews spoke first, outlining the police concern regarding Ellie and noting, in particular, the importance of anyone in the vicinity of Rowan Wood making contact with police as a matter of urgency. My picture of Ellie was displayed behind me, her smile incongruous with the solemnity of the conference.

Andrews asked me to speak then and I glanced at the page, hoping to make my way through it without mistake. The room was silent save for the whirr and click of camera batteries charging and discharging with each flash.

'My Ellie is a good girl,' I said. 'She's such a good girl. I just want her home. I just need her to come home to me. My baby . . .'

The words dissolved into tears, despite my promising myself I would not cry. Everything seemed suddenly heightened, each sound, each word, each feeling, as if the hothouse effect of the room had intensified every sensation until it was almost unbearable.

I felt Glenn put her arm around my shoulder and draw me lightly towards her in a show of sympathy, the most explicit since I had met her.

No one spoke while I cried, but I was aware of their hush, of the increased barrage of camera clicks, the sense that the room itself was leaning in towards me as the gathered reporters strained to get the best shot of my distress.

Andrews spoke again, but I could not be sure what he said, for I could hear only the rushing in my ears, as if someone held a conch up to them. I could hear my own pulse.

He had clearly invited questions though, for all of a sudden, hands were raised, voices calling out, overlapping and rising above each other in competition to be heard.

'One at a time,' Andrews said, pointing to a young, blond journalist in the front row who smiled at being chosen first.

'Is it true someone was arrested this morning?'

Andrews straightened in his seat. 'I can confirm that a male in his forties is assisting us in our investigation. We are following a line of inquiry at present and hope to be able to take forward a file to the prosecution service in the near future.'

'Follow-up,' the blond said, before Andrews could select the next speaker. 'Is it true that the male in question is a relative of Ellie?'

Eyes glanced at me and I heard their thoughts, their admonitions that I had failed my child. They knew. They could use all the jargon and vagueness they wanted, but they knew it was Eamon.

I was suddenly aware of a fourth chair, set off to one side, behind the desk. I'd seen these things before, grieving parents, supporting one another, flanked by the police. Yet here I was, on my own, highlighting my husband's absence, Ellie's father's absence. The police wanted people to know.

As we moved back out of the room afterwards, Glenn's hand on the small of my back, directing me away from the journalists, she asked me how I felt.

'Humiliated,' I said.

Chapter Twenty-Two

The humiliation deepened when I returned home, having been given my keys back. While the officers who had searched the house had done so without causing too much upheaval, I could tell where they had been, where things were sitting out of place, dust rings now visible.

I went straight to Ellie's room, but they seemed to have taken most care here, perhaps realising that this space, of any in the house, was one where any disturbance would only cause greater pain.

In our room, they'd gone through my drawers and wardrobe space, I could tell, but had made some effort to keep it neat. Eamon's side of the room was different; clothes hung off the hangers or had slid to the wardrobe floor and I could see a gap where they had lifted the floor of the wardrobe to search beneath it, the wood returned not quite flush.

The idea of hands going through my belongings, touching my underwear, my sanitary items, all because of Eamon, left me feeling violated, as if bereft of my own dignity. I considered tidying Eamon's things, as a distraction from my thoughts, but couldn't bring myself to do it.

I sat that evening, waiting for the report to appear but, at the first sight of myself, I turned it off, unable to look at the wreckage of my life displayed for public consumption. The reporter, whom I recognised as the blond, then gave a further report to camera, underscoring that the man being questioned by police was understood to be Ellie's stepfather, Eamon Condron.

Within minutes, my phone buzzed to life with texts, missed calls, messages through Facebook, most supportive, some enquiring, all prurient. I turned off the TV and my phone and sat in the quiet of the house.

How had I not seen what Eamon was? How had I not noticed before? Or had I? I thought again of journeys in the car with him, passing groups of schoolgirls, his quick glance right, looking too long. I thought of him with Ellie when she was just beginning to develop a chest, insisting on tickling her, finding cause to hug her. At the time, I'd imagined he was being supportive, trying to show her that she wasn't changing to him, that he was a constant. Now, I wasn't so sure. Then there was the knocking on her door and his annoyance when I took her side.

How had I not realised? And even if he had nothing to do with where she was now, I could not imagine sharing my home, my bed, myself with him again. He had spied on my daughter. What had he been doing as he watched that footage back? I felt physically sick again, though realised that I'd eaten nothing since the morning, and had no appetite to do so.

I heard a rattle at the door and, initially, assuming it was some ghoul, looking to feast on my despair, I ignored it. I heard a second rattle, then Brenda's voice, calling, I realised, through the letterbox.

I opened the door to her and she hurried in, her face already drawn in pity, a dish of pasta bake in her hands.

'God love you,' she said, half hugging me. 'I just saw it. Why do they think it was Eamon?'

She moved past me into the kitchen and placed the dish on the counter, then turned to face me.

'I . . . He was filming her getting changed, without her realising,' I said. I needed to tell someone, someone who would understand that the fault lay with him, not me, that it was his sin to bear, not mine.

'Oh, sweet Jesus!' Brenda said, one hand covering her mouth as she gripped the counter as if to support herself from falling. 'Sweet Jesus,' she repeated.

I shrugged. 'I never knew,' I said.

'Of course you didn't,' she said. 'Of course not. No one thinks that. No one.'

'They do,' I said. 'I know how people think.'

'Fuck them!' Brenda said. 'Let them think what they like. People who know you, people who matter, know that you'd nothing to do with it.'

'Thanks,' I said, slumping in the seat, exhausted now, the weight of my shame shared and, for a second, lessened.

'But they don't think he'd anything to do with poor Ellie going missing, do they?'

'I don't know,' I said.

'He couldn't have,' she said, surprising me with the assertion. 'I mean, it's not credible to think he'd hurt her, whatever else about him.'

'I thought that,' I said. 'But I didn't know him at all. I'm not even sure I know Ellie the way I thought.'

'We all know her,' Brenda said. 'She was a sweetheart – is a sweetheart,' she corrected herself quickly, the flush rising along her throat.

'Don't worry,' I said. 'I've done that, too.'

Brenda took the seat opposite me. 'Why do they think he took Ellie, though?'

The past days had made me wary, even of my friend's interrogations. 'He was in the area where she went missing that night,' I said. 'He told me he was at yours, but it turns out he was near the woods instead. But he came home before she was last heard from, so I don't know. I don't know anything, Brenda. They don't tell me anything.'

'It couldn't be him,' she repeated. 'I just know it couldn't be Eamon. He'd not have hurt poor Ellie.'

She sat with me until almost seven, insisting that I eat, warming the bake for me in the oven and presenting it to me with sugary tea and biscuits. 'For your blood-sugar levels,' she said.

After she left, I went upstairs to sort through Eamon's clothes, as much to keep myself busy as anything. I noticed now that Eamon's travel bag was missing and with it, presumably, the clothes he'd worn while away. I assumed the police must have taken them to examine more closely.

It was then that my anger began to flare as I thought of what he had done to my child, watching her in her most private moments. I tore out one of his shirts in anger, tossing it onto the bed, then kept going, pulling out each item of clothing he owned, piling them on the bed. There was something cathartic about it, creating space in the wardrobe, tearing his shirts, so carefully ironed over the past years, from the hangers, balling them up and tossing them onto the bed too. Then his trousers, checking the pockets for money or keys, for anything I could not afford to lose, before they too joined the pile. It was in one such search that I found the condom, in the pocket of a pair of black jeans that were rolled into a ball on the floor of the wardrobe.

In a strange way, it almost confirmed what I had expected. Eamon and I barely had sex anymore, mostly due to my waning interest, partly due to his increasing disregard for my enjoyment of it. Either way, we rarely did so. Still, on those occasions when we did, he insisted that he would not wear protection. It ruined it for him, he said. It wasn't natural. Instead, he'd insisted that I go on the pill. And I had.

The condom then, was not for use with me.

In some ways, I'd always suspected Eamon was capable of sleeping around even if he wasn't actively doing so. His job, being away from home for periods at a time, must surely have presented him with opportunities. And, while I had not admitted it to myself before this, in my heart I knew he would not be able to resist temptation if it presented itself. So the condom came as a substantiation of an unformed thought.

As I gathered up the clothes from the floor, I recalled that the ones he'd worn while away were with the police. These trousers had not been those. Something flickered into life at the edges of my consciousness, some sudden awareness. He'd been wearing these the night Ellie went missing, the night he'd told me he was at Brenda's. And Brenda had been out at the City Hotel, working with a client at one of her motivational talks.

The flickering coalesced as something struck me. I recalled when Brenda had first spoken to me about working with her, she had talked about meeting one of her clients off the plane. He'd flown the whole way in from Dublin to see her, she said, as evidence of her reputation and that of the team I'd be joining. They'd met in one of the rooms and he'd headed straight home again on the return flight. I recalled it because she'd joked about him, about how she'd been tempted to book the room for the night and convince him to rearrange his flight. I'd laughed, believing it to be a joke among friends. Now, I wondered if I'd been misguided.

I googled the number for the City Hotel and called it.

'This is Brenda Logue,' I said, when the receptionist answered. 'I was booked into one of your conference rooms on Friday night and I think I forgot my laptop charger. Would you know if it was found?'

'One moment, please.' The voice was young, professional. After a moment, she returned. 'There's nothing sitting around here. Which room were you in?'

'I can't remember,' I said. 'Can you check the booking for details?'

I could hear a clatter of keystrokes as she checked the computer. 'There's nothing here for Brenda Logue. Would you have booked under a different name?'

'Logue Consultancy,' I suggested, the name of Brenda's company.

Another brief clatter of keys. 'No, nothing, I'm afraid. Are you sure it was Friday?'

'My mistake,' I said. 'Thank you anyway,' I added, then cut the call.

I repeated the call to the Airport Hotel this time, which lay on the roadway out towards Rowan Wood. 'We have your booking, Mrs Logue, but there's been nothing handed in. You stayed in a bedroom on the third floor, is that right?'

'That's right,' I said.

'I'll check if the cleaning service found anything and give you a ring right back,' the voice, male this time, efficient, said. 'We have your number on file.'

I knew that, when he called her back, Brenda might suspect what had happened. I did not want her to be forewarned.

Chapter Twenty-Three

'Is everything okay?' Brenda asked. She opened the door when I arrived and stepped back to allow me entrance. Instead, I remained on the step, not wishing to bring my suspicions into that house, to Amy and Harry who'd done nothing to warrant what I believed I now knew.

'Dora?' she asked. 'Is everything okay?'

'You didn't mention that you'd seen Eamon's car at the Airport Hotel,' I said.

Brenda took a second, her expression frozen, then stepped out to me, pulling the door closed behind her.

'I didn't notice it, I suppose,' she said.

'You told me you were at the City Hotel,' I said. 'Why?'

She shook her head lightly, staring into the space over my shoulder, as if to search her own memories. 'No,' she said. 'I don't think . . . You must have misheard me.'

'You said the City,' I repeated. 'But that's not where you were.'

'That's right,' she said. 'You're right. I was meant to be at the City but they double booked and I had to take a conference room in the Airport instead. Why? I didn't see Eamon's car, but then I was inside the whole time. Apart from going home. What's wrong, Dora?'

'You booked a conference room?'

Brenda nodded, her mouth slightly open in an expression of confusion. 'Why? What does it matter?'

'Not a bedroom on the third floor?'

She swallowed dryly. 'I don't . . . What has this to do with Ellie, Dora?' she asked. 'We need to focus on getting her home.'

'Don't mention my daughter,' I warned, stepping towards her with enough aggression that she took a step back from me. 'Don't mention her name.'

Brenda held her two hands up in a show of surrender. 'I don't know what's going on, Dora,' she said.

'Eamon was there, wasn't he?'

She glanced beyond me, then back towards her own house. From inside, I could hear the shrill urgency of the telephone ringing and guessed it would be the Airport Hotel returning her supposed call.

'I found the condom in his pocket,' I said. 'The trousers he was wearing that night.'

The flush rose along Brenda's throat again and blazed onto her cheeks.

'Is he . . .?' She tried to pantomime shock but it didn't quite land.

'I know he was with you,' I said. 'Your perfume. I've only noticed it these past few days, but I've smelt it before. On his clothes nights when he came back from a night out.'

'Everyone wears it,' she said. 'That doesn't—'

'Please don't lie to me,' I said. 'Everyone has been lying to me. I don't know my daughter; I don't know my husband. I thought I knew my friend.'

'You do know me,' Brenda said suddenly, reaching out to take my hands in hers. I stepped back from her, out of her reach.

'Then tell me the truth. If I know he was with you on Friday night, at least I know he didn't have anything to do with Ellie.'

She glanced wildly about her, as if to see who else was in earshot. At that the door opened and Harry appeared.

'The hotel called there about your laptop charger—' he began, then saw me too. 'Hey, Dora,' he said, stepping down gingerly in his socks and coming to where we stood on the driveway. 'Are you not coming in?'

'Not tonight,' I said. 'In case Ellie calls and I'm not in.'

He nodded sympathetically. 'How are you managing?'

I nodded. 'As you'd expect.'

'I was sorry to hear about Eamon,' he said, his gaze dropping to his own feet. 'Whatever way it works out, I was shocked to hear about it.'

'Thank you,' I said, admiring his restraint in not asking for details. 'I mean it, Harry. Thank you.'

In that moment, even in my own anger, I felt desperately sorry for him. Like me, he'd been deceived by his partner and by his friend. I could see from the look of abject terror frozen like rictus on Brenda's face that she was afraid I was going to tell him the truth. But that was not my task to do.

We stood for a moment in silence, Harry looking at the ground, me at Brenda, Brenda at the space to the left of me, then Harry nodded, as if agreeing with an unspoken thought. 'I'll leave you to it, so,' he said. 'Take care, Dora. Call if you need anything.'

He shuffled back into the house, closing the door softly behind him.

'Well?' I asked.

Brenda stared at me a moment. 'Thanks for not saying anything,' she said, smiling sadly.

I waited and did not speak until finally she nodded.

'What does that mean? The nod?'

I needed her to say it. I needed to be clear, to be certain.

'He was with me.'

'*With* you?'

A nod.

'How long?'

'A few hours.'

'No. How long has it been going on?'

She shrugged lightly. 'About a year,' she said. 'Once or twice before that, but a year.'

I felt winded, despite having expected the admission. Eamon had been spying on my daughter, sleeping with my friend and I had suspected nothing. Had I been sleepwalking through my own life? How could I not have known? What did it say about me as a wife, as a mother?

'You need to tell Harry,' I said.

I could see her begin to panic now. 'Dora, please. It'll destroy our family. Things are just getting back on track. Friday was to be our last time. I told him—'

'He deserves to know,' I said. 'You tell him or I will.'

'Think about Amy,' she said, tears spilling. 'It'll break her.'

'She needs to know who her mother is,' I said. 'And you need to tell the police.'

'Why?'

'Because they think Eamon did it. They think he was to blame for Ellie.'

'After what he's done, why would you want to help him? Say nothing.'

I had considered this, thought about little else since I'd heard that Brenda had been in the Airport Hotel.

'Because so long as they think it was him, whoever actually took her from me is getting away with it.'

I turned to leave, then realised that I did not feel as though I had said all that I needed to say, but I could not articulate everything that I felt satisfactorily.

Instead, I walked up to Brenda and slapped her hard, open palmed, across her face. She stared at me in disbelief, the mark of my print white against the flushing on her cheeks while, beyond, Amy watched from her bedroom window.

Chapter Twenty-Four

I could not be sure that Brenda would tell the truth to either Harry or to the police, for to do the latter would inevitably mean having to admit what she had done to her husband. Had the circumstances been in any way different, I would have been content to leave Eamon on his own. But, as I had told Brenda, the longer the police spent looking at Eamon, the less effort they were making in finding Ellie. And so I called Glenn to tell her what I had learned.

'I'm actually on my way to you now,' she said when she answered. I could hear from the level of background noise that she was in the car and so I waited for her arrival, boiling the kettle for tea, habit being so strong.

She arrived with a bag of items which the team had taken from my house that morning and which I had not even missed, among them Ellie's toothbrush.

'For a DNA profile,' Glenn explained as I took the brush out. 'But I knew you'd want it back. We did keep a few things we found, including items of underwear we believe to be Ellie's which we found in Eamon's lorry.'

She handed me pictures of the items: a bra and two pairs of pants.

'Ellie did have ones like those,' I said, handing her back

the images. 'I've not seen them in some time though and I do all the washing in the house.'

'She'd not have been wearing them on Friday, then?'

I shook my head. 'I don't think so. Those were things she was bought years back.'

Glenn grimaced and I knew that she was thinking the same as me: Eamon must have taken the items when Ellie was even younger than she was now.

'You'd something to tell me about Eamon,' Glenn said, taking a seat.

I made tea while I explained what I had learned about Eamon and Brenda and the alibi that their affair had provided.

She listened without interruption and I got a sense that she was waiting to speak. I set the cup in front of her and took the seat opposite.

'I'll get someone to speak to her,' Glenn said. 'We'll need a statement but that's useful.'

'Something's wrong,' I said.

Glenn angled her head a little as she raised her shoulders briefly. 'We've had a lot of responses to the press conference this morning,' she said. 'We've a huge amount of things to follow up, but there have been a few developments that you need to know about.'

I straightened in my chair, my mind racing. I could tell from her tone, and the care with which she seemed to be picking her words, that none of the developments were going to be good.

'We managed to track down how Ellie's bag ended up in the layby on the A5. A youth who was at the rave found it while leaving. One of his friends corroborated his story. The young lad's father brought him in. He claimed they didn't know who it belonged to and the nature of the woodland rave meant there was no lost property or that, so they kept it. They searched through it, took the purse and sixty pounds that was in it and used it to buy a takeaway. They parked up in the layby to eat, then dumped the bag along with their rubbish when they were done. There's no evidence that Ellie was in the car or with the two boys in question. The dad returned her purse and offered to repay the money.'

'I don't care about that. What's going to be done to them?'

'Probably nothing,' Glenn said. 'They were opportunistic, taking money from a bag they found, but it's not something they'll be charged with, I'd imagine. It would only be considered theft if they could have taken reasonable steps to return it to her and didn't: finding it in a woodland would have made that difficult.'

I nodded. The money didn't matter that much – at least I knew Ellie hadn't been taken in a car somewhere. She must still be nearby which meant, to my mind at least, that she could still be found.

'We also got a report of a fire spotted in the woods the night that Ellie went missing. There were several actually. We've been able to discount some of the areas of fire damage as kids lighting a campfire after the rave. But we did find one site that is further out than the rest. We've found scraps of burnt fabric in the fire. I'm afraid they match the description of some of the clothes you said Ellie was wearing.'

It took me a moment to fully understand the significance of what she had told me but even then, I needed to ask her to be sure.

'Someone burned her clothes?'

Glenn nodded. 'I'm sorry, Mrs Condron,' she said. 'It has changed the focus of our investigation though from Missing Persons to a murder investigation.'

The room tilted from me and I knocked over the mug of tea as I reached out to steady myself.

'She's not coming home,' I managed to say, feeling my throat constrict, my lungs seeming to seize.

'I don't think so,' Glenn said. 'I'm so sorry, Dora.'

From the living room, the clock began to chime. Eight o'clock. I saw again Ellie standing at the living room door, saying goodbye. It had been three days since last I saw my daughter. Three days that marked not an aberration from the normal, but the start of a new normal; one in which I was completely on my own.

Three Months

Chapter Twenty-Five

Andrews took a seat on the sofa, Glenn on the armchair. I took my seat opposite, a cigarette balancing on the edge of the ashtray next to my wine glass. I saw Andrews' gaze sliding from one to the other, then to Glenn. Almost defiantly, I took a mouthful from the glass and waited.

'We wanted to update you,' he said. 'As you know, we've been exploring various avenues, but I'm afraid we've just not managed to get the breakthrough we wanted.'

He looked again to Glenn, perhaps in the hope she might corroborate the extent of their efforts, for she nodded, her face a mask of pity.

'At this stage, we have no further lines of inquiry to follow,' he said. 'And, despite the best efforts of the recovery teams, we've sadly not been successful in locating Ellie's remains.'

'Maybe that means she's still alive,' I said.

Andrews shook his head, his gaze not meeting mine. 'We're confident that she's not, I'm afraid.'

'Why?'

He sat back, taking a breath as if to speak, then looking across to Glenn once more. Despite his seniority, he seemed to rely on her when dealing with me. I wondered whether it was because she was a woman, or because her role meant that she'd more experience dealing with the bereaved. I took another drink and waited him out for a response.

'We've traced Ellie's movements through the woods that night,' Glenn said. 'We suspect she was in the company of someone. We suspect something happened and that person contacted a second person to help them dispose of her remains.'

'Dispose,' I said, swallowing a second mouthful. 'She wasn't a bag of rubbish.'

'I understand, Mrs Condron,' she said. 'I don't mean that disrespectfully. We have evidence of communication between the two individuals of interest but not the content of that communication.'

'Can't you seize their phones?'

'We tried. The devices used that night were destroyed. Both parties claim they were stolen, along with a car, which we found, subsequently, burnt out on Old Farm Road. We have no way to prove otherwise and, unless either party decides to confess, or Ellie is found, we've hit a brick wall.'

'So that's it?' I said, guessing the nature of their visit now. I'd seen Glenn with less frequency as the weeks had given way to months and the season had turned from summer, through to late autumn.

'The investigation won't end,' Andrews said. 'But it will be scaled down, I'm afraid. As will the searches for Ellie. Unless we have credible information about the possible location of— her possible location, we'll be standing down our recovery teams. I am sorry.'

'The investigation is still very much an active and open one,' Glenn said. 'It's really just an operational change. But we wanted to let you know.'

'You're not looking for her anymore,' I said. 'Behind all the fancy words, that's what that means, isn't it? You've given up looking.'

'We've not given up,' Glenn said.

'You've stopped looking.'

'We're reallocating resources,' Andrews said. 'Look, Mrs Condron, I understand how you feel—'

'No, you don't,' I said. 'You have no idea how I feel. Neither of you do. Ellie was my life. She was part of me, and I was part of her. And someone took her from me. I don't know where or how. I don't even *know* that she's gone because I have nothing: no grave, no body, nothing to know for sure. I'm lying awake at night, making up all kinds of stories for her, where she is, what she's doing, because I don't know. You said you'd find answers.'

'We said we'd do our best,' Andrews replied. 'And we have, ma'am. We can't force people to talk.'

'Why not?'

Andrews looked again at Glenn.

'What are you looking at her for?' I snapped. 'She doesn't know any more than you do.'

'This isn't a good time,' Andrews said, seeming to nod towards the glass I held. 'I understand how angry you must feel, but please believe me: we've done everything we could.'

'I don't believe that,' I said. 'If you'd done everything you could, you'd know what happened to my girl.'

'Knowing and proving are two very different things, Dora,' Glenn said. 'But if it helps you to find some sort of closure, I can tell you with some degree of certainty that Ellie met her death at the hands of someone in those woods.

By the time you realised she was missing, she was already dead. Whether it was an accident or something else, we don't know. But she died in Rowan Wood. I'm sorry.'

I finished my drink, suspecting that her repeated use of dead and died was to leave me in no doubt.

And I had been in doubt. What I'd told Andrews had been true, but had not fully encapsulated the enormity of the stories I'd created during those sleepless nights. I tried to imagine where she might have gone, if she made it out of the woods. In one such fantasy, she'd decided she needed to escape, to get away from Eamon. She'd taken a change of clothes, or borrowed ones off Nicola Ward, her friend, and walked through the woods into the next county. She'd taken a bus then to London. She was working in a café, living in an apartment, studying nights at the local college. She had a cat – she'd always wanted a cat, but Eamon's allergies (and my aversion to them) had meant we'd not bought one. But she had one now. She was happy.

Other nights, that fantasy had soured. She'd made it to London but was homeless. I saw her sleeping on cardboard in a shop entranceway. I imagined some faceless stranger going into the local corner shop and buying her a can of Coke and a pre-packed sandwich. He'd give her enough to find a shelter. Or, on darker evenings, he'd take advantage of her.

She'd amnesia and been taken in by an old couple one night. They didn't have TV so didn't know who she was. But they had a grandson and they'd introduced her to him. He was kind.

These fantasies swirled together, night after night, playing like shadows across my bedroom ceiling. And with them, images I could not unsee, of Ellie lying naked in a woodland. Or in the river. I imagined her, buried, dirt in her mouth and ears, and felt the irresistible compulsion to spit it out and the frustration at having no agency to do so.

One night, the first frost of the coming winter fell. The house was cold, even with the heating running. I'd seen her then, frozen in the ground, and wanted, more than anything, to take a blanket and find her resting place so that I could warm the earth above her.

These and other thoughts would finally bleed into my dreams and I would doze listlessly until dawn broke and the furniture of the room took shape once more, distinct from the shadows.

Chapter Twenty-Six

Over those twelve weeks since Ellie went missing, I'd found myself almost instinctively aware of when it neared eight p.m. on Friday evenings, as if I was mentally marking off another full week since last I'd seen her. I relived each word, each look, reconsidered what I could have said had I known that this would be the last time we'd speak. I looked for signs, something that would mark it as different, as if on some level we had both known this was our final conversation together and that I'd said something in which Ellie had taken comfort in her final moments.

'All right, love. Have fun.' Perhaps the word 'love' had registered more than all the rest. She would have known, in the familiarity with which I had said it, the depth of love I had for her, how much she meant. Or *had* it been drained of all significance, so frequently had I used it, not just to Ellie, but to her friends, to Eamon, to strangers at times. Why couldn't I have had something that signified to her that she was different?

Even her name, Ellie. I'd always liked it for no reason other than it pleased me to say it, the sound and shape of it. When Ellie was seven she told me she wanted to change it.

I'd collected her from school. It was raining, so Eamon had driven me; we'd just started dating and he'd spent the morning with me because Ellie was at school and we'd time together without her catching us.

'How was school, love?' I asked, glancing over my shoulder at her.

Her lip wobbled as she tried, without success, to hold back the fat tears that were already rolling down her cheeks.

'What's wrong?'

I twisted in my seat, holding out my hand for her to take. She placed her hand lightly in mine, her voice rising with emotion as she spoke.

'They all call me Elephant,' she said.

'What?'

I could see no reason; she was willow thin, even then, delicate and precise in her movements. Nothing about her suggested the nickname.

'We had singing today and the teacher taught us a new song. "Ellie the Elephant".'

'Nellie!' I said, laughing, thinking the misunderstanding rectified would ease her. It did the opposite.

'I know!' she shouted. 'But they all sang Ellie. Even Miss laughed at it. They all laughed at me.' Then the tears began in earnest, smearing her cheeks as she sobbed uncontrollably.

'Let me in beside her,' I said to Eamon.

He'd been laughing to himself at the rhyme. 'Don't pander to her,' he said. 'She needs to be able to take a teasing.'

'I don't need advice on how to parent,' I snapped. 'Now stop so I can get in beside her.' Reluctantly, he pulled over, and I climbed in next to her, cradling her head against my chest.

'They'll soon stop,' I said. 'Don't show them you're annoyed, and they'll stop.'

'I hate my name,' she said, suddenly, her voice half muffled against me. 'I wish you'd never called me the stupid thing.'

'Try being called Dora,' I said. 'Dora the Dormouse, my old dad used to say.'

She blurted out a teary snort. 'That is worse,' she said.

'The names don't matter. It's the person inside that counts,' I said to her, holding her against me all the way home.

Ellie did not mention it again. Eamon, on the other hand, hummed 'Nellie the Elephant' for the rest of the day as he moved around the house and let me know his annoyance at my refusing his advice.

The memory caught me unaware, and I thought I could still feel, even now, the pressure of her head against my side, her breaths keeping time with the rhythm of my heart.

It was half seven. I lifted my coat and walked down to Madge's to pick up some things. I'd stopped buying in a weekly grocery shop, there being little point when there was only me in the house, so I picked up items every day or two. I didn't mind Madge's; she understood the situation and did not pry. I'd been foolish enough to go to the supermarket once and ended up leaving my trolley, half filled, abandoned on the aisle after being stopped and quizzed by well-wishers for the fourth time.

This evening was no different. Madge scanned through my bread, milk, wine, cigarettes with nothing more than a brief comment on the weather. She smiled sympathetically as I searched for my purse. The door chimed behind me and, turning, I felt my innards constrict when Amy walked in. She moved across to the fridge, lifted milk and came and joined the queue behind me.

'How's things, love?' Madge asked, waiting for me to fish for change.

'All right,' Amy said.

'How's Dad?'

'I'm not sure,' she muttered.

I picked out the correct coins and handed them to Madge, then took the bag from her. She'd been looking past me at Amy as I'd looked up, I sensed. Something told me that their shared look was about me.

By the time I'd made it halfway up the street, Amy was already alongside me and looked to bypass me.

'How are you, love?' I asked. That word again. Love.

'Fine,' she said, pacing on.

'Are you not speaking to me?' I asked.

She slowed a little, as if considering whether to stop, then turned to face me. 'Why did you do it?'

'Do what?'

'Mum and Dad. Why did you make her tell him?'

I could see the hurt in her eyes, the pain.

'I'm sorry, love,' I said. 'I thought it was the right thing to do.'

'Why? Why was that your choice to make?'

'What's happened, Amy?'

She seemed to slump a little then. 'Dad's moved out,' she said.

'I'm so sorry,' I repeated. I was aware that eight p.m. was nearing, that I wanted to be inside to mark the moment. 'Come with me, love. Come on.'

Amy walked back towards the house with me, but hung back at the door, as if afraid to enter.

'Will you come in?'

'Mum says I'm not allowed to.'

I shrugged and nodded. She seemed to reconsider, perhaps realising the absurdity of the comment, herself an adult now. She tapped the milk carton against the side of her leg once or twice, then nodded.

Chapter Twenty-Seven

I poured myself a glass of wine from the bottle I'd bought in Madge's. It wasn't chilled, but no matter. It would be enough to take the edge off hearing the clock chime eight once more. I realised the moment had become the twisted equivalent of her birthday in some ways: not a marker of the time passed since her arrival in this world, but instead of her leaving me.

'Do you want one?' I asked, raising the bottle towards Amy who stood in the hallway.

'I'm okay, thanks,' she said.

I nodded, grateful in a way that she'd refused.

'We'll go into the living room,' I said, leading her in, then taking my seat, just where I'd sat the night she'd gone. I glanced at the wall clock. Seven fifty p.m.

'Is it strange?' Amy asked, sitting down. 'The house without her. It must be so strange.'

'I turn to speak to her sometimes,' I said. 'I'll hear something on TV that I know she'd like and I turn to tell her and remember she's not there.'

'I'm like that with Dad,' Amy said, raising her chin a little.

'I didn't mean any harm, Amy,' I said. 'I never meant to hurt you or your daddy. God knows, you were such a good friend to Ellie. Hurting you is the last thing I'd want.'

She accepted the comment with a brief nod.

'Where did your daddy go?'

'He's moved into a flat out at Beech Grove,' she said. 'It's pretty nice, but there's only one bedroom so I can't stay with him.'

'Is he okay?'

'I think he was heartbroken,' she said. 'Maybe more at Eamon than Mum.'

'I understand that,' I said, sipping as I watched the clock.

'I'm sorry I didn't tell you sooner about Ellie going to the party,' she said suddenly, and I wondered if that had really been the cause of her reluctance to speak to me. 'I should have said.'

'It wouldn't have mattered,' I said. 'She was already dead by the time I realised she was gone, the police said.'

She nodded, her hands clasped between her legs, her shoulders hunched. I could tell she wanted to leave. It was 7.55 p.m.

'Did you know she was . . . Did you know she liked girls?'

Amy seemed taken aback by the question and initially seemed too flustered to speak.

'It's okay,' I said. 'I worked it out afterwards. But I felt like I'd let her down by not knowing. I learned more about her, and about Eamon, since I lost her than I ever thought possible.'

'I didn't know for sure. But I heard that she'd told people in art college that she was bi. I thought when she was talking about Nicki that he was a boy. It was only afterwards that someone told me it was Nicki Ward.'

'Do you know her?'

She shook her head. 'I know of her brother. He's a bit of a scumbag, to be honest.'

'I've been told that her father is a drug dealer,' I said.

'I don't know about that, but apparently the brother is.'

'Was Nicki Ward her girlfriend?'

Amy shrugged. 'I don't know. You hear things.'

The clock chimed eight. I turned instinctively towards the door, imagined Ellie standing there, her hand raised in farewell. I wanted to reach out to her, to take her hand and have her lead me wherever she was going. But she did not. I finished my drink, cradled the glass, lingered a moment too long, seeing her once more in my imagination.

'Are you okay?' Amy asked. 'Mrs Condron?'

'Sorry, love,' I said. 'You said you hear things? What things?'

Amy shook her head. 'It's nothing.'

'Please,' I said. 'I know nothing. I hear nothing. The police don't tell me anything. Please.'

She seemed to gather herself to speak. 'I heard that she went to the rave with Nicki because she thought they might hook up. But when Nicki realised what she was looking for, the two of them had a row. I heard Nicki got really upset and Ellie headed off on her own.'

'Who told you this?'

'Just rumours,' she said. 'People talk.'

'Any other rumours?'

She shook her head again. 'Nothing. Just that. I felt sorry for her. If she liked Nicki and wanted to be happy, it's shit that it didn't work out for her before she . . . you know. I don't know what I mean.'

'I try to imagine her happy,' I said. 'I try to picture her somewhere happy. And that makes me feel better, even if to be happy, she needs to be away from me.'

'She was always happy with you, Mrs Condron. She only ever said good things about you. Said you could be a bit mental sometimes, but who can't?' she added and laughed.

The sound, alien to the house for three months, sounded good. Like the first cracking of ice in the early spring. I found myself joining in it, warmed a little by the wine.

'What about Eamon? Did she talk about him?'

'Not so much,' Amy said. 'She thought he was a bit of a creep.'

'Did she know he was spying on her?'

'He what?' Amy said, sitting forward. I realised I probably shouldn't have said it, but I was at ease in her company. The truth was, I felt closer to Ellie with Amy there and I wondered if she had lingered in the doorway as the clock chimed as much to be near her friend as her mother.

'He had set up a camera in her room when she was younger without anyone knowing,' I said, draining my glass.

'Jesus,' Amy said, her expression one of disgust. 'She never mentioned that.'

I thought for a moment, wanting to ask but not sure how it would be received. 'Why did you fall out?' I managed, finally.

'I don't know if we fell out as such. But we definitely drifted.'

'Did something happen?'

She shook her head. 'But I wondered if maybe she found out about Eamon and Mum.'

'Why?'

'It happened around the same time Mum said to Dad that they started sleeping together. She used to come over to ours and one night, when I invited her, she wouldn't come in. She didn't say why. Mum was in the house on her own that night – Dad was away. I wondered after Mum admitted what had happened whether Ellie found out about it. Probably not, but it would explain it. Maybe I'm just looking for excuses. Maybe we just went different ways.'

I nodded. 'Maybe.'

Amy stood then. 'I best get back. She wanted milk for her coffee. I was just glad to get out of the house for ten minutes.'

I got up too, using the armrest of the sofa to help me stand, and followed her out to the hallway.

'Thank you, Amy,' I said. 'For being such a good friend to Ellie. She was lucky that she had you.'

Tears sparkled in her eyes again and, despite myself, I found myself welling up at the sight of it.

She moved towards me and embraced me quickly. Her shape, her form, was so like Ellie's that, for a second, I closed my eyes and imagined it was her. But her scent was different. Just as quickly, we had parted and she was gone.

Chapter Twenty-Eight

I woke early the following morning, as I usually did, and listened to the silence of the house build, punctuated only with a few groans from the water pipes and, eventually, the distant firing up of the central heating boiler and the creaking of the radiators as they began to heat.

Moments like this were always the most difficult. Wakening early, knowing that the day lay wide before me, something to be endured that a few more hours of sleep might have shortened, made more manageable. I had no reason to get up, no purpose. No one to make breakfast for, no one to get out to school. No one.

My head pounded as I moved it, even the touch of the pillow making it seem tender. My mouth was dry and furred and I told myself I'd not have any wine that evening. I wasn't an alcoholic, I was sure of that, but I was aware that my intake had increased over the past three months. With no company in the evenings, no distractions from the thoughts that assailed me and twisted me with anxiety, I'd found a glass or two was enough to take off the edge. Then I'd been finishing bottles each night, always making sure there were two in the fridge so I could start on the second if the night was still early and the voice of the dead still loud. I knew I shouldn't be mixing it with my anxiety medication but felt incapable of facing the evenings without the crutch it provided me.

I thought back over what Glenn and Andrews had said, what Amy had said. The only time in all of this that I'd done something for myself was in finding out the truth of Eamon and Brenda. I'd waited for everyone else to help me, to advise me. And it had reached this point. No one was any closer to finding Ellie. Life had stalled for me while around me it continued, unabated, for everyone else. I knew then that the only way I could hope to find the truth, to find Ellie, would be to take things into my own control.

So, by eight thirty that morning, I was already sitting at the bus stop opposite the art college, waiting for the students to arrive. I knew that the car Ellie had been pictured getting into was a green VW Golf. Therefore, I watched and waited for one to appear. As a result, I almost missed Nicola Ward when she arrived, for she alighted from a red BMW, which stopped at the traffic lights a few hundred yards up from the college. I only recognised her from the self-portrait that she'd taken with Ellie. She was a little taller than me, I guessed, thin, a little androgynous, with the same spiky hair I'd seen in the images, though now dyed a silver colour.

'Miss Ward?' I called, running out into the traffic to try to catch her before she reached the college doors and disappeared inside.

Cars blasted their horns as I weaved my way across the two lanes towards where the girl stood, two other friends having joined her on the way in.

'Excuse me!' I shouted, managing to make it across. I saw

the driver of the BMW stare at me as it passed. He was in his twenties, perhaps, his face raised defiantly.

The three girls looked at me as I approached with a bemused detachment that seemed the preserve of their age.

'Nicola Ward?' I asked as I drew level with them.

She smiled, a little uncertainly, and nodded her head. 'Who are you?'

'I'm Ellie's mummy,' I said. 'Ellie Condron.'

The smile froze on her face while her two friends turned to look at her. 'What are you doing here?'

'I know you were with Ellie the night she disappeared,' I said. 'I want you to tell me what happened that night.'

She became suddenly agitated, looking around her as if to see who might be watching. 'You can't be here,' she said, pushing past her friends and hurrying now towards the front door.

'Please,' I said, following after her. 'I just want to know what happened. You had a fight with her. Is that right?'

She pushed on now, through a group that were waiting just at the entrance, but her folder caught between them, slowing her progress, allowing me to catch up with her. I put my hand on her arm and she reacted as if I'd burned her.

'Don't touch me,' she snapped.

'Please. I need to know the truth. Why did you fight?'

'We didn't . . .' she began, then with some heft, pulled the folder free and moved on inside.

I followed after her, calling to her as she weaved her way through the students drifting in for the morning class. 'Please. I need to know what happened! Where's Ellie?'

She had made it as far as the security desk and I saw her say something to the man who sat there.

'Where's Ellie?' I screamed.

The foyer had gone silent now, the students all turned, looking first to me and then following my gaze to where Nicola Ward stood.

'You know where she is. Please, give me my daughter!'

'I don't know,' she said. 'Leave me alone.'

'Give me my daughter!' I shouted, all sense of self-awareness gone. Why would she not tell me? 'Give me my daughter!'

I saw the security man rise and direct the girl in through a set of doors towards the back of the foyer while he came towards me.

'Give me my daughter!' I screamed as he tried to shield the girl from me, stepping between us, his hands raised. 'Tell me where my daughter is!' I shouted again.

'No wonder she wanted away from you!' Nicola Ward shouted back, her face flushed and slick with tears. 'Bitch!'

The comment winded me almost physically. I stood, my mouth ajar, but no sounds could come out, no words would form.

Then the girl disappeared through the double doors and I was left standing, facing the security guard as, around me, mobile phones were held aloft, recording the whole encounter.

Chapter Twenty-Nine

'Mrs Condron,' the security man said, blocking me from moving any further into the building after the girl. 'Do you remember me?'

'Of course,' I said. 'I'm not stupid.' I glanced at his name badge to remind me: Philip.

'Are you okay, Mrs Condron?'

'I just wanted to ask her where my daughter is.'

He moved to put his hand on my arm and I twisted from him, causing him to raise his hands in a show that he was not imposing himself on me.

'This probably isn't the best way to do it,' he said.

'I just want my daughter,' I stated, staring him full in the face in the hope that he would recognise the simplicity of this fact.

'I know. But you can't really be in here, with the students,' he said. 'It's not the place for it.'

'I don't know where else to go,' I said, and realised in saying it that it was the truth. I had nowhere else to go, nowhere else to look for Ellie. Nicola Ward was my only hope. And she wanted nothing to do with me.

'Come on and sit down,' Philip said, motioning to guide me towards the security desk. 'Come on.'

He led me past the desk, past the staring faces of the students, like spectators at a zoo, and into the control room whose doors were set in the wall behind the security desk.

Inside was an old table with three chairs spotted around it and a fridge humming noisily. The room was stuffy, partly due to its size and partly the bank of security screens set into one wall, offering a variety of views of the college building and those moving freely through it.

'Sit down,' Philip said, 'if you like. I've the kettle not long boiled.'

I took a hard-backed chair opposite the bank of images and stared up at them. Ellie had walked through those same corridors, I thought, and I found myself scanning each screen lest I catch a glimpse of her somewhere among the students.

'How are you doing?' Philip asked, bringing across two mugs of tea and then handing me a carton of milk and a bag of sugar with the teaspoon stuck inside it.

'Fine,' I said, aware at once of the ridiculous nature of the comment. 'I just want to know what happened to Ellie.'

'I'm sure you do,' he said. 'That's totally understandable.'

'The police have stopped searching,' I said. He was the first person I'd told this to, possibly because he was the first to ask how I was.

In the early days of Ellie's disappearance, my phone had buzzed constantly with messages of love and support, notifications from Facebook of people sharing my request for help in finding my girl. But after Eamon's arrest, I noticed a change. It was as if people became less sympathetic, as if they suspected that I was partly to blame for my own misfortunes because of Eamon, because I'd failed to protect my daughter from my husband. Even after the police had issued a statement saying he was being charged with offences not related to Ellie's murder, that distance remained. The searches stopped, the vigils ended, the tone of the notifications changed. Rumour had indicted Eamon, and I was his accomplice.

'I'm sorry to hear that,' Philip said, and it took me a second to remember to what he was replying. 'We're still encouraging the students here to share any information they have.'

'It's not working,' I said, then realised it was unkind. 'But thank you.'

He nodded, spooning two sugars into his cup.

'Look, Mrs Condron, by rights I should contact the police about what happened here, but I don't want to. I need you to promise me that you'll not come in here again after one of the kids. They have a right to be safe, too.'

'Safe? She was with Ellie the night she died. She knows something.'

'I'm sure if she did, she'd have told the police.'

I snorted derisively. 'The police?'

'I'm just saying, Mrs Condron. The police have spoken with a lot of these kids. You can't be coming in now and shouting after them in the corridors.'

'That's not true, what she said about Ellie wanting to get away from me,' I said, more for my own benefit than his. 'Ellie was happy with us. With me.'

'I'm sure she was,' he said, with a brief smile of sympathy that did not quite reach his eyes.

'Why would she say that?'

He shrugged. 'I think maybe she was upset. You know kids; they lash out when they're angry.'

'Ellie didn't,' I said, though even as I'd said it, I knew it was not true.

The day she'd got her hair cropped short, she told me she was going to the hairdressers. She'd showered before coming down for breakfast and, when she finally did, her beautiful hair was tied up in a ponytail.

'I'm thinking of getting my hair cut,' she said.

I'd grunted some form of agreement, assuming she meant a trim.

'Short,' she added.

'*Short* short?'

'Short. Cropped up. Pixie style.'

That had got my attention then. I'd never taken more than an inch or two off her hair from when she was a child. It was only in the past two or three years that she'd even being going to the hairdressers at all; until then I'd cut it for her.

'No. That wouldn't be nice. Your hair's lovely.'

'If you're ten,' she said. 'I'm not a child anymore.'

'You are to me. You wouldn't suit it. Your face is too round.'

'Are you saying I'm fat?' she asked.

I laughed a little, assuming that she was joking, the comment mock-offended. I was wrong.

'Your face is too wrinkled,' she'd retorted. 'No wonder—'

'Mind your tongue, girl,' I snapped, all good humour in the room suddenly gone. 'You'll be going nowhere.'

'You called me fat. How do you like it when someone calls you names?' she said, moving towards me.

'I didn't say you were fat. I said your face is too soft featured for short hair. You suit your hair as it is. That's all.'

'Soft featured? That's just as bad.'

'What's wrong with you? I was trying to be nice.'

'Fuck me if that's you being nice.'

I'd lifted my hand and slapped her before I was even fully aware that I was doing it. It wasn't hard, but it was sharp, and swift, and unexpected for both of us. Apart for the odd slap across the legs when she was being a madam as a child, I'd never hit her. I could not fully explain, even to myself, why I did so now.

'Don't use talk like that in my house.'

'I hate this place,' she said, with a quiet that unnerved me. Tears shone in her eyes, the mark of my hand flushing on her cheek. 'I hate you. No wonder Eamon's away all the time.'

'You're a spiteful bitch,' I said, even as I wanted to apologise for what I'd just done, wanted to take her in my arms and kiss the red welt I'd left on her and be again her mother. 'If you don't like it here, you can move out.'

'I just might,' she said, turning and grabbing her jacket. 'I'll be glad to be away from the fucking pair of you.'

'Good riddance,' I'd shouted as the front door slammed shut. To my shame, I was more concerned about what people might think when they saw the mark on her cheek, what she might say about it, than I was about the fact I had struck my child.

'Had she wanted away from me?' I said, now. I was wounded by the memory, not so much because of what had happened, for I knew all families had their fights, but because, in the weeks after she'd gone, any thought I'd had of her, any recollection, had been so positive. In fact, I realised, I'd not even really remembered anything specific. It had been more the impression of Ellie that I'd missed, the idea of her formed from her best qualities and the sheer ferocity of the love I felt for my child, translated into grief.

I felt like I'd betrayed her, struck her a second time, in remembering such an incident now.

'I'm sure she didn't,' Philip repeated.

Ellie had arrived back around midnight that night, her head shaved. We did not speak of it again. After a few weeks of letting it grow out, she kept it in the pixie cut she'd wanted.

Philip coughed lightly. He'd been glancing at the security console and I realised now he'd been waiting for the halls to clear before bringing me back out into the foyer. My immediate suspicion was that it was to keep me away from the students, but I realised, with a brief flush of gratitude, that it also meant there would be no footage of me being escorted out of the building.

'I'll go,' I said, pre-empting his asking me to do so, and he nodded.

'Thank you,' he said.

'Thank you. You've been very kind. Today and . . . the day she went.'

He lowered his gaze from mine and I sensed the compliment embarrassed him.

A thought shook clear from my fog of memory and confusion and came more sharply into view.

'Did she get rid of her car?'

Philip seemed bewildered by the random nature of the question.

'Nicola Ward. She drove a green VW Golf when Ellie went. You were the one told me the make. She got a lift in a BMW today. Does she not have the green car anymore?'

'I don't think she has a car,' Philip said. 'That Beemer belongs to her brother. I think the green one was his too, but I've not seen it in a bit.'

I thought once more of the police's comment about the burnt-out car.

'What's her brother's name?'

Philip shook his head. 'Mrs Condron. For the students' sake, I have to tell you to stay away from Nicola Ward. But for your sake, stay well clear of her brother.'

'Why?'

'He's not a good fella,' Philip said, seeming to pick his words with some care.

'In what way?' The atmosphere in the room had changed and I felt nausea building, even as my throat tightened.

'He's tied up in all kinds of things,' Philip said.

'Drugs?'

'I'd rather not speculate,' he said. 'But you're not too far off the mark there.'

'I should wash this,' I said, lifting my cup.

'I can do that,' Philip said, and I sensed that he wanted me to leave, that the conversation had taken a turn he'd rather it not have.

'Thank you,' I said. 'I'm sorry about this morning.'

He shook his head. 'Not to worry. But, please, don't be following the kids in here again or I'll have to report it on. Even if I don't want to.'

I walked out into the foyer, which was quiet now, bright and spacious, the light of the weak winter sun beyond seeming to have been intensified by the glass walls and ceilings. I looked across to the display panels of work, but the exhibition had been changed and I could not see Ellie's pictures anywhere.

'Her portrait's gone,' I said, feeling more saddened by it than I could fully understand. 'The picture she drew.'

Philip glanced across to the displays. 'I can ask around and see if some of the tutors still have it, if you'd like it. I can't see why they wouldn't give it to you.'

I thought of the girl in the picture, torn in two, pulling herself apart.

'Thank you,' I said, again.

Chapter Thirty

I took the bus home, walking the last stretch from the shops to my house. Some of the neighbours nodded as they passed, one or two even managed a curt, tight-lipped smile, but none stopped to speak, to ask what news there was since. My head throbbed again, a searing sharpness seemingly driving through my right eye and a reciprocal pain seemed to have settled at the base of my skull.

I was glad to get indoors, away from the brightness of the winter glare. I went back to my bedroom, pulled the curtain, lay under the covers, hoping that the pain would subside. I must have dozed, for when I woke, the shadows in the room had shifted, the light slanting now through the gap in the curtains where they'd not quite met.

It took me a moment to remember what day it was. My eye still ached, and my mouth felt dry and coated. Then I realised that the house phone ringing must have woken me. I half fell from the bed and struggled downstairs. Each movement caused the pain at the back of my skull to sear.

I could not quite place why the house seemed so silent. I'd dreamed, I realised, of Ellie, for when I woke, for a second or two, I'd forgotten that she was gone. The realisation now, that she was not coming home, tore me and I had to grip the bannister for support.

In my dream, she'd been next to me on the sofa. Her hair was long, as it had been before. She was crying. I'd wanted to comfort her, to hug her, but had not been able to reach her. Each time I moved closer, something happened, someone spoke, even though we were alone, just us two, and when I looked to her again, she was as far from me as before. She'd spoken one word: 'Mummy'. I knew she was looking for me, needed me, was calling for me from wherever she now found herself.

The phone began ringing again and this time I made it in time to answer before the caller hung up.

'Hello?'

There was a moment's silence. 'Is that Dora Condron?'

'Yes,' I said. The voice was male, local, muffled.

'Keep the fuck away from the Ward girl.'

'What?'

'You heard. Stay away from her if you know what's good for you.'

'Who is this?' I said. 'Who are you?'

But they had hung up.

I stood a moment, the receiver in my hand, stunned at the nature of the call. Then a scream tore itself free from me, without any effort on my part to contain it any longer.

'Cowards. Bastard!' I shouted down the dead line. 'Bastard.'

I sat afterwards in the kitchen, having a smoke to try to settle my nerves. Nervous energy coursed through me, leaving me jittery. How had they got my number? And my name? Dora. Not Pandora, the ridiculous name my parents had saddled me with. Dora. As if they knew me or had spoken with someone who did.

For a moment, I wondered whether Philip, the security guard in the art college, might have been behind it, but I found that hard to reconcile with the man who had twice now shown me such kindness.

The smoke was leaving me lightheaded but doing little for the lightning flashes of adrenaline surging through me in waves. I opened the half-empty bottle in the fridge and poured a glass. The first mouthful was enough to relax me a little, enough to let me think more clearly.

He'd warned me, Philip, about the brother. That he was bad news. Was that her brother who'd phoned? The voice had gravel to it, heft, which did not seem like that of a youth.

I got up and double-checked that the front door was locked and chained, then double-checked the windows in the house, now that I was able to consider what had just happened.

I thought about phoning Glenn to report it, but to do so would only involve my having to admit to going to the art college. I suspected the police would not look kindly on that. Besides, all they'd do is try to trace the call. I realised that I had not done so myself and went in and dialled for the last caller's number, but it was withheld, perhaps unsurprisingly.

I went in and finished off my drink, then poured a second to empty the bottle. I'd hit a raw nerve, I decided. Something had annoyed someone when I went to see Nicola Ward, badly enough that they'd phoned to threaten me. And what could they do to me, anyway? Kill me? So what? I had nothing: nothing to live for and nothing to lose.

I smiled, grimly, as I realised the mistake that they'd made. They'd shown me that I'd been on the right track. Nicola Ward did have something to hide. And it went beyond her, to whoever had made the call. Her father, maybe? Leo, was that what McBride the journalist had said he was called?

Either way, they had shown me that I was on the right track. And, with their threats, they had helped me see clearly for the first time that I no longer feared them, for the only thing to fear was death and, in death, I would see Ellie again. My dream, I knew now, was simply to show me that what kept me from her was this world. Leaving it would only bring me closer to her.

I went upstairs to the chest of drawers next to my bed and took out the picture of Ellie taken outside the art college the night she went missing. The green car that had pulled up next to her was visible, its registration number clear. I wondered whether it might have been the car found burnt out on Old Farm Road; the car in which had been the person the police suspected of taking Ellie from me.

There was, I knew, one possible way to find out.

Chapter Thirty-One

I called Ann McBride, the reporter from the *Herald*, the following morning. She was out interviewing someone but promised to call later. It was nearer lunch by the time she did. I made her coffee as she took off her coat and set down her phone on the table top, already recording.

'How are you managing since?' she asked.

I handed her the cup, then sat opposite her and gathered myself. I'd lain awake from after five, wondering what best to say, how much I could reveal. I'd decided to err on the side of caution for now, simply because that was what I'd always been taught. Least said, soonest mended had been one of my own mother's favourite phrases; something reflected in her own quiet nature and was, perhaps, why she'd let my father treat her the way he had. More than once, when I'd seen the purpling of a bruise beneath the concealer she'd applied to her cheek, her jaw, her eye, I'd sworn that I'd never marry a man like him, that I'd not repeat my mother's mistakes. But, while Eamon had never hit me, I was beginning to see how much he'd controlled me, told me what to do, what to wear. I'd have been able to cope with it, had accepted it as normal, as what his love looked like. But what he'd done to Ellie was something I could never forgive.

'The police have stopped searching,' I said.

McBride nodded as she blew across the surface of her coffee before taking a sip. 'I heard.'

'What did they tell you?'

She shrugged and put down her mug. I suspected the coffee wasn't right; having rarely drunk it myself, I could never gauge how strong or weak it should be. 'Probably less than they told you.'

'I think they know who was with her when she . . . when she went,' I said. 'But they can't prove it.'

'I got that from the subtext of their statement,' McBride said. 'In the absence of a confession or the discovery of Ellie's remains, I think they feel they've hit a brick wall.'

'Do you know who the suspect is?'

McBride's eyes glinted. 'Do you?'

'I know who she went to the rave with.'

'Leo Ward's girl. You told me that the last time we spoke.'

'I went to see her yesterday.'

'The Ward girl? What did she say?'

'Nothing,' I said. She didn't need to know the comment about Ellie wanting to get away from me, I reasoned. It would only muddy the waters.

'I'm not surprised. Her father would be a "No comment" type of guy. I'm surprised he let you see her.'

'I went down to the art college and caught her on her way in.'

McBride sat back in her seat. 'You doorstepped Leo Ward's daughter?'

I nodded. 'I didn't know Leo Ward. The girl was with Ellie when she went missing. She must know something about what happened that night.'

'*Didn't* know?'

I took a moment, wondering as to the wisdom of telling her. But I realised that I'd wanted to tell someone, needed to tell someone, if only to know that it really happened, that I'd not imagined it.

'I got a phone call after I came back here, warning me to stay away from her.'

'You're kidding!' McBride said, even as she leaned a little towards me, interested now. I could tell her expression of surprise was anything but. If she knew Leo Ward to be the type of man she said he was, threatening phone calls would hardly have been out of character.

'And how did that make you feel?'

'Scared at first,' I said. 'It was a violation of my home.'

I knew what to say, what was expected. It was what McBride would want me to say.

'But then it made me realise that I must have hit a raw nerve. If they have nothing to hide, they'd not be warning me off.'

She nodded now, though not with the same certainty I had felt the previous evening. Saying it now, forming the thought into words, I was not even wholly convinced myself that I was right. Perhaps he was just a father protecting his daughter from a stranger shouting at her in front of her school.

'So, I contacted you.'

McBride sat back again, lifting her cup and raising it to her lips, almost from instinct, then stopped before tasting it and put it back down.

'I'm really sorry this happened to you, Mrs Condron,' she said. 'But I don't know how much of it I'll be able to use. I can't accuse someone of making threatening phone calls. And I'd be hauled over the coals if I published Nicola Ward's name in connection with the case, or even implied she was involved in what happened to Ellie. You need proof.'

I nodded and handed her the CCTV screenshot of Ellie standing at the green VW Golf. 'That's the last image of Ellie, getting into that car.'

'I'm not underestimating your grief—' she began.

'No. That car. I think it belongs to Nicola Ward's brother. He's changed it now and got a red BMW. I saw him in it yesterday.'

McBride reached for her phone and I could tell I was losing her.

'Please. The police told me that the main suspect they have claimed his car was stolen and burnt out up on Old Farm Road the night Ellie went. Twenty-third of July. I need to know if it's the same car.'

'And you thought I would know if it was.'

'I thought you might have reported on it. Taken pictures, maybe.'

McBride shook her head. 'We did report it, now that you mention it to me, but I think it was in a bigger story about a spate of joyriding. And I didn't take any pictures. I wasn't even up at the site.'

'Would you know someone who was?'

She shook her head, but I could tell she was thinking. The information was clearly something the police hadn't shared with her, something she could follow up.

'No,' she said. 'But I might know someone who could help identify the car.' She reached out and I passed her the picture. She lifted her phone and, turning off the recording, made a call.

I could hear the tinny ringing on the line, heard the soft timbre of a male voice answer.

'Hi Joe . . . Good. How are you? I need a quick favour, if you can. I'm looking for the owner of car.'

The soft rumble of a reply and then a pause. He must have asked for the number for McBride read it out to him, then thanked him. She waited for a moment.

'Do you want another coffee?' I asked.

She shook her head, reinforcing the refusal with a raised hand.

'No problem,' she said suddenly. I could hear the man speaking but it was indistinct. McBride lifted her pen and jotted down something on the back of the picture. The gesture annoyed me, even if she was helping me; the lack of value she'd placed on that final image of my girl, using it as no more than scrap notepaper. She must have realised my annoyance for she glanced at me, then mouthed an apology.

'That's great. And does he still own it? Really? On what date?'

Again she jotted down something on the page, wincing as she did so but perhaps feeling that the damage was already done.

'I owe you, Joe,' she said, laughing lightly. 'I know. More than one.'

She put the phone down and looked first at the details on the page and then to me. 'The car was registered to Adam Ward,' she said. 'That's Leo Ward's son, Nicola's brother.'

I nodded, feeling a brief flicker of something. Vindication, perhaps. 'That proves it.'

'It proves that he picked her up,' McBride cautioned. 'But the police would have known that already. What's more interesting is that he reported the car as "written off" on 25 July, which means he made an insurance claim against the vehicle being destroyed.'

The brief feeling of vindication soured in my stomach and hardened into anger.

'He killed my Ellie,' I said and surprised myself with tears. I felt as if a weight had simultaneously been lifted and laid on me, a momentary feeling of relief at knowing a little more about what had happened to my girl and horror at the fact that nothing could be done with such knowledge.

Chapter Thirty-Two

I needed to get out of the house so I went for a walk around the block. Our estate was on the outskirts of town, not far from the river. The area between the two was now a football pitch, around the edges of which ran a dirt track. I picked my way through the traffic running along the road separating the estate from the pitches and began a first lap of the route. It had been a while since I'd exercised, and I found myself out of breath quicker than I'd expected.

The earlier headache was blooming again behind my eyes and I suspected that either the painkillers or the wine had worn off, allowing the sharpness to bite through. I sat on a park bench, set just behind the goal posts at one end and closed my eyes for a moment.

'It's her,' I heard someone say and, looking round, spotted a couple coming towards me, their terrier snuffling in the undergrowth that lay behind where I sat.

'You sure?' the man asked, his lips barely moving.

'I can hear you, you know!' I said, glaring at them and gaining, in return, a pretence of confusion. 'I'm sitting right here. I can hear you.'

They hurried their pace, the man tugging on the lead to call his dog, which had stopped behind my seat to go to the toilet. It got dragged away, half finished.

'You need to clean up after your animal!' I shouted, standing now and pointing to the pile of dirt.

The woman of the couple turned her head towards me, even as her husband shepherded her onwards.

'Do you want a picture?'

They moved off and I turned to sit, only then noticing another couple who'd been walking not far behind them, who now stood, watching me, as if wondering whether it were safe to pass.

'I can hear them,' I explained, then retook my seat as they, too, hurried past, barely glancing in my direction.

I sat a moment longer, as if in defiance of them all, their gossip and rumour, their judgement. Then I gathered myself and set off back up to the house, the climb up the roadway leaving me breathless by the time I made it home.

If I saw the vehicle parked there, it did not register with me. The first I knew something was wrong was when I went to put my key in the door and found it already unlocked. I was sure I'd locked it before I left; at least, I was fairly sure.

I stepped into the hallway, feeling as if something in the house had shifted. The living room and kitchen were empty but I could hear someone moving around upstairs.

'Who's that?' I shouted, taking out my mobile and dialling 999. I stood with my finger poised on the call button, then shouted again. 'Who's that?'

Eamon's head came into view as he looked down over the edge of the upper bannister. 'It's me.'

'Why are you here?' I managed, after the momentary shock of seeing him passed.

'I'd my hearing today. I'm out on bail until the trial.'

'But why are you here?'

'This is my home.'

'Not anymore,' I said.

He muttered something, then came down the stairs towards me. I did not press the call button, but left the phone screen on in case I needed to.

'Look, Dora. We should talk.'

'There's nothing to say.'

'We've not spoken since Ellie went.'

'Don't use her name. I don't want to hear it.'

'Ellie?'

'Don't! I don't allow you to say her name.'

He glanced at me askance, then moved into the living room. 'Come in and sit down,' he said. 'We need to straighten this out.'

I followed him in but refused to sit, standing instead in front of the hearth. 'I'm listening,' I said.

He looked up at me from where he sat on the sofa, then straightened himself a little and took a breath. 'I know you're hurt, about Brenda and that.'

'Brenda?'

He nodded. 'It just happened. We didn't plan nothing. It just happened one night.'

'I don't give a shit about Brenda,' I said.

'Then what?'

'You were filming my daughter,' I said, incredulous that it even needed to be stated.

'That?' he said, dismissively. 'The police blew that out of proportion.'

'I saw some of the images,' I said. 'They were from years ago. She was just a child.'

'I didn't know the laptop was recording,' he said. 'You know how hard those things are to use. It must have been recording without anyone knowing. I'd not be spying on my own stepdaughter.'

'My slutty stepdaughter,' I said. 'Wasn't that one of the porn videos you were watching?'

'Everyone watches it, Dora,' he said, standing now, trying to reset the balance in the room. 'It's harmless.'

'It's not harmless. Someone's daughter was in that. Someone just like my daughter.'

'Our daughter.'

'She was never yours,' I snapped. 'She was mine. And you spied on her. Were you thinking about her when you were watching that filth?'

'I wasn't thinking about you for sure,' he said, his mood darkening. 'What did you think I'd be doing? Our sex life died years ago. Is it any wonder I had to use porn? Do you think I wanted to?'

'And Brenda?'

'At least she's not afraid to be herself.'

'What does that mean?'

'Dora the Dormouse. Creeping around, afraid of her nerves,' he said, his hands gathered under his chin, mincing and mimicking a pretence of a small animal.

'Don't call me that,' I said. 'I'm sick of you calling me that.'

He'd continued doing it after I'd first told them about the nickname on the day Ellie had been taunted about Ellie the Elephant. I remembered clearly one particular summer when we went to Alton Towers for a holiday. Ellie had been of an age when she'd wanted to go on the rollercoasters and begged one of us to go with her. I wouldn't, afraid of being trapped, afraid of falling, afraid. Eamon had offered to take her instead.

'Your mam's nervous,' he'd told Ellie. 'Like a wee dormouse. Dora the Dormouse!'

Ellie had roared with laughter at the name and Eamon, pleased at the response, had repeated the name again. I'd joined in the laughter, despite feeling just a little hurt, so glad was I to see Ellie and Eamon getting on so well. I'd watched as they stood in line for the third time to go on a ride and Ellie had briefly hugged into him with excitement. The name was worth it to see her happy.

'If you'd even tried to make me happy, none of this would have happened,' he said now.

'None of it? Ellie going too?'

'Who knows? Maybe she'd have been happier here too.'

'She was happy,' I said.

'Aye, she was,' he scoffed. 'Her dropping out of school to get to art college quicker. Looking to grow up and you holding her back.'

'That's not true,' I said, cursing myself as I felt tears of frustration welling. 'She was happy here. Until you showed up. You videoed her.'

'Change the record,' he said. 'I told you it was an accident.'

'I don't believe you.'

He lunged towards me then and, despite myself, I winced.

'There she is. Dora the Dormouse. I'm not going to hit you, you basket case.'

'You're not staying here.'

'It's my fucking house. You don't like it, pack your stuff and get out.'

'It's both ours,' I said.

'Do you pay the mortgage all of a sudden?'

'I'll manage. I want you to leave.'

'Make me,' he said, his arms folded across his chest. He squared his shoulders, drawing himself to his full height.

'You're out on bail,' I said. 'I'll tell the cops you were going to hit me.'

'I'll actually fucking hit you if you threaten me,' he said, losing his temper and lunging at me again, grabbing me this time by the material of my jumper. The thin gold necklace I wore under my top was gathered in his grip too and I could feel the links digging into the back of my neck.

At one time, I would have been terrified. Before Ellie.

'Go on,' I said. 'Do it then. And I'll be on the phone to them straight away.'

He stared at me and I could feel the thin metal cutting into my skin, but I was determined not to show him I was hurting. Finally, he released his grip and shoved me backward, causing me to stumble a little at the edge of the hearth.

'You're a bitch,' he said. 'A pair of bitches, the two of you.'

'You can take your things and get out,' I said.

'I'll burn this place down, if you speak to me like that again,' he said, but he turned and went upstairs to gather his things.

'Do that,' I said. 'I'll gladly sit in it while it burns.'

Chapter Thirty-Three

Whether it was the exhilaration of standing my ground with Eamon or the sheer sense of relief I felt after he had left, I couldn't tell, but as I sat that evening, it seemed clearer to me than ever that I needed to confront Adam Ward face to face. I knew there was no point in trying to speak to him; he would not stop at the college for any longer than it took to drop off his sister. Besides, I suspected that both of them would be well warned to avoid me. I confess now, it did not strike me then as odd that I was confronting two youths. To my mind, one of them had taken my Ellie from me, the other knew about it and had done nothing to protect her. I needed to get his attention, I reasoned. I needed him to stop.

I could barely sleep that night. My mind raced, thoughts of Eamon, of my own father, of Adam Ward, someone whom I had only glimpsed once and yet who merged with the other men in my life who had taken things from me. I thought of him, sitting back in his chair, confident in the safety of his car, sure of himself. Getting away with murder. And I had no doubt that he was a murderer. I had looked into his face. I had seen the final face Ellie saw. I had stood so near to him. How had he looked at me? How had he faced me?

I ran through various scenarios in which I stopped him and confronted him. I could bring a knife in my bag, force him out of the car, force him to confess. But I knew that I would not; that was not me, no matter how satisfying the fantasy seemed in those early hours. But I needed to do something, to let him know that I knew. To let everyone know who he was and what he had done to my child.

I was in town early that morning, waiting at the paint shop not far from the art college. I'd everything bought and ready long before the college was due to open.

I walked down and took my seat once more at the bus stop opposite the art college, the can of red paint I'd bought opened and sitting on the ground next to me in a plastic bag to conceal it from view. I was waiting for the red BMW this time, knew whence it would come and at what time and so I spotted it in a queue of traffic while it was still some distance from the college.

I steeled myself, then stood and, lifting the pot, prepared to step out onto the roadway. I could see some of the students near the door of the college looking across, spotted a few raising their mobile phones. Perhaps they had recognised me from the previous morning: perhaps they thought it was some form of installation art. Either way, they were recording, just as I had hoped they would.

I saw Ward pulling in along the side of the road, a hundred yards or so, then pull out again, even as his sister, looking across the road over the roof of the car, spotted me stepping out onto the roadway. She rushed forward, thudding on the roof of the car, hoping to stop her brother, but in his haste, he pulled into a gap in traffic just as I stepped out in his path. He had only time to stop and register who I was when I emptied the paint pot over the windscreen and car bonnet.

The windscreen wipers came on automatically, smearing the red paint across the glass, flicking think globules of it onto the road on either side of it, spattering Nicola Ward who had run out alongside her brother's car to stop him. In a moment, Adam Ward was out of the car and running towards me, his face flushed with anger.

'What the fuck are you doing?' he screamed. 'You mad bitch!'

More cameras were appearing with each second, focused on this performance in the middle of the street.

'Murderer!' I shouted at him. 'You've my girl's blood on your hands. Murderer.'

'What the fuck are you—' he seethed as he grabbed at me, pulling me towards him.

'You're being watched,' I said, motioning towards those standing on either side of the roadway, filming us. 'This is Adam Ward,' I shouted. 'He's a drug dealer. He killed my daughter. Ellie Condron. My daughter is Ellie Condron. This is her killer.'

I could see him blanch as I spoke, could tell that I had been right. He had killed Ellie. He'd believed he could get away with it. He was wrong. Now he knew how it felt, to have no power. Now they all knew.

'I didn't . . . I didn't kill anyone,' he said, releasing me and directing his words to the spectators. 'She's mad.'

I glanced across at his sister who stood watching, open mouthed, tears shimmering in her eyes, her hands held out to her sides as she looked at the red paint, like blood spatters on her clothes.

'And you knew,' I said. 'Ellie trusted you and you let her down.'

'Leave us alone,' she screamed, the tears spilling now. 'You don't know anything. Leave us alone.'

Adam Ward had backed away now and was climbing into his car, his phone already wedged between his shoulder and his jaw.

'His name is Adam Ward,' I shouted again for the benefit of the cameras. 'He is a killer and a drug dealer. He murdered my daughter, Ellie, in Rowan Wood. The police know but can't prove it.'

Nicola Ward was in the car beside her brother now as he tried to negotiate his way past me. I placed my hand into the pool of paint on his bonnet and pressed it onto the windscreen, a bloody handprint above his face, that he could not ignore.

Then he was past me, weaving in and out of traffic to escape me. I lifted the pot and walked calmly back towards the bus, even as the sirens began to build in the distance.

Across the road, at the door of the college, I could see Philip standing watching me, his expression one of shock and sadness in conflict. I raised my hand in salute to him, then took my seat at the bus stop and waited for someone to arrive.

Chapter Thirty-Four

When the police came, one officer took me across to their car while another had a word with some of those standing around. I watched as several of them shared their footage of the incident with him on their phones. Every so often, while watching it, he would glance across at me, his expression unreadable.

Meanwhile, the first officer, a young woman with striking blue eyes, stood at the open door of the car where I sat, her hand resting on the radio attached to the upper chest piece of her uniform. I could hear the conversation unfolding as the person at the other end first agreed to check my background and then promptly buzzed back with a burst of static to tell her who I was. Her expression was clearer than her partner's – that furrowing of sympathy and dread that had become commonplace on the faces of those dealing with me.

I felt like I was a burden; an added responsibility for those whose working lives intersected with me. I sensed that people hated to see me, that I reminded them of the worst elements of our humanity, made them face things they did not want to face, force themselves into a show of sympathy when, in fact, many of them may have felt I was the cause of so many of my own problems: the woman who did not know her daughter, her husband, her friend. As if I'd been sleeping while the world turned. So this, this day, was a marker that I had taken back control of my own life. I had no regrets and I told the officer that, even as she first led me across to the car.

'I'm sorry about your daughter,' she said, when she'd finished her radio conversation.

No, you're not, I thought.

'Thanks,' I said.

She nodded. 'Give me a minute,' she said, then, closing the door softly, as if afraid to disturb me, she moved back across to where her colleague stood. I could see them talking, could imagine the tone of the conversation as they looked to where I sat. Perhaps they felt I needed to be handled carefully, or shown some clemency, being Ellie's mother. Perhaps they thought I would want clemency. The truth was, they were wrong.

Finally, the young officer with the bright eyes came over and, opening the door, squatted down so she was speaking at my level, as one might with a child.

'We're going to take you down to the station,' she said. 'Obviously, what you did here this morning broke all kinds of laws, not least criminal damage. But the person whose car you attacked has yet to make a complaint and has left the scene of the incident, so we'll need to speak with them. You also made some pretty strong accusations, publicly.'

'I called him a murderer,' I said. 'He is.'

'We don't know that, ma'am.'

'You do. You just can't prove it. I don't need to prove it.'

'You attacked a young man, ma'am.'

'Paint on his car seems less serious than blood on his hands.'

She sighed then, her hands resting on her knees as she puffed a strand of hair from her face and looked over her shoulder towards her partner.

'I'd like to speak to Constable Glenn,' I said. 'She was the Family Liaison for my daughter's case. She'll know the background.'

The girl nodded, as if grateful for the escape route my request provided for her.

When they had booked me in at the sergeant's desk, they took me to the interview room where Glenn had last met me. This time a uniformed officer stood, waiting for Glenn to arrive. When she did, she nodded to him and he left.

'Mrs Condron,' she said. 'You've had your rights explained to you.'

'Have I been arrested?'

'Was that not explained?'

I shrugged. 'Have I been charged?'

'Not yet,' Glenn said. 'We have to speak with the victim, too.'

I scoffed. 'The victim? You don't think there's something wrong when the only person who might be charged with what happened to Ellie is her own mother.'

'Your husband has been charged with a number of offences, too,' Glenn snapped. 'So there's that. Besides, this isn't about Ellie.'

'Of course it's about Ellie,' I said. 'It's all about Ellie.'

'You threw paint over someone's car.'

'It was him, though. Wasn't it? Adam Ward?'

'It was him what?' Glenn said, her gaze not meeting mine.

'He was the one who was with her when she went. He was the one who contacted someone for help, whose car was burnt out.'

'I'm not sure what you mean,' she said, and I began to suspect that she and Andrews had told me more than they should have the day they called off the search.

'He had a green VW Golf on the evening Ellie went,' I said. 'He declared it written off several days later. Around the time that a car was found burned on Old Farm Road. A car that may have been used in whatever happened to Ellie.'

'How do you know that – about the car being written off?'

I held her stare now and did not answer.

'So the attack was what? Revenge?'

'I threw paint on his car. Do you think that's an equivalence for what he did to Ellie?'

'We don't know that he did anything to Ellie,' Glenn said.

'You let her down, you and Detective Andrews. She was counting on you to find her and you didn't. She was counting on you to catch whoever hurt her and you didn't.'

'We did our best, Mrs Condron,' Glenn said, suddenly. 'I'm sorry we haven't been able to bring charges against anyone directly in connection to Ellie's disappearance, but we are working at it. And stunts like this one this morning don't help. Nor does going off investigating people yourself on some half-baked rumour or misunderstanding. Now, we have every sympathy for you and your situation, but you attacked a young man in the street after harassing a teenage girl two days ago—'

'I don't want your sympathy!' I shouted, unable to control myself. 'All I have is sympathy. People looking at me, tiptoeing around me like I'm a wounded dog. I don't want sympathy; I want answers. I want my daughter back. I can't even bury her. I have nowhere to go to think of her, to visit her. She vanished off the face of the Earth and no one can tell me why. There's nothing. I have nothing. I am nothing now.'

'I understand—'

'Everyone understands!' I said. 'But no one does. You don't know. If you did, you'd have found her by now.'

'This won't bring her back,' Glenn said, softly.

'And parading me in front of the press after you arrested my husband, did that bring her back? Hoping I'd cry so people would feel bad for me and might help, did that work? No one cares.'

'We got a massive response to that appeal.'

'Then where is she?'

Glenn raised her shoulders but did not reply.

'Exactly. Now people know. They know who killed her. His face is on every camera that was pointed at me this morning. Her face too. Everyone knows who they are now.'

'Nicola Ward had nothing to do with Ellie.'

'She let her down,' I snapped. 'Ellie trusted her and she failed her. She didn't protect her.'

Glenn pursed her lips but did not speak. But I could sense what she was thinking. I'd failed her too. I had brought Eamon into our house, into our lives. I had exposed her to him.

'Nor did I,' I admitted. 'Before you say anything.'

'I wasn't going to say that. I was going to ask, what if you're wrong? What if neither of them had anything to do with Ellie?'

'Then I've let her down again,' I said.

Chapter Thirty-Five

I was allowed home later that afternoon, after accepting a caution for my behaviour that morning. Adam Ward and his father had been contacted and had declined to press further charges, in light of what had happened to Ellie and her friendship with Nicola Ward.

'It's because they *know*,' I said. 'They'd have to prove that what I said wasn't true.'

'They wouldn't,' Glenn said. 'But perhaps Mr Ward realises how bad it would look to press charges against a grieving parent. You've had a lucky escape, but it won't happen twice. You need to stay away from the art college, stay away from the Ward children. And their father,' she added, perhaps reading more in my expression than I'd hoped. 'If we get reports of you harassing them again, you will face charges.'

'Does this make you feel good?' I asked, aware of the unfairness of the question, even as I asked it.

'Nothing about any of this makes me feel good, Mrs Condron,' she said. 'But we're working on a reduced team, still looking for Ellie, and I've wasted a good part of a day when I could be doing that dealing with this instead. I'm happy to keep you updated with what we're doing, and any breakthroughs we have, you'll be the first to know, but the more you waste our time dealing with stunts like this morning's, the longer it will take us to bring Ellie home to you and to bring whomever harmed her to face the courts.'

I considered what she had said all the way home. But I felt no regret at what I had done. After weeks of feeling only numb, facing Ward, seeing his panic, had sparked briefly to life something in me, some sense of exhilaration that had simply highlighted the emptiness to which I had become accustomed.

Yet the emptiness surged back as I stepped into the hallway of the house. The stillness hanging, like dust motes suspended in the stream of winter sun shining through the landing window, the silence so imposing, the loneliness almost a physical form so palpable was it, a constant companion for the past months. But then, it was always with me, even when others were there. It had sat next to me in the interview room as Glenn had questioned me, it had shared my seat on the bus, and now it stood beside me in the silence of the hallway and I felt as if all the colour of the house drained in its presence, as if it swallowed all around it, leaving everything hollow and insubstantial. Yet I was also afraid that one day I might wake up and it would be gone. For what would I do then? What would be the point of continuing, for it filled the absence torn by Ellie's loss.

I went to the chip shop that evening; the fridge was empty and, for the first time in weeks, I'd felt hungry enough to eat more than cereal or toast. It was relatively quiet, perhaps because it was mid-week. The two customers who were there both looked up when I entered. One, whom

I did not recognise, turned his attention straight back to his phone. The other, a woman who lived a few streets down, offered a tight smile of pity, then dropped her head. Likewise, the girl who served me who, when she handed me my change, took my hand in both of hers. 'I threw in an extra fish,' she said. 'We're all thinking of you and poor Ellie.'

I nodded and managed a thank you, took my food and was grateful to get back out to the fresh air, escaping the suffocation of sympathy.

So keen was I to get back into the safety of the house, to the company of my loneliness, that I did not spot the car parked across the street, nor did I pay much heed to the sound of the car doors opening and shutting behind me. I'd just pushed the door open when I felt the hands grip my neck and upper arm, shoving me into the hallway and causing the fish supper to spill onto the floor.

I fell awkwardly, twisting as I did to try to escape the grip that held me. Two figures stood in the gloom of the hallway above me, both dressed in dark clothes, one in a balaclava, one with his hood pulled up and a scarf wrapped around the lower half of his face.

'You stupid bitch,' the man who had grabbed me said, his mouth a tight, cruel line visible through the gap in his face covering. 'You were warned.'

He leaned down towards me and grabbed my hair in his gloved hand. I thought at first he was going to pull me up to my feet but instead he held my head off the ground a little then struck me full on the face with his other fist. Light bloomed in explosions of white and red with the impact and I felt the back of my skull smack off the hall floor. Something had cracked and I felt the warmth of blood from my nose, and a second later the taste in my mouth, like old pennies.

I felt myself lifted up once more and another punch. I tried to raise my arms, to protect myself, to dislodge his grip on my hair, then felt a searing pain and something solid struck my elbow. I glanced across to see the other man had a bat in his hand and was trying to angle to strike me again, the hall's narrowness saving me from further violence for he could not get the swing he wanted.

'Move,' I heard him say, felt the release of pressure as the first got up off me. I curled myself into a ball, my hands over my head, as the blows and kicks began, Ellie's name my prayer, my mantra, as if hoping she might intervene from wherever she was.

One blow hit my hand and I felt an electric pulse shooting along the bone to my elbow. Then my attacker relented and the first man squatted down next to me, his face so close to mine I could smell the cigarette smoke from his breath.

'You're lucky you're not joining that bitch of a daughter of yours.'

I stared at him, my eyes tacky with blood, my field of vision tinted green and blue for some reason. I could still feel each blow, could feel the blazing agony of my arms, my legs, my hand, my head.

The man pushed himself up to his feet and delivered one final kick to my stomach, which caused me to vomit, almost instantly, onto the carpet and his shoe where he stood.

'Dirty bitch,' he said, then wiped his foot on me.

I heard the sound of the two of them leaving and, a few seconds later, the slamming of doors, the car's ignition, the sound of their engine receding as they drove off.

The hall light above me seemed to be spinning out of all control, the floor sliding from beneath me. I vomited a second time but had little to bring up. The retching, however, was so severe, it seemed to drain me of all that I had, and I longed to sleep. I closed my eyes for a moment.

The touch of a hand on my shoulder made me jerk awake and, for a second, I thought they had returned. A face floated near mine and I tried to move away from it, in case it was my attacker, but my arm had not the strength in it to help me push myself back and it shot electric currents of pain to my shoulder each time I tried to move.

'Mrs Condron,' a voice I ought to recognise said. 'It's me.'

The face took form, soft featured with long brown hair. 'Ellie?' I said and smiled, feeling the corners of my mouth tear with the movement. 'I knew you'd come for me.'

One of my teeth felt loose and I prodded at it with my tongue, could feel it give beneath the pressure, could taste afresh the blood in my mouth.

'No, Mrs Condron. It's me, Amy,' she said and her features sharpened into a more recognisable form.

'Amy, love,' I said, trying to raise myself up on my elbows and being rewarded only with more pain.

'What happened?' Amy asked. I felt her hand touch the back of my head, felt her raise me up a little, then lower me again onto a pillow of some sort. 'I've called the ambulance.'

'I'm okay,' I said. The room was still shifting and Amy's face seemed to slope and shift as I looked at her. I closed my eyes, but could still feel the motion, so opened them once more, chose a spot on the ceiling and stared at it, while everything on the edges of my field of vision continued to spin.

'I saw your door standing open,' Amy said. 'I was coming back from the shop and saw it. I thought something had happened to you.'

I felt her hand take mine and I tried to give hers a squeeze, but was unable to. Instead, I laid my other hand on top of hers, hoped she could at least sense the pressure I had intended to show my thanks.

'You're a good girl, Ellie,' I said, then closed my eyes again and welcomed the darkness.

I don't know whether it was the action of the adrenaline, or relief at it being over, but as I lay there, I began to giggle, albeit only briefly, for it hurt to do so. I was in agony, my limbs felt on fire, my head spinning, my centre aching. But I could feel everything, every individual pain. And for the first time in weeks, that was enough to distract me from the emptiness, the numbness that I had lived with for too long.

I could feel. The shock of the sensation surprised me.

Chapter Thirty-Six

Despite my protests, Amy called her mother and they both drove behind the ambulance as I was taken to hospital, having locked up the house for me.

The paramedic sat next to the stretcher on which I lay, holding one of my hands lightly in his. I wanted to sleep, could feel my eyelids heavy, but he kept talking to me, asking me what seemed pointless questions; I could feel my irritation growing with each one. I wanted him to stop talking, to allow me to rest. I wanted to tell him how I had not slept properly in weeks and now, when finally I felt ready to, he would not let me. It was only afterwards that I understood that had been the point.

Even with that, I only remember fragments of the conversation, as if from a dream. He'd bought a new house for him and his girlfriend. They were expecting a baby. But I do not recall his name, or that of his partner and, if I'm honest, I do not even remember his face, only his voice, soft and steady and unrelenting.

My memories of the hospital that night are similarly elusive. I remember primarily sounds, and smells, and light: clatters and raised voices and mechanical beeping; the glare of fluorescent bulbs that lined interminable lengths of corridor; the intrusive spot of thin torch beams flitted across my field of vision; the sharp, chemical smell of disinfectant. I remember questions and concerns, shared looks when I told the doctor and nurses that I'd fallen on the stairs. I remember a uniformed police officer appearing, hovering beside my bed, but I could offer her nothing that seemed to satisfy her. I remember being sick, repeatedly. I remember the coldness of the sheets on the bed, the sense of relief that I had handed myself into the care of others, how glad I was that, though the pain relief took the edge off my injuries, I could still feel something there, ragged and loose, like the exposed wound left by a pulled tooth. Finally, I remember that I welcomed the quiet that sleep finally brought.

I was woken through the night for observation, so by six thirty the following morning, I was already awake and alert, surprised to find my right arm was in a plaster cast that I only vaguely had recollection of being fitted.

'Good morning,' the nurse who came in to take my blood pressure offered, cheerily.

I grunted a response, suddenly aware again of the aching that seemed to flare in every fibre of my body with even the simple act of sitting up in the bed.

'Wait a minute,' she said, putting down her tray on the small bedside cabinet and, moving across, putting her arm around my back and helping me. In that movement, the air sweetened with the smell of her, her clothes, her body spray, and I knew it instantly as one Ellie wore. For the briefest second, Ellie was there, her arm around me, her scent in my mouth and nose. I breathed deeply, despite the pain, hoping to capture and hold that smell a little longer, but it was elusive as memory.

'Are you feeling better this morning?' she asked as she fixed the pillow behind me. I could see her nametag – Susan. 'You were in a bad state last night.'

'I don't remember last night,' I said.

'You'd taken a fair knock to the head. Concussion, for sure.'

She lifted my elbow, gently, and wrapped the monitor cuff around my unplastered arm.

'Is it broken?' I asked, trying to lift the damaged arm but with limited success.

'In a few places,' she said. 'Can you remember what happened?'

The question was so casual, asked while she busied herself with the monitor. I felt the steady pressure of the cuff inflate.

'I fell down the stairs.'

'That's what you said last night, too,' she said. 'You don't remember anything else?'

Her face, beneath the kindness, the sincerity, betrayed a steeliness with the question.

'Like what?'

She shook her head, turned to look at the monitor as it beeped. 'That's a little high,' she said. 'We'll keep an eye on it for a bit. The doctor will be in with you soon.'

The time crawled that morning. I felt like the tablets were wearing off too quickly and every shift in the bed caused pain to flare across my body. My head hurt, my mouth felt dry. Each nerve ending tingled and fizzed so that my hands shook even as I tried to drink a glass of water.

The door opened and, rather than a doctor, a uniformed police officer I thought I ought to know came in, her face a sort of déjà vu. She looked drawn, tired.

'How are we this morning, Mrs Condron?' she asked.

'Sore.'

'I'm not surprised. I wanted to ask you a few questions. I was here last night, but you were a little out of it.'

I offered a light raising of my plastered arm as explanation, then instantly regretted the unnecessary movement.

'I understand,' she said. 'Can you tell me what happened? How you ended up . . . well, here?'

'I fell down the stairs.'

She nodded, grimly. 'That's what you said last night, too.'

'That's what happened.'

She pulled up a chair next to the bed and sat.

'The thing is, according to the doctors, your injuries are not as consistent with a fall as they'd expect.'

'I can't explain that.'

'I understand it can be difficult, Mrs Condron,' she said. 'But you're safe here.'

'Everyone says they understand,' I said. 'That's all I hear from people: they understand. No one understands.'

'Then help me to understand. Did someone hit you?'

I looked at her, sitting next to me, her notebook on her lap. Her hair was frazzled and had escaped the clip she'd used to hold it up so it sat easily under her cap. Her face was pale, her eyes heavy with bags, the blood vessels on her cheeks spidery red lines. I suspected this was the end of a shift for her.

'I fell,' I said.

'Is your husband at home?'

'You people don't even check your own records, do you?' I said, laughing lightly at the absurdity of it.

'There's no need to get upset, Mrs Condron,' the officer said.

'I'm not upset. Just check your own files.'

'Can you please not shout, ma'am,' she said.

I stared at her, bewildered. I wasn't shouting. Why couldn't she understand that I wasn't shouting? So I told her that.

'Ma'am, please,' she began as the door opened and the young nurse, Susan, came in.

'Everything okay, Dora?' she asked.

'No one's listening to me,' I said. 'I fell. No one's listening to me.'

Susan came across, her eyes on the young policewoman. 'Dora, we're listening. That's okay. If you fell, you fell. Don't be upsetting yourself.'

'I'm not upset,' I said and was surprised to see them both wince at the comment.

'That's okay,' Susan said again, her hands outstretched as she approached me, warily. 'We need to keep your blood pressure under control, Dora. Just try to relax. I'm going to get the doctor.'

'I can come back later,' the policewoman said to me as Susan left. 'Is there anyone you'd like me to contact?'

I stared at her, knowing that she didn't mean anything by it. 'I don't have anyone left,' I said.

'I'm sorry to hear that, Mrs Condron,' she said. 'You've been through the wars.'

She stood now, her hands resting on her belt, as she waited for the medical staff to return. I realised they were afraid to leave me on my own.

'I'm fine,' I said. 'You can go. I'm fine.'

'I know,' she said, her brief smile strikingly insincere.

Chapter Thirty-Seven

In fact, it was Glenn who returned later that day. She took her spot opposite me, her hands folded in her lap as she waited for Susan to finish checking my blood pressure once more.

The bed was warm, the room stuffy. I felt like there were small insects crawling just beneath the surface of my skin but itching one area just caused the sensation to move to somewhere else. I needed to get back to my own house. And yet, I was acutely aware that home now had changed once more: the two men standing in my hallway had violated whatever security, safety, I had felt there, even if I knew that I had invited them in, in a way, through my actions with the paint.

'Ward says it wasn't him,' Glenn said, when Susan had left.

'I never said it was.'

'No, you said you fell down some stairs.'

I nodded, lightly, my brain feeling untethered inside my skull.

'Yet your arms carry defensive wounds. Were the stairs attacking you as you fell?'

'What difference does it make?'

'If whoever attacked you said something that would lead to Ward, that would be useful.'

'No, he said it wasn't him,' I explained. 'What difference would someone saying something make?'

Glenn shrugged. 'He and his family were out for a very lengthy, public dinner last night during the period when you were attacked. Not that that doesn't mean your attackers weren't working on his instructions.'

I stared up at the ceiling, willing her to go.

'Would your husband be capable of this?'

'Eamon?' I asked, surprised, for I had not considered him as a possibility.

'You asked him to leave the family home,' she said. 'He may resent it.'

'This wasn't Eamon,' I said. 'He'd want to do it himself.'

'Have you someone who could stay with you? When you get home?'

I shook my head. 'No one,' I said. 'I don't need anyone either.'

'It might be best—'

'Whoever did this had a chance to do more and didn't,' I said. 'Why would they come back?'

'That depends on you not doing anything that might kick the hornets' nest,' Glenn said.

'What's the worst they can do?'

'Kill you.'

I glanced across at her. 'Is that all?'

They allowed me home the following day with pain medication and a warning not to drink while taking it. Several times the staff had attempted to convince me to tell the truth about what had happened to me. When it had become apparent that my story had not changed, they furnished me with leaflets on domestic abuse and a helpline number, should I need it.

The house was chilled when I arrived back. The temperature had dropped that day but the heating wasn't on automatic, so I'd sat in the kitchen with my coat on, draped over my right shoulder while my arm nestled in a sling. I negotiated making tea, then moved back out to the hallway and picked up the congealed remains of the fish supper I'd dropped, then came back out to clean the bloodstains out of the carpet.

It was around eight o'clock that same evening that I heard the doorbell ring. I peered out through the curtained living room window. A heavyset man, whom I did not recognise, stood on the step. I opened the window a fraction and called across. He ambled over, his movements neat and careful, as if he considered each before making it.

'Mrs Condron. You don't know me,' he began. 'I'm Donal Kelly.'

I shook my head, the name meaning nothing.

'I'm a . . . Well, your daughter, Ellie, sent me to you.'

My stomach lurched with the comment. I rushed out to the hall, almost unable to breathe, fumbling with the keys so I could open the door. The man stood now, more visible in the hall light. He was middle aged, with sandy hair combed over to the side, round penny glasses that looked a little too large for his features.

'Where is she? Is she hurt?'

'Can I come in, Mrs Condron?'

'Where's Ellie? Have you taken her?'

He shook his head, a little sadly. 'I should explain,' he said. 'I'm a . . . Well, I have extra-sensory intuition.'

I had the impression he was nervous, whether because of the verbal tic or the way he twisted one hand in the other as he spoke.

'What does that mean?'

'I'm a psychic, a medium, whatever you like.'

I felt the last flicker of the hope his first words had kindled die in my breast.

'Go away,' I said, starting to close the door.

'The name Leo is important,' he said, quickly. 'And water.'

'What?' I stopped, holding the door ajar, caught by the name.

'The name Leo. I can't work out why. Is it a toy, maybe? A lion or a teddy bear of some sort, perhaps.'

I shuddered, involuntarily.

'I see things,' he said. 'Pictures, words, places. When I think of someone who has died. But only if they want me to do something for them.'

'You said Ellie sent you to me,' I said, trying not to let him see what impact his words had had. In the room above, I knew Leo sat guard on Ellie's bed, waiting for her return.

'Leo seemed too personal to be intended for anyone else but you,' he said. 'I did speak to the police a few weeks back, when I first got the image of water but . . . well, they thanked me but I heard nothing more. Can I come in?'

I stood back, allowing him to pass me, then directed him towards the kitchen.

'Are you okay?' he asked, looking at the half washed out bloodstains on the floor, then looking to my own injuries, clearer now in the light.

'I fell,' I said.

He did not believe me, but had the good grace to say nothing. 'I read about Ellie going missing a few months back,' he said, moving into the kitchen and taking the seat opposite mine, but only after stopping and considering all available choices. The seat he had taken was where Eamon usually sat.

'I'll not sit in Ellie's seat,' he said, then laid his hand gently on the wooden back of the chair she habitually used.

'How did you know that was her chair?'

He shrugged in a quick, curt movement. 'Like I said ... well, I have these intuitions.'

'I don't believe in mediums, or whatever you call yourselves,' I said, taking the seat opposite him.

'That doesn't matter,' he said. 'What's the old saying about God – even if you don't believe in Him, He believes in you.'

'Do you believe in God?'

He considered the question, his head tilted lightly to one side. 'I do,' he said, after some thought. 'I've seen too much from the other side to doubt that there's more beyond what we can see.'

'Why me? Why Ellie? You're not from here.'

His accent was heavy; Birmingham, I guessed.

'I don't choose,' he said. 'The dead choose me. Ellie chose me.'

I stifled a sob. 'So she is dead?' I asked.

He nodded. 'I'm so sorry. I only get images from the dead. It's how they speak.'

'What did she say to you?'

'I saw water first, dark water.'

'She vanished near a river,' I said.

He shook his head. 'I know, but I don't think it's a river. It's dark, like water contained, like a tank of some sort. I told the police then.'

'Detective Andrews?'

A nod. 'He said they'd follow up if I had anything more.'

'Did you?'

'I saw fire and water. And the word Leo kept coming back to me, over and over. But the word was warm, like something she loved, not something she was afraid of. That's what made me know I had to see you.'

Despite my scepticism, I felt compelled by his words.

'Why fire?'

'I think something was burned around the time she died. I get a smell sometimes, of burning oil or petrol.'

I felt the skin on my arm prickle beneath the cast.

'Who put you up to this?' I asked.

'There's not . . . well, I mean, no one. I'm not looking for anything, beyond being useful. Ellie wants to be found; she'd not be revealing these things to me if she didn't. I want to help you find her, to bring her home.'

'Why not just go back to the police?'

'I have,' he said. 'But depending on the detective, they can sometimes be a little . . . well, scoffing of my gift.'

'So you want me to speak to them? I'm not sure they'll listen to me over you,' I said.

He shrugged. 'It's also sometimes easier to hear what the one who has passed wants to say if I can touch something that was important to them. I get clearer pictures, sharper pictures, with that connection.'

'What will you do with it?' I asked. 'Whatever it is you want.'

'Nothing. Simply touch it. That's enough usually.'

'Wait here,' I said, then went upstairs to Ellie's room. I did not want him in here, in this space that held air that she had breathed. I lifted Leo from the bed, gently, inhaled the scent of him from his fur and saw Ellie again, more sharply in focus in my mind's eye than she had been for weeks, then carried him downstairs and presented him to Kelly, with the care one might use with a sacrificial offering.

'Leo,' he said with a nod, as if this confirmed all that he thought. 'May I?' he asked, then took the toy in his hands, held him against his breast and closed his eyes.

The room stilled and I was afraid almost to breathe lest it disturbed him. I could feel my tears begin to rise, had a sensation that Ellie was standing in the room next to me, a feeling so strong, I glanced over my shoulder, fearful that she might be there, fearful that she would not.

We remained like that for a few moments, or maybe longer, I cannot recall. Finally, Kelly opened his eyes and nodded once, then handed Leo back to me with a gentleness that surprised me.

'Anything?' I asked.

He smiled. 'That's not . . . well, it doesn't always work straight away. Sometimes it takes a moment or two for the images to become clear. Like old film developing, the picture takes shape over a while.'

He stood and pushed in his chair. 'Thank you for speaking with me,' he said. 'I've booked into the City Hotel for the evening,' he said. 'I'm going out to Rowan Wood tomorrow. You could join me, if you like, before I go back home.'

He stared at me, blinking mildly behind his outsized glasses. If he was the connecting point between Ellie and me, how could I refuse?

Chapter Thirty-Eight

Kelly collected me just before nine the following morning. I'd not slept, not been able to sleep, my mind a swirl of images of dark water and fire. The skin beneath my plaster cast felt scalded and I could not find comfort. I'd taken two painkillers before bedtime but it had not helped. Even a nightcap had not taken the edge off much. Perhaps because of Kelly, I imagined Ellie was calling to me; sought through the myriad images conjured by my imagination for any that would have meaning, that would allow me to hear her voice once more.

'Thank you for doing this,' Kelly said as he drove along the A5 before turning down towards the river to where the expanse of woodland stood. It stretched for miles, right into the next county, though I remembered Eamon telling me on a walk we'd taken with Ellie, years ago, that there were actually two woods that had merged over time.

Ellie had been around ten then and was just beginning to stretch. She'd picked some berries off one of the trees, its bough heavy with the small orange fruit, and had popped one in her mouth.

'Don't eat those,' Eamon said to her.

She spat it out instantly, the skin still unbroken, but then continued to spit for some moments after in case any taint of it remained.

'Are they poisonous?' she'd asked, her eyes wide with fear and wonder at how close to death she'd been.

'No,' Eamon said, gathering a handful himself. 'You can cook them and they make nice jam and things. But raw, they're not very nice. They'd leave you with a yucky taste.'

I'd linked arms with him then, leaned against him a little as we walked, proud that I had brought this man into our lives, who could teach Ellie about the world, about things I would never have known.

'The rowan is a witch tree,' he'd said as Ellie, who for most of the walk had been trailing behind us, as if embarrassed to be in our company, now kept pace with us. She affected disinterest, but I could tell by the way she quickened her pace that she wanted to hear.

'It's supposed to offer protection, which is why you know that you'll never come to harm in this wood; the good witches will protect you.'

'Are there good witches?' Ellie asked.

'Some people think so. They make potions from berries and tree bark and cast spells to keep you safe.'

'Like Mum with her herbal tea,' Ellie had said, then she and Eamon shared a laugh and she ran ahead, the berries she'd picked still clutched tenderly in her hand.

I found them that night under her pillow. I'd allowed them to stay there for a day or two until they burst and stained the case, then I'd thrown them in the bin. I regretted that now.

'This must be an old woodland,' Kelly said as we pulled into the parking bay at its entrance. 'The rowans were considered magical.'

I looked across at him, surprised by the comment, as if he had somehow seen my own memories.

'That was a long time ago, though. A different life,' he said, causing the goosebumps to rise along my arms.

'They were meant to protect,' I said.

'Indeed. They . . . well, they were thought to protect. Now we believe they're a portal to a different place, between this world and the next. Ellie is standing at that portal, Mrs Condron. Last night I dreamed of her standing in a doorway, waiting. I think she wants you to find her, then she can pass on.'

His words elicited a mixture of renewed grief and renewed resolution and I swallowed back my tears at the thought that she had visited him but not me. I'd longed to see her once more, in my dreams, had looked for her, but without success.

'It was Leo,' he said, simply, pushing his glasses up onto the bridge of his nose. 'I knew he would bring me closer to her. Her voice is strong, Mrs Condron. That's a good thing. That means she'll make sure that she's heard. We need to find her, for all three of us to find peace. Whatever it takes.'

'Whatever it takes,' I agreed.

We walked in silence through the woodland. Though called Rowan Wood, it was a mixture of various different types of tree. While most had shed their leaves by that stage of the year, a few still clung on and here and there an evergreen was spotted, offering bursts of colour among the monotony of the lines of thin trunks, standing stark against the backdrop of decaying leaves. The ground was soft, almost buoyant with the cushion of mulch. The air was sharp and tannic and heavy with moisture running up off the river. I felt washed by it, could swear that Ellie was near, as if just beyond my line of vision, waiting for me to catch up. Unbidden, I saw her again, aged ten, walking ahead of us, turning and waiting for us, the berries in her hand unblemished.

We broke into a clearing, a natural bowl in the land. Kelly half slid, half stumbled down the low incline into the centre of the space, then stood and, turning in a circle, took in the area.

'This was where the dance was held,' he said. I glanced around for anything that might confirm his assertion. Sure enough, a strand of crime-scene tape remained attached to the low branch of one of the trees at the far side, fluttering in the light breeze. I felt suddenly exposed, felt a chill creeping through me as if seeping up through the decaying forest floor. I shuddered, wrapped my arms around myself.

'Do you feel it?' Kelly asked, the briefest of smiles flickering on his lips. 'Do you feel her?'

I nodded, not trusting myself to speak.

'She was here. And she's glad now that we are. She's with us.'

He climbed up the other side of the incline and followed a path worn in the leaves, moving deeper into the forest. In the distance I could hear the soft suspiration of the river, could smell the dampness rising.

We walked for almost a quarter of an hour before he stopped once more. The river ran close by now, its flow clearly audible. The ground was sodden, water rising around our feet when we stepped too heavily.

Kelly moved across to a huge rowan tree that stood on its own, its boughs thick with fruit.

'We're here,' he said, softly. 'This is the place.'

I felt as if the breath had been sucked from my body. My hands tingled with pins and needles, my head light, my legs began to shake. I needed to sit. Instead, I leaned against the lower limb of the tree next to me and tried to settle myself.

We stood in a small clearing. The rowan at the centre provided some form of shelter with the expanse of its upper limbs spread. To one side, it had grown over a boulder, its ancient roots curled around the rock as if pulling it in towards the tree's core and I felt panic rise again with that feeling of being trapped, of being pulled inexorably towards something.

'This is the place,' he repeated.

'Is she here?' I asked. 'Is this where she's buried?'

He shook his head. 'No. But this is where she passed over. And it was a good passing. She wants you to know that. She didn't feel any pain.'

I started to cry then, big sobs of pain that shook me and broke open once more the healing wound on my cheek.

Kelly stood silently, his head bowed. He did not offer sympathy, did not console me, could not.

'Thank you,' I said, when the first wave had passed. I looked around more slowly now, wanting to know the place, wanting to see what Ellie had seen in her last moments, to share that with her.

A ragged circle of trees stood spaced out around the rowan, like a crown with it at the centre. To my right, a low lichen-covered stone broke free from the earth, like a headstone. I moved across and realised it was the county boundary marker. The police had said they believed she had died near the county line. I pressed my left hand to my mouth, then touched the stone marker with the gentlest kiss, as if it would somehow reach Ellie that way. Through the trees, down to the right, I could glimpse water.

'Water,' I said, pointing to it. 'You said you saw fire and water.'

Kelly nodded. 'But not here. This is where she passed, but not where she remains. This is a portal spot – the best kind too – a county boundary and a rowan standing alone. Take comfort in that.'

He stopped suddenly, raised a finger in a gesture that I wasn't to speak, then closed his eyes and inhaled deeply. He inclined his head to one side, then turned and sniffed at the air, as if following a scent. He opened his eyes and looked around, checking in all directions as if for signs of others coming.

'What is it?'

Kelly raised his shoulders lightly. 'I keep getting the scent of a man,' he said. 'Just the hint of aftershave, but I can't place it. But I think it's his.'

'Who?'

'The man who killed Ellie.'

I surprised myself with a scream, so primal in nature it felt as if it was ripped from me against my wishes. I could not stop it, could not control it; it was as though someone else screamed through me and I was an observer in my own skin.

Then it was past, and I felt exhausted all of a sudden.

'I can't go on,' I said.

'You must,' Kelly said. 'You're almost there.'

Kelly dropped me back home. We sat in the car together and I felt absurdly nervous, like someone at the end of a date. I felt he expected something from me, felt I should offer him something in return for the gift of his sight that he'd shared with me, all scepticism long since gone.

'Would you like to come in?' I asked.

He shook his head. 'I feel like I'm so close,' he said. 'I wish I could stay a few more days but, well . . . I need to get home. I can't afford any more time.'

'I can pay,' I said, without even thinking. 'If that's what you need.'

He shook his head. 'That's very kind, Mrs Condron. No. I couldn't.'

'Please,' I said. 'If you're so close. The aftershave. Maybe you'll find what it is.'

He nodded. 'I'm planning on going to the local chemists and trying the samples, to see if I can find it.'

'Please,' I said. 'I'm alone in this. You're the only one who has offered to help. Please let me help you to help me.'

He flushed with embarrassment. 'I need money for the hotel,' he said. 'And a small stipend to allow me to eat.'

'I have money,' I said. 'If I covered those costs, could you stay?'

'Perhaps a day or two more,' he said. 'But I'll pay myself. I can see how important it is for you that Ellie is heard.'

'Wait here,' I said, then got out and went straight into the house. We had a small moneybox, disguised as a soup can to fool thieves, in which I kept cash when Eamon was away, in case we needed any basics and I couldn't get to the bank. He travelled with our card in case of emergency. I topped it up each time he left, to the point that it now had almost £500 in it. I removed it all and, keeping £20 for myself, took the rest back out to Kelly's waiting car.

I thrust it into his hand, with my left hand.

He took it, held my hand in his, his eyes flushed with tears. 'Thank you, Mrs Condron,' he said. 'Thank you for believing.'

Chapter Thirty-Nine

I was watching television that evening when I heard the doorbell ring. I suspected it might be Kelly, perhaps returning having found the scent he'd smelt. Instead, it was Glenn.

'You,' I said, opening the door a fraction.

'Mrs Condron,' she said. 'I was just calling to see how you were since.'

I was, momentarily, taken aback by her comment. 'Have you news?'

She shook her head, her expression pained. 'Nothing, I'm afraid.'

'Then there's no point in being here.'

She held my gaze for a second and I could tell I had hurt her.

'Just so long as you're okay,' she said, turning to leave.

'Wait,' I said, relenting and regretting my harshness. 'Come in.'

She stopped and looked at me. 'I best be going. My shift's done; I was just checking on you.'

'I'm sorry,' I said. 'Thank you.'

She in turn seemed to reconsider. 'How are you? Still sore, I'd imagine.'

'I've met someone,' I said, suddenly, as if compelled to share what had happened with someone, anyone.

'That's good,' Glenn said, her smile frozen on her lips.

'Not like that. Someone who can hear Ellie speaking to him.'

The smile faltered now and her shoulders dropped. 'What?'

'A man called Donal Kelly,' I said. 'He's a medium.'

'Christ,' Glenn muttered. She came back up towards me now, stepping into the hallway and facing me. 'Did you give him money?'

'He knew where she died,' I said, feeling those earlier tears rising again in my earnestness for her to share my belief.

'Did you give him money?' Glenn asked again. 'Dora?'

I felt my conviction falter, felt anger build again towards Glenn for causing me to doubt.

'He said he told you what he'd seen and you ignored him,' I said. 'You've done nothing to find Ellie and when someone who can help appears, you ignore him.'

'We didn't ignore him,' Glenn said. 'We searched in three different areas that he provided tip-offs for. Because we can't take a chance that some scam artist, claiming to know something, isn't actually the killer playing with the police. So every time Kelly offers his opinion on any case we run, we have to assign resources to a wild goose chase.'

'He knew things no one else could have known.'

'Like what?'

'He knew where the rave was held. And the post where he said Ellie was, down by the county marker, just as you said.'

'Kelly was at our crime scenes,' Glenn said. 'We keep an eye out for him now.'

'What?'

'He comes to crime scenes, stands with the reporters and watches what we do.'

'Maybe he's drawn there.'

She shook her head. 'He's a con man, Dora,' she said. 'Did you give him any money?'

'He didn't ask for any,' I said.

'But did you give him any?'

I couldn't look her full in the face. 'I want you to leave now,' I said.

'How much?'

I felt my face blaze and was once more sitting at the centre of a press conference, Glenn beside me, my husband arrested, my daughter lost, my humiliation made public.

'It doesn't matter,' I said. 'I trust him. He knew about her teddy bear, Leo. He knew that name. She told him the name Leo.'

'Like Leo Ward? The person who ran the rave she attended the night she passed? Like that name?'

I held her gaze then, surprised at the anger I could feel building. I was sick of being treated as if I was stupid. First by Eamon and Brenda, then by the police, now by Kelly apparently.

'It's not about the money,' I said. 'I don't care about the money.'

'He stole from you,' Glenn said.

'Everyone has stolen from me; my dignity, my marriage, my child.' Tears broke despite my best efforts to withhold them. 'And now you, stealing what last bit of hope I had.'

Glenn's expression softened. 'I'm sorry, Dora,' she said, laying her hand on my arm. 'I don't mean to do that. I'm looking out for you.'

'Eamon used to say that,' I said. 'Every time he told me what to do, what to wear, what to spend. Every time someone looks out for me, I end up worse than I was.'

'I'll chase him up, get your money back.'

'He's staying in the City Hotel,' I said.

'I doubt it. He lives about fifteen miles from here, up past Wickham. I'll get your money back.'

Glenn left soon after, seemingly having convinced herself that retrieving my money would somehow make me feel better, despite what I had said.

I considered what she had told me; I did not want to believe her. Kelly had been so sincere, so kind. I decided to warn him that she would be calling, to tell him that he was to tell her I wanted him to have the money.

But, when I called the City Hotel to speak to him, the receptionist there told me that no one of that name was booked into the hotel.

Chapter Forty

I'd had a drink before bedtime to try to settle my nerves, but instead of helping me sleep, I found myself paralysed in a sort of fever dream in which I was assailed by images of woodlands, of fire, of water, of Ellie calling for me, of rowan berries, of Eamon, of Brenda, smiling, of Andrews and Glenn, of Adam Ward, of burning cars, of Nicola Ward, of my child tearing herself in half.

Since Ellie's disappearance, everything I had done had been for nothing, serving only to further humiliate me without helping me find my child. I was sure that Adam Ward had killed her. If the police would not convict him, bring him before the court of justice, I had no choice but to drag him into the public court.

I called Ann McBride just before eight the following morning and told her I had a story for her.

I could tell when she saw me that she was conflicted between pity for my physical state and excitement at the story she knew she could generate from it. We spoke first. I'd offered her coffee, out of habit, but she declined. 'What happened?' she asked, gesturing towards the cast, her eyes on my face. The bruising around my cheek and eyes had darkened overnight and was starting to yellow around the edges, making it seem more pronounced, my stitches thick with dried blood.

'I was attacked in my home a few nights ago. Two men followed me into the hallway and attacked me; one punched me in the face while the other attacked me with a baseball bat,' I said. 'I broke the bones in my hand and arm trying to protect my skull.'

'That's desperate,' McBride said, unable to hide her eagerness to hear more. 'Why would someone do that?'

'Earlier that day, I'd confronted the person the police believe killed my daughter.'

'Confronted?'

'I poured red paint over his car outside the art college. People filmed it.'

McBride's eyes widened and she looked down to her notes. 'And you think these two events are connected?'

I thought carefully about what to say. My attackers had been careful not to say anything that would connect them directly back to Ward, and Ward's family had clearly created an alibi for the duration of my attack, meaning the police could not do anything to them. But inference and implication would never be enough.

'Yes. They told me to stay away from that person. They said they'd been sent by his father who is also a well-known drug dealer.'

'Allegedly,' McBride added.

I shrugged as best I could. 'They said that the police would never be able to prove that he had arranged it; that he and his family would have an alibi for the time of the attack. The police have since told me that that's the case. They can't touch them. But, likewise, I won't be silenced.'

'Mrs Condron, this is off the record,' McBride said. 'But if they assaulted you for confronting him in the street, what might they do if you make a public accusation against him?'

'I don't know,' I said. 'But the worst they can do is kill me, and I've no fear of that. So all the threats and beatings will not stop me from making sure everyone knows what happened to my Ellie. I will not stop until the person who killed her gets what they deserve. And that's on the record. I want him to know, I'm not afraid of him and I'm not going to stop until I get answers to what happened to Ellie. Until I bring her home.'

The story appeared online later than evening. McBride had left out the accusations about drug dealing and the finer details about my attack on Ward's car, perhaps afraid that the latter would leave the paper open to being sued. Still, it was clear enough that I had blamed the family of the person who had killed Ellie for arranging for me to be beaten.

Around ten p.m. the phone rang. I'd been expecting the call, hoping for it.

'Mrs Condron?' It was a man's voice, though light and softer than I'd expected. 'This is Leo Ward. I think we need to talk.'

'I've nothing to say,' I said. 'Get your son to hand himself in.'

'I've something to say, though. I'd like the chance to meet.'

'So I can be attacked again?'

'I'm not— Look, can we meet somewhere public, tomorrow? Somewhere you feel safe. I can help you find the answers you're looking for.'

'All I want is my daughter.'

'I understand that. I would too, in your shoes.'

I had nothing to lose in meeting the man; in fact, I'd wanted to meet him, to let him know, from one parent to another, what his child had done to mine. Had done to me by extension. I told him the name of a café, The Boston Tea Party, where Ellie and I used to go for lunch sometimes when she'd a half day at college if I was downtown. The staff knew me well enough, would keep an eye.

'Would ten a.m. be too early?' he asked.

'I don't sleep,' I said, then hung up.

Chapter Forty-One

It took me a moment to recognise Ward when I went in the following morning. Several couples sat at tables and, on one side, a group of workmen were eating fried breakfasts, clearly having already done a few hours. The café was stuffy, the windows damp and misted with condensation, due in part to the chill of the morning, as if winter had arrived all at once.

Ward sat on the far side of the room, at a table by the window. Despite my arriving ten minutes early, he was already halfway through a cup of coffee. He rose when I entered and stayed standing by his chair until I joined him and sat myself.

'Tea or coffee, Mrs Condron?' he asked. 'Or something more? Have you had breakfast?'

'Tea,' I said, then added, 'please,' habit being so strong.

He returned a moment later. 'They'll bring it down,' he said, then sat, gathering his hands together in front of him on the table and regarding me carefully. 'Thank you for meeting me.'

'I was interested to see who you were,' I said. I was a little surprised by the man. I'd imagined someone intimidating, someone with weight and heft. By contrast, Ward was a small man, only a few inches taller than me, I guessed. His frame was narrow, his arms wiry rather than muscular. His trousers were ill fitting and hung baggily on him when he stood. His features were fine, his hair shorn fairly neat but unmistakably greying, as was the thin beard he wore, despite his being around the same age as me, in his late thirties at most. I understood now why he'd had to hire men to attack me. He did not have a body capable of violence, I believed.

The server arrived with a tray. I knew her from having been in here before, but could not recall her name. She laid the cup and saucer, pot and milk jug carefully on the table in front of me, trying not to look at my injuries.

'Good to see you again, Dora,' she said. 'We were all devastated by what happened to poor Ellie.'

I could have sworn she glanced at Ward then before she turned and left and I suspected she knew who he was, perhaps had seen McBride's story and made the connection. That thought comforted me; the staff would be watching Ward carefully on my behalf, I hoped.

'I'm sorry about what happened to you,' Ward said, when she was gone. 'Not just your daughter, but this too.' He indicated my broken arm with a light gesture of his hand.

'You're sorry?' I scoffed. 'You did this.'

He nodded. 'I did,' he said.

I was taken aback at the frankness of the admission. He didn't try to hide behind it or convince me I was wrong.

'You weren't one of them.'

'No. But they acted on my orders.'

'Why?'

'You know why. Look, let's not insult one another by lying. You were trying to blame what happened to your child on mine. I understand why you did it – we'd do anything for our children. But you have to see that I will protect my children just as violently as you want to find yours.'

I swallowed back what I had planned to say. After weeks of platitudes and lies, here for the first time was someone telling me the truth, treating me with enough respect to be honest to me.

'Though I don't believe for a second that they told you it was me who had hired them.'

I smiled. 'They didn't. I made that up, for the paper.'

He stared at me, as if re-evaluating me, then nodded. He laid his two hands flat against the table surface. 'Adam did not kill your daughter,' he said.

'The police think so.'

'Then they're wrong.'

'Of course they are,' I scoffed.

'They are,' he insisted. 'Look, I understand you need to find answers, that you want someone to blame. But you're blaming the wrong person.'

'I don't think I am. And the fact you're here only convinces me more of that.'

'I'm here,' he said, his voice with a edge of something darker now, 'to get you off my family's back. Adam had nothing to do with what happened to Ellie. I swear on my life, on my children's lives, Adam did not kill your daughter.'

'How do you know?' I asked, a little taken aback by the vehemence of his claim, though still sure he was lying.

'Adam was with me,' he said. 'I arranged that rave with him and he was with me. He did not kill Ellie.' He emphasised the assertion, jabbing his finger against the table on each word.

'The police—'

'The police,' Ward scoffed. 'The police couldn't find their own arseholes with a compass and a map. The police want to pin something on me. This was their chance to do it.'

'That's convenient.'

'It's really not from where I'm sitting,' Ward said. 'I thought you of all people would know what that's like. Didn't they spend the first few days trying to pin it on your husband? Instead of chasing down the real killer, they found someone they wanted to blame and focused on that. They wasted those vital first hours, first days.'

I said nothing, despite having harboured the same suspicions myself.

'Then, when they found it couldn't have been him, they turn on me and my boy, simply because they knew we were there.'

'Ellie was friends with your daughter.'

'I know she was. Nicola and Ellie were very close. Do you really think if Nicola knew what had happened to her, she'd say nothing?'

'I think Ellie was in love with her,' I said. I'm not sure why I revealed that; perhaps I hoped, if the girl heard, if she knew, it might be the catalyst she needed to tell the truth.

'And Nicola was very fond of her,' he said, moving on. 'Adam's car was stolen that evening: he'd used it to carry equipment for me and left it parked up at the entrance to Rowan. When we went looking for it at the end of the night, it was stolen. We reported it to the police and that was it: once they knew I was there, they looked to blame me or one of the kids in some way. They ignored everything else. The thieving that was going on that night, the joyriders, people off their heads.'

'Your customers.'

'These raves started out as an exclusive thing. We kept the numbers small, invite only. It meant we had a good crowd, people who knew one another and just wanted to party. The past few, word has leaked out and we had uninvited people turning up. Undesirables.'

I stared at him, almost in disbelief that he was sharing with me his complaints about his business.

'Look, my point is,' he said, 'there were people there that no one knew. People that wouldn't normally have been. There were pickpockets, all kinds of things. We told the police this at the time, that it could have been that someone tried to steal from Ellie and she tried to stop them. Or someone took her somewhere. Her bag was stolen, isn't that right?'

'It was found,' I said. 'The person came forward.'

'It was "found"?' he echoed. 'Really? Adam's car was "found", too. The police didn't look at that at all.'

A thought struck me. 'How do you know so much about the case? The bag? Eamon? Have you someone telling you?'

'It pays to know what's happening,' Ward said. 'And, if I were you, I'd not be happy with how the police have been conducting things since Ellie went. I'd not be happy at all.'

'I'm not,' I agreed. 'Your son should be in jail by now.'

His frame jerked a little and I could tell, when he spoke, it was through gritted teeth. 'I've told you, Adam had nothing to do with it. I've sworn that to you.'

'I don't know you,' I said. 'So your word, or your oath, means nothing to me. People will do anything for their child.'

'They will,' Ward said.

'They will,' I agreed. 'I'm not going to stop until I get the truth.'

Ward took a breath, held it, straightened himself in his seat, glancing around as if to see who was listening, then leaned forward a little towards me, inviting my confidence.

'The police aren't going to find your daughter,' he said and, for a moment, I felt as if the winter's chill was in the room with us, encircling us. I felt sick, felt an admission of some sort was imminent.

'But I can,' he continued. 'I know a lot of the people who were there. I've heard all the rumours.'

'So have I,' I said. 'I know she and your daughter fought.'

Ward accepted the comment with a nod, pursed his lips lightly, as if reconsidering what he was saying. 'They did. Ellie misunderstood their friendship. She tried to kiss Nicola. When Nicola told her she wasn't gay, apparently Ellie got upset and ran off. That was the last time Nicki saw her.'

'And she didn't go after her?'

'Would you? Break someone's heart and then go after them to make it worse? Nicki was pretty upset herself at what had happened.'

The story pained me more than I wanted to admit. My poor girl. I just wanted to hold her in my arms, comfort her. In all the fantasies that I'd had, night after night, the ones where her last moments had at least been happy ones had brought me some solace. With these words, Ward had taken even that from me.

'I'm sorry,' he said. 'I can see that's hurt you and that wasn't my intention.'

I shook my head, but could not look up at him.

He reached across the table then, his hand inches from mine.

'I want to help you, Mrs Condron,' he said. 'I can find whoever killed your daughter for you.'

'Then why haven't you before now? Hand them over to the police.'

He shook his head, lifted his spoon and stirred the cold remnants of his coffee.

'The way I'd ask those questions, I couldn't go to the police with it. If you want me to find who did it, I'll make them pay. But there's no going back from it, and there's no going to the police.'

The cold enveloped me then and time stilled. He held my gaze so there could be no misunderstanding.

'Do you want me to find who did this?'

For three months, I'd wanted nothing less. Everyone who had offered to help me had let me down or lied to me. But here, in this man, I believed I had found someone who had as much reason for the truth to be known as I, if his child had not been involved, as he claimed.

'I'd want to hear them say it. I'd want to look into their eyes and know they'd done it,' I said.

'Of course.' Ward nodded. 'I'd want the same thing if I were you.'

'How will you—?' I began, but he raised a hand.

'Leave it with me. I'll be in touch when I have anything for you.'

He stood then and laid a ten-pound note on the table.

'Thank you for meeting me, Mrs Condron,' he said, and then he was gone, before I had time to reconsider the wisdom of the agreement we had just reached.

Chapter Forty-Two

I sat that evening, waiting for his call. I had not, I realised, any idea of how long it might take for him to find the person who had taken Ellie from me. Did he already know who it was? Would his children tell him truths they had not told the police? And, beneath all that, how could I even trust him? Still, I also believed that he had as much reason now as I did to find the truth – to protect his child, if his child was innocent. If he was guilty, he'd not be able to convince me otherwise.

My arm ached that day, the pain seeming to drill through the very bones, exploding at each nerve ending so intensely that I had to double the dose of painkillers, but it did nothing to dampen it. I couldn't settle, turning on and off the television again, making cups of tea that sat cold on the kitchen counter because I forgot I'd made them. I picked up a magazine that had belonged to Ellie, hoping that reading it might allow me to connect with her in some way, offer me some insight into how she thought, what she felt, but the words jumbled on the page, seeming to shift from their proper place each time I moved on, so I found myself re-reading the same line over and over, trying to make sense of it. She'd seemingly bookmarked an article with a page torn from her scrapbook, on which she'd done a sketch of a cityscape. The magazine article into which the sheet had been tucked was 'How to Spot a Liar'. I did not manage beyond the opening paragraphs.

I knew how to spot liars for they were all around me: Eamon had lied to me; Brenda lied to me; Ellie had lied to me (though I could understand why, it didn't make it less hurtful); I was sure Adam and Nicola Ward were lying to me; Amy had lied to me the night Ellie went; Kelly had lied to me; the police had lied to me, saying they would find my child and letting her down, letting me down. I realised then the problem: if all of these people had lied, then the common denominator in all of it was me. Me. If people lied to me, it was because they could, because I was stupid enough to believe what they told me. The only person who had not lied to me, who had been honest even when it could have cost them something, was Leo Ward. He'd told me the truth about the beating; he'd respected me enough not to lie. So, while I did not trust him, I would at least allow him the chance to do what the police had failed to do. I would know, I told myself, whether he was telling the truth. The experience of the last months meant that now, at least, I knew how to spot a liar. They were everywhere.

The call came at around eleven thirty p.m. I'd had a glass or two of wine to settle my nerves, locking the front door and turning off all the lights to the front of the house so that no one else might disturb me, before the shrillness of the ringing phone shocked me from a slumber on the sofa in front of the fire.

'I'm coming to collect you,' the speaker said, and it took me a second to place the softly spoken voice as Leo Ward. 'I've found him.'

I'd almost decided not to answer the door by the time he arrived, so sick was I at the thought of what lay ahead. My arm was aching and I'd taken two painkillers, and then, because my nerves were ragged, had drunk the last glass of wine left in the bottle too.

The knock at the door was light and quick. Ward stood back a little down the driveway when I answered.

'Will I need a coat?' I asked, absurdly, never having been in this situation before and unsure whether we would be indoors or out.

'It's coming into winter,' he said. 'You always need a coat.'

'I've told someone I'm going with you,' I lied, realising for the first time what a dangerous position I was voluntarily putting myself in.

'That's why I collected you,' he said. 'All your neighbours will see me here; I'll be the first person the police come to if something happens to you.'

I nodded, accepting the logic of his explanation, then went in and lifted my coat. 'Where are we going?' I asked, following him down the driveway to his car, which was parked, engine running, on the kerb. It was a black sports car and, between this one and Adam's, it was clear that Ward was making quite a bit of money; I assumed that McBride's description of him as a drug dealer was probably fairly accurate.

'Not far,' he said.

* * *

He drove for around twenty minutes, almost in complete silence. The wine I'd drunk burned in my throat and stomach, acidic and sharp. The heat of the car, and the darkness and motion lulled me into a stupor of sorts so that I felt once more removed from myself.

Glancing across at Ward, this man whom I'd only met once, driving me to face my child's killer, was both terrifying and absurd. I started to speak, to force myself back into the moment, to be present there in the car, but no words would form, my tongue feeling heavy and shapeless in my mouth.

I saw Rowan Wood pass on the right-hand side of us, then Ward took a turning up to the left and I could feel the road steepen. In the headlights' glare, I could see the road eventually narrow to a dirt path. There were no lights visible around us, no houses this far out of town. Finally, we pulled into the left and the car beam illuminated, ahead of us, an old barn.

Ward turned off the engine and climbed out. I sat, as if pinned to the seat, unable to move.

'Come on,' he said.

'I've changed my mind,' I said. 'Take me home.'

He leaned down at his side of the car, his arm resting on the open door. 'Not a chance. I told you when you asked me to find him, I said you couldn't back out.'

'Please,' I said. 'Don't make me do this.'

Ward spat on the ground, then shook his head. 'You do know the person who killed your daughter is in that building. A hundred yards from you. After everything you've been through, put me and my family through, the answer you wanted is sitting just in there.'

'I can't do it,' I said.

'Tough,' Ward said, then slammed the door and walked away. I saw him enter the barn through a side door, just as the headlights of the car cut out and I was plunged into darkness. That panicked me even more than the thought of what lay before me.

Unsteadily, I got out of the car and made my way across to the barn. The ground was uneven and an evening frost had hardened the tractor tracks in the earth so that I stumbled as I walked. The sudden chill in the air after the heat of the car left me dizzy while above me the stars seemed to stretch for ever, tumbling away from me constantly, so that I felt as if I was still in the moving vehicle.

Light leaked from the edges of the barn door and I had to push it hard to open it, the hinges having come loose and the bottom grating against the cement floor of the building.

Inside, two men stood – Ward and another man who seemed familiar somehow despite my not recognising him. It struck me that he may have been one of the men who attacked me, but I could not be sure.

They turned when I entered and moved towards the rear of the barn. Not for the first time, I wondered whether the whole thing was a set-up, to kill me. Ward may have collected me in view of the neighbours, but in reality, how many of them would have been looking out at the street at that time of night? How many of them, indeed, would care to take notice?

Yet, I also knew that the worst Ward would do to me was kill me. And that threat held no fear for me anymore.

I followed them then, the cement floor feeling spongy beneath my feet, and I realised my depth perception was off so that the ground seemed slightly further from me than I expected as I took each step.

Towards the back of the barn, stacks of hay bales on each side rose to the rusting rafters of the ceiling. Moving between them, I reached a more open area to the back where the two men now stood and, between them, a figure sat on an old kitchen chair.

He was, perhaps, in his late teens. He wore grey tracksuit bottoms and a white T-shirt, though both were stained with dirt and blood. His hands were bound behind him, a strip of tape across his chest and arms, holding him in place. He bled from a cut over his left eye, the blood seeping down his neck and onto the collar of his T-shirt. His right eye was swollen shut and a bruise stood livid on his jaw. One of his shoes and socks had been removed and I could see a long metal nail had been hammered into the foot. His head hung, seemingly limp, as if he had passed out.

The air was thick with blood and excrement. I felt a flush of acid in my throat and vomited up the wine I'd drunk onto the hay-strewn floor.

'This is him,' Ward said, slapping the youth on the side of the head, rousing him enough to regard me with his open eye. A strip of silver tape had been placed over his mouth. 'This is the scum who stole your girl from you.'

Chapter Forty-Three

'His name is Mark Dean,' Ward said. 'He's a druggie, a thief, a joyrider – anything you can think of, he's involved in it.'

I regarded the youth more closely, in the hope that I might recognise him, that I might have seen him at some stage before, his life and Ellie's intersecting in some significant way. But I did not know him.

'Mark!' Ward shouted, but with no response. 'Mark!' a second time, accompanied by a kick to his shod foot which roused the young man enough that his head lolled round and he blinked up at me.

'I don't know him,' I said.

'You're the better for it,' Ward said. 'He's a dirtbag. Aren't you, Mark?'

'But I don't know him,' I repeated. I'd been sure that I would recognise something in the man that would indicate some meaning to Ellie's death, something understandable. If Mark Dean had killed her, for what purpose? A random act of violence? An accident? The senselessness of it infuriated me.

'He's confessed,' Ward said. 'It took a bit of effort, but he told us the whole story. He stole her bag while she was dancing and she chased after him, into the woods. She caught up with him and he says he panicked. He says he lifted a rock and . . . then he hit her.' Ward glanced sideways at me, then laid a hand on my arm. 'I'm sorry. But you did ask me to find out.'

There was something anticlimactic about it, something unfinished. I don't know what I had expected, but it had not been this. For months, during sleepless nights, I'd created so many versions of what happened, had populated so many of them with Nicola and Adam Ward once I'd seen them, could impose their faces on the demons of those dreams. This now was so completely alien to what I had seen, what I'd imagined.

'I don't believe you,' I said. 'That's not how Ellie died.'

Ward kicked the young man again, causing him to lift his head once more. Blood dripped from his fringe onto his cheek. Ward pulled the tape free from his mouth with a quick, sharp action, causing the youth to wince.

'Mark. Tell this woman what you told me.'

He tried to speak, opening and closing his mouth, but without sound, as if his lungs had failed him.

'Louder, Mark.'

'I took the bag,' he muttered. 'I took the bag.'

'The one that looked like an owl?' I said.

He blinked against the light. I moved closer, squatted next to him and could smell where he had soiled himself at some stage.

'The bag that looked like an owl?' I repeated.

His open eye focused on me a moment, his pupil seeming almost to pulsate in size. He nodded. 'The owl bag. I took it.'

'What then?' I asked.

He didn't speak, his vision seeming to settle on a spot just beyond us, his expression quizzical, as if he'd seen something he did not expect.

'What then?' I repeated.

'I dumped her,' he managed, his eyes not lifting from the spot on the floor. 'I dumped her. I dumped her. I dumped her.' The words began to jumble together and I realised he was crying. 'I dumped her,' he shouted.

'Where?' I asked, desperate now to know, to bring her home.

'Uppa allake,' he mumbled, his head dropping again.

'Where?' I was desperate now, pushing at him with my good hand, trying to rouse him to speak once more. 'Where did you dump her?'

'The lake,' he muttered. 'The lake.'

'Black Lake,' Ward said. 'It must be. There's no other lake around here.'

Black Lake lay up beyond Old Farm Road. At one stage it had been a quarry but that had fallen into disuse and so the lake became a local walk and a place where the younger people went to swim in the summer when the weather improved. It was near where Ward's green car had been found burnt out.

'Dark water,' I said, Kelly's words now making sense to me.

'What?' Ward asked.

'Someone told me Ellie would be found in dark water. They didn't know what it meant.'

'Black Lake? Dark water?' He nodded. 'Who told you that?'

At that, Dean began to cough, a fit so violent, he slumped forward off his seat. Instinctively, I moved to catch him, his head and upper chest falling against my body. He was taped to the chair and would not have fallen anyway, I realised, and in moving to help him, the coat I wore was badged with his blood.

'So, what do you want to do?' Ward asked. 'You have him now.'

I stared at the man, sitting there before me, offered to me.

'I . . . I don't know,' I said. And I didn't. I'd been so long focused on wanting to know what had happened to Ellie, who had taken her, that I hadn't thought about what I wanted to happen next, had not considered what life would look like after that point was reached. 'We should take him to the police.'

Ward shook his head. 'That's not going to happen,' he said. 'I did tell you that when we met. I did you a favour, finding someone the police couldn't. I'm not going to jail for this,' he added, gesturing towards the young man and the injuries he carried.

'They need to find Ellie.'

Ward shrugged. 'I'll have someone call in a tip-off about Black Lake. Though I know they've already searched up there because that's where this arsehole burned out Adam's car after he stole it to move Ellie's body.'

I tried to think about the practicalities of what he was saying, about how likely it was that this boy could move my child, could take a car, could—

'He raped her,' Ward said, refocusing my thoughts instantly. 'I didn't want to tell you, but you deserve the truth. I'd want to know if it was me.'

The comment winded me. 'What?'

'He and his mate. There were two of them there. They went to the cops afterwards and claimed they'd found Ellie's bag, so the cops didn't look at them. They backed up one another's story. But his mate bummed about it to some of his junkie friends.'

'Where is he? Why isn't he here?'

'He overdosed a few nights back. A dirty mix.'

I tried to make sense of all that he had said. I remembered Glenn saying that the person who took Ellie's bag had come forward a few days later, that their friend had corroborated their story that they'd found it. The bag had been dumped on the main road back into town from Black Lake. There was enough of what he said to be true, that could mean it was all true.

'Did you . . .? Did you hurt my girl?' I asked Dean.

His head hung forward and he did not react.

Ward kicked the chair, rousing him once more.

'Mark. Answer the lady. Is all this true?'

His head lolled a little, then he nodded, as if too exhausted to speak.

'Say it,' I said.

Nothing.

'Say it!' I screamed, grabbing his hair and raising his head to look at me. He stared beyond my shoulder, as if at someone standing behind me and I had a thought that Ellie might be there.

'Say it. Say it's true.'

His mouth worked a moment before the words rasped. 'I'm sorry.'

I stared at him, unsure how to react. My anger, my hatred, my frustration, my loss, my grief, my humiliation, all traced back to this man, to his actions. Then, instinctively, I spat on him.

I felt Ward take my hand, and for a second, thought it a gesture of comfort. Then I realised that he was pressing a gun between my fingers, holding it in place there when I automatically tried to let it go.

'This is what you wanted,' he said. 'I told you there would be no going back, no going to the police. The minute you asked me to find him, you started this. You can't unring a bell.'

I looked at the gun: I'd never seen one in real life before at such close proximity. The metal body was dull, a blue sheen catching the light from the fittings above us. The barrel was stubbed, the whole thing smaller than I'd expected. I could see the small, snub noses of the bullets in the chambers of the cylinder.

'I can't,' I said.

Ward shrugged. 'One way or the other, he's not leaving here alive. He took your daughter. He stole from my son and left him in the frame for it.'

I looked again at the gun.

'He raped your daughter,' he said. 'Which means he'll do it again. You can't let that happen. If you couldn't protect your own girl, you can protect someone else's. Take control of this now.'

I looked at the man. Mark Dean. What had I expected? A monster? And yet, what he had done had been monstrous. He had destroyed my life, I realised. My marriage, my family, my life, all in ruins. Because he wanted to steal a bag which might have had £60 in it if even that. And then he took what he wanted and kept taking.

Any sympathy I felt for him was as a result of the condition he was in now at this moment, yet he deserved everything he had got. More, in fact.

And I knew that I had caused this; I had asked Ward to find him, had known what would happen, had wished for it to happen. And now, when I had the chance, the choice, I was debating the rights and wrongs.

I thought of Pandora, my namesake, in that moment, holding open a chest while evil escaped.

I raised the gun in my left hand, which shook as I held it. I tried to steady it with my right, but the cast restricted my movement.

Unbidden, I saw Ellie, her face flashing so vividly in my mind's eye that it almost imposed itself over the scene in front of me. Ellie, who had made a choice with her body of whom she would love. And he had deprived her of that choice. The child, her hand outstretched, the berries unblemished. He had killed her, taken her from me. Her future taken, my future taken.

I felt my finger tighten on the trigger, felt the resistance.

I thought of her hair, cropped short, saw in it now the injury he had caused, the wounding of her perfect features, the theft of her laugh, her light, her smile, her beauty, her kindness, her joy, her sadness, her care, her touch, her love, her life.

'Bastard,' I blurted out, my hand shaking all the more violently now as I squeezed on the trigger, my eyes instinctively shutting.

And in that darkness, I saw her, tearing herself in half, and felt her conflict, felt that fight between duty and desire, between what she wanted and what she felt was the right thing to do. I wanted to touch her, to cup the two halves of her in my hands and hold her back together until the tear healed and she was whole once more.

I felt my hand shudder, tried to pull the trigger but something stopped me, some resistance so strong that I had not the power to overcome it.

I opened my eyes and looked again at Mark Dean, the bleeding crown of his head, the swollen eye, the gashes.

'I can't,' I said. 'I'm sorry.'

I felt Ward take the gun from my outstretched hand and then the room was suddenly alive with the sharp pop of the gunshot, the air heavy with smoke and a smell almost of rotten eggs. Dean's body jerked and then blood began to seep from his temple, dripping onto his trouser leg.

My ears momentarily blocked with the sound and I could hear only a ringing as the barn seemed to still. Then the adrenaline hit me and I felt my arms and legs begin to shudder with the effect. My stomach turned and I was sick yet again.

Ward stood and waited for me to stop. Then he nodded at Dean.

'That's for your girl. That's for Ellie.'

Chapter Forty-Four

The events of the rest of that evening are strangely both incredibly vivid to me and yet feel as though they happened to someone else who relayed them to me, like a false memory.

Ward brought me back out to the car where I broke down and cried to be allowed to go back, cried for Ellie, cried for myself. I begged him to take me to the police, to allow them to take Dean's body, but he refused.

'We're going to get rid of him,' he said. 'He didn't tell you where he put Ellie, so why should he get anything better.'

'His family—'

'His family gave up on him a long time ago. No one is going to miss Mark Dean.'

'I need to tell someone,' I said.

'Why?' Ward asked. 'You wanted revenge for Ellie. You got revenge.'

'Not like this,' I said.

'This is the only way,' he said. 'Do you think the police would have dealt with him? They had him in for questioning and released him. What good is there in telling them now?'

'They might . . . They . . . I don't know,' I admitted.

'I need you to understand,' Ward said, leaning across and gripping my chin in his gloved hand with such force it scared me into listening. 'You did this. I found him for you, because you asked. You brought him to this.'

'I didn't want him dead.'

'You did,' Ward said. 'The moment you asked me, you put that bullet in his head as much as if you'd pulled the trigger yourself. And be clear, if you do go to the police, or feel the need to tell your priest or your best friend or whoever, the gun that shot him has your fingerprints all over it. Your prints, not mine.'

He held up his hand, gloved, for me to see. 'I trusted you enough to bring you here this evening. I need to know that you won't go blabbing about what happened here to anyone. Or Dean won't be the only one who doesn't make it away from this barn.'

'I'll not say anything,' I said.

He dropped me home and I remember nothing else of the night save for the two bottles of wine I took to help me cope. I stripped and washed my clothes in as hot a wash as I could, then showered twice to ensure not a drop of Dean's blood remained on me.

By the time I was finishing the first bottle, I had found the electric clippers I'd used to cut Eamon's hair and sheared off my own as best I could.

At some stage, around three a.m., I think, I found myself in Ellie's room, lying on her bed, weeping as I tried to reclaim once more her scent from the nightdress she'd balled up under the pillow.

I woke at some stage just after dawn and made it to the bathroom, but not the toilet, before I was sick once more.

When the doorbell rang after one the following afternoon, I was still lying on the bathroom floor, having finally fallen asleep there, the hard, cold surface of the lino helping mitigate the spinning of the room I still felt.

I was sure it must be the police. Dean would have been found by now and his killing traced back to me. Truth be told, I didn't mind. I was ready for them; what else did I have?

I was both relieved and disappointed then, when I looked out of the living room window, to see Donal Kelly standing on the step, a bag in his hand.

'Mrs Condron,' he said when I answered, then recoiled a little, perhaps at the state I must have presented.

'I'm tapped out,' I said. 'I've no more money.'

He blushed lightly at the comment. 'Can I come in?' he said.

'You've made a fool of me already,' I said. 'What more do you want?'

He nodded, pushing his glasses onto the bridge of his nose. 'I wanted . . . well, I had to leave at short notice the other day,' he said. 'Something came up at home. So I didn't need your money for the hotel after all. It's in there.'

His comment caught me off guard. I wondered if Glenn had spoken with him. Or if the hotel receptionist had told him I'd called looking for him, even though I'd not given my name.

I took the proffered bag from him and opened it. Inside was a bundle of notes, bound by an elastic band, and a bottle of aftershave, which I took out.

'That's the smell I was picking up in the woods,' he said. 'It took a while, but I found it eventually. I used some of your money to buy that bottle. I've included the receipt in there. I hope that's okay,' he added.

I thought again of what Glenn had said about him. He was an odd type of con man, giving me back my money.

'Did the police speak to you?' I asked, sure Glenn must have gone to him.

'No,' he said. 'Have you said to them about what we felt up at the county line?'

I shook my head. Had I felt something? I couldn't quite recall, though at his suggestion, it seemed to me that I had experienced a closeness with Ellie there. I opened the aftershave bottle and sniffed. There was something instantly familiar about the smell and I found myself wondering if I too, unbeknownst at the time, had smelled it, standing in Rowan Wood. Or since, perhaps? In the barn the previous night? Had I smelt it then? Or was that too a false memory?

'Hugo Boss,' Kelly said. 'There were a few different types, but that's the one.'

'Thank you,' I said.

He nodded. 'You've changed your mind. About me,' he said. 'You think I'm playing you for a fool.'

'No,' I said, though it was pointless, for I had said as much when he arrived.

'That's okay,' he said. 'Belief is like the tide: it comes and goes. But when Ellie is found, and she will be found, there will be dark water. I thought it was a lake or the river at night, but I think she's in a container of some sort; a septic tank, an oil drum, something like that.'

I shivered then, as if his words had connected with

something deep inside of me, something about which I was not even consciously aware, like a divining rod, twitching.

'If I can be of any further help, please do let me know,' he said, turning to leave.

'I'm sorry,' I said, moving out after him. 'The police—'

'The police don't . . . well, they doubt my gift. But they also come to me when they're stuck. I can't make people believe; I can only tell you what I hear and see. And smell,' he added with a forlorn laugh, gesturing towards the after-shave bottle. 'But I wish you peace, Mrs Condron. Ellie wants you to be at peace. She wants you to know that.'

I reached out to him with my free hand. 'Wait,' I said, my throat thick with incipient tears. 'I need to know something.'

He nodded, smiling mildly. 'You want to know why she speaks to me and not you,' he said: a statement, not a question.

The tears began to spill then. 'I go to sleep praying that I'll dream of her, just so I can see her face again, hear her voice. But so often there's nothing.'

'It's not personal,' Kelly said. 'Your love for her is so strong, it drowns out the images she needs you to see. Why does she speak to me? Because I didn't know her, so the images are not clouded by any feelings, any memories, any preconceptions. I receive what she sends to me unfiltered, if you like. Sometimes it takes a little distance to see and hear clearly. Your love is a cloud-gatherer that blocks your vision.'

I nodded, feeling suddenly exhausted by it all, feeling torn in so many directions. I thought of Ellie's portrait and knew now how she felt.

'Well, I hope you find peace,' he said. 'And remember the dark water.'

With that, he turned and left me standing, riven in ways I can still not fully articulate.

Three Years

Chapter Forty-Five

'Time doesn't heal, no matter what people say, but perhaps it allows you to reach an accommodation of sorts with your loss, to carry it with you. And for those of you who are struggling, that is a cause for hope. And we must always try to find hope.'

I looked around the room. We were sitting in a conference room attached to the local library, soft-cushioned metal seats and chipped Formica tables the only furnishings, beyond a whiteboard on a stand positioned in the corner.

I could tell almost instinctively the different stages of grief at which my listeners had arrived. There were one or two who had wept consistently since entering forty minutes earlier, the freshly wounded; there were those who'd remained impassive, arms folded, legs outstretched, the polystyrene cup of tea cooling next to the leg of their seat, who were at the same stage as me by then; and there were those, part way between the two, who nodded with fervour at my comments, smiling mildly perhaps at the hope my words offered, that their pain might, someday soon, be lessened.

Just as I had started speaking, I'd seen someone slip in at the rear of the room and take a seat. I felt sure I knew his face, but could not place him. He was a little older than me, I guessed, tall, thin framed but carrying the soft roundness of a belly. I found myself drawn to him as I spoke and could see him nod at one point, as if in acknowledgement of mutual recognition.

'Look, that'll do us for today,' I said, in conclusion. 'Thanks, everyone, and see you at the next meeting. First Thursday of the month, seven p.m.'

Some left straight away, some lingered to talk. The man who'd arrived late waited a moment, sharing a few words with Mary, the widowed woman beside whom he'd sat, then he stood and came across to me.

'Mrs Condron,' he said. 'I didn't expect you to be here.'

I smiled, struggling to remember who he was and fearing I could not ask his name without appearing rude. His face was as one recalled from a fever dream and I felt sure I'd met him in the time after Ellie had gone missing.

'Philip,' he said, pressing his hand to his chest. 'We met—'

'The art college,' I said. 'You're the security officer there.'

He nodded and smiled mildly. 'That's right. It's been a while.'

'Three years,' I said. 'A little longer, even.'

'And you're doing this now? That's great.'

I nodded, glancing around the empty room, the final stragglers continuing their conversation outside where they could have a smoke as they chatted.

'Once I got myself straightened out a little, I thought it would be helpful, for me and for others.'

'That's great,' he repeated, his hands shifting into his pockets as if he was not sure what else to do with them.

'What about you?'

'I'm still at the college,' he said. 'Keeping busy.'

I'd meant what was he doing at the group. It was an informal grief management session, which I'd started running about six months earlier and which was growing in popularity. Initially, I'd felt a bit of a fraud setting it up but, in ways, it ran itself – everyone sharing their own story, their own experience, and we were learning from each other. I was, at least, not an imposter in my own story.

But I suspected he'd known that I meant the meeting, and he had chosen not to answer. I knew well enough to respect that until he was willing to talk.

'Do you need a hand to lock up?'

'I've just to stack the chairs . . .' I said, then nodded. 'Thank you, that would be great.'

The chairs had been positioned in two loose semicircles, one enclosing the other, the room's relative narrowness meaning having a full circle was impractical. He started lifting chairs at one end of the outer line and I moved from the opposite direction along the inner one, so we met in the middle.

'How are you doing since?' he asked. 'This is such a good idea,' he added before I could answer. 'The group, I mean.'

I shrugged. 'I thought it might help people who were finding things tough. I know I struggled quite a bit after Ellie,' I said, then added with a grim laugh, 'Not that I need to tell you that.'

'It was a hard time for you,' he said.

'And you were very kind,' I replied, remembering now more clearly the different ways in which he had helped me back then.

'It was nothing,' he said. 'Anyone would have done the same.'

'It wasn't nothing to me,' I said. 'And plenty of people didn't, including people I thought I could count on.'

He lowered his head as he moved on past me, stacking the seats.

'How are you doing?'

'I'm okay, I guess,' he said. His presence at the group at all suggested that he had lost someone, though he was working to avoid the subject for now.

'I'm going to get a cup of coffee across the street,' I said. 'Would you like to join me?'

'I best be getting home,' he said. 'I don't want to intrude.'

'You'd not be intruding,' I said. 'But if you're busy that's—'

'No, I'm not busy at all. You know what? That would be nice,' he said. 'Thank you.'

The cafés were closed by that time of the evening, so we went to a wine bar further down the road.

'Would you like something stronger?' Philip asked when we went in. 'Wine?'

'No, thanks,' I said. 'I'm off it. Tea would be perfect.'

After a few minutes he returned with two cups, milk and sugar on a tray and I gave him a hand to place them on the table. He sat opposite me and carefully took a spoonful of sugar, tapping the loaded spoon against the bowl as if to dislodge excess sugar before putting it in his coffee. His movements were mannered, careful.

'So, how are you?' I asked again. 'You're at my group,' I added, as a prompt.

He nodded but did not look at me as he added milk to his cup. 'I lost my wife,' he said, finally.

'My God, I'm so sorry,' I said.

He nodded his thanks. 'It's been over a year now. I thought I was managing okay. People tell you that after the first year it should get easier, but that's not how it's been for me. I saw a poster for the group and thought I'd come to see what it was. It couldn't hurt, after all.'

I shrugged. 'Who knows about grief but those who've lost someone? Had your wife been sick?'

He shook his head, cleared his throat, stirred his coffee.

'I'm sorry,' I said, softly. 'And how are you doing?'

It was his turn to shrug and I apologised.

'I know,' I said. 'It's one of those questions that people ask and you think, if I told you, you'd be sorry you'd ever spoken to me.'

Philip laughed at that. 'That's true,' he said. 'But you're doing okay?'

For a moment I was back in the art college foyer that first morning. The vividness of the memory, the intense anguish of that day, flooded through me and I felt as if I'd shunted suddenly sideways and was sitting next to myself watching this conversation now, this dancing around the reality of our losses for fear of opening wounds.

'The truth is,' I said, 'the wounds are always open, aren't they? They're always raw.'

Philip nodded as if he had been privy to my thoughts and this comment had been the obvious response to an unspoken conversation.

'Things unravelled for me after . . .' I began, then corrected myself. 'Once the police scaled down the investigation. The winter after Ellie went was pretty rough.'

I'd been arrested for assault. How do you tell someone that?

Chapter Forty-Six

In the days after Mark Dean's killing, I'd imagined I would find peace. I did not sleep for several nights but put it down to adrenaline and fear and the expectation that the police would arrive at my door at any moment.

When I was out at the shops, the merest sound of a siren caused me to panic, to abandon shopping baskets in the middle of aisles and run home. I felt everyone knew, that everyone was watching. I recall one morning sitting in the kitchen at breakfast and a bird landed on the windowsill over the sink and stared in through the glass at me. Its head swivelled from side to side, the black beads of its eyes focused on me. In the weeks after Ellie went, such visits would have been welcome, a sign, to me at least, that Ellie was watching over me, making contact with me. But not now.

I remembered taking Ellie to see a movie in the cinema when she was young. Eamon and I had promised to take her over the school holidays. The day we'd planned it, we'd had a row – I don't recall over what – and he refused to go. Ellie and I had gone together anyway and I'd been grateful for the chance to escape the anger of the house for an hour. But once there, I'd started to cry, in the dark of the cinema, and could not stop. Ellie had sat next to me, trying to comfort me, while other children, in rows nearer the front, had laughed at the movie. It had been about a group of birds who were spies during the war. On the way back on the bus, while I'd run through various scenarios that might unfold when we returned home, Ellie had stared out of the window, then turned to me and said, 'What if all birds are really spies? What if they're watching us all the time?'

I'd laughed, not really thinking about what she said. But I thought about it now, with this bird, staring in at me, as if aware of my guilt, watching me.

I'd run to the window and banged on the glass, shooing the bird away. Later that day, I'd gone and bought rat poison and left it lying around the yard, hidden in chunks of bread so that, the following day, the garden was littered with the carcasses of birds.

Looking back at it now, I can see the tricks that paranoia had played on me, yet at the time it had seemed perfectly rational and, even now, I can understand why I reacted as I did.

Within weeks, I'd spread my campaign to the common, a patch of green area at the centre of the estate. One of the neighbours must have worked out what I was doing, and for months afterwards I suspected it was Brenda, for on one such occasion, when I went out in the early dawn to pepper the green with poisoned bread, the police arrived.

I'd not slept and my drinking from the previous evening had continued through the sleepless hours into the morning. I don't recall the series of events, nor do I wish to, but between the police arriving and us all leaving with me in the back of their car, restrained, I still have flashes of conversations and an image of my punching at one of the officers. I remember the smell of the earth, the chill of the frost, the hardness of the frozen ground as they pushed me down to restrain me. I remember faces, almost disembodied and gloating, staring in the windows of the car as we passed.

When I woke later that day, I was lying on a thin blue plastic-covered mattress in a cell. The room was unbelievably hot, the walls tilting and spinning, and I was soaked with sweat. Glenn sat on the raised platform that served as a bench and bed while I lay on the floor where, presumably, I'd thrown the mattress when first I was brought in.

She handed me a bottle of orange juice, chilled and damp with condensation.

'I thought you'd need something to rehydrate you,' she said.

I refused the bottle, staring around me, trying to reconstruct the events that had brought me here.

'Do you remember being arrested?' she said.

'Bits of it,' I managed. I groaned as an image of a young man, his face livid with three bloody streaks from my nails, formed fleetingly in my mind, then vanished.

'I'm sorry to see you like this, Mrs Condron,' she said.

'You can stick your sorry,' I snapped.

'I understand your anger, ma'am,' she said. 'We are still looking for Ellie. We're doing our best.'

'It's too late,' I said. 'You're too late.'

Glenn misunderstood my comment for she nodded. 'We won't be able to bring her home alive,' she said. 'And you don't know how sorry I am that that's the case, but we will do everything we can to bring her back to you so you can lay her to rest. And we will get her killer eventually.'

'No, you won't.'

'We'll do our best.'

'You're too late,' I said again. 'You can forget about it now.'

Glenn frowned quizzically. 'What do you mean, Mrs Condron?'

I shook my head but my brain felt rattled by the movement. My mouth was dry and I regretted not taking the juice but felt I could not do so now, having refused it.

'Why were you putting out poison on the common?'

I knew the question to be a trick. If the birds were spies, the police would know. I said nothing.

'One of your neighbours said you're killing birds in your garden.'

Again, nothing.

'They were concerned when they saw you putting the same stuff out on the common, where the local kids play and where people walk their dogs. Were you trying to hurt someone's child?'

'Why would I hurt a child?' I asked. Mark Dean looked up at me, blood dripping from his hair, his eye swollen closed. I swallowed, tried to see past him, but Glenn appeared as if out of focus.

'Why would you poison animals?' Glenn asked.

I shook my head, more gently this time.

'You assaulted an officer,' she added. 'Do you remember that?'

'Is he okay?'

'He's off getting a tetanus shot,' she said.

'I'm not dirty,' I snapped.

'It's a standard precaution,' she said. 'Besides, you'd been handling rat poison. They found boxes of the stuff in your kitchen.'

'You'd no right to go into my house.'

'They needed to lock up,' Glenn said. 'You'd left your door open while you were out killing the local cats.'

'Birds,' I said.

'Birds,' Glenn repeated.

We sat in silence for a few moments. Glenn offered me the juice once more, wordlessly extending it towards me, and I took it with the slightest nod of thanks and drank it. I instantly regretted doing so.

'What happens now?'

'You need to look for help,' Glenn said. 'None of this behaviour is normal, Dora. We all have sympathy for you here, but you can't keep going like this.'

'I don't want your sympathy,' I said. 'I wanted you to find who killed my child.'

'Do you not want that still?'

'It doesn't matter now,' I said.

Glenn sat forward, her hands on her knees as she looked down at me. 'What have you done, Dora?'

'Nothing.'

'Dora, if you—'

'I'm not your friend,' I said. 'Don't call me Dora.'

'Mrs Condron. If you know something about Ellie or about what happened to her, you need to tell us.'

'What good would it do?'

'It's the law,' she said. 'But it would let us find justice for Ellie.'

'Justice? There is no justice,' I snapped. 'Nothing you do or I do will change what's happened now.'

'I hope that's not true,' Glenn said. 'Or I'd have no reason to do this job.'

'Look in Black Lake,' I said. 'That's where you should be starting.'

Glenn nodded. 'We already have,' she said and, for a moment, I wondered whether Leo Ward had told the police what had happened. 'Donal Kelly contacted us about his "dark water" vision. We dredged the lake, but there was nothing there, I'm afraid. He tells me he returned your money.'

I nodded. 'You were wrong about him.'

Glenn accepted the comment. 'Perhaps. In this case.'

We sat another moment in silence and I could tell Glenn was considering something. Finally, when she spoke, I thought I would be sick.

'Does the name Mark Dean mean anything to you? Mark Dean?'

I did not trust myself to speak and so shook my head, immediately enflaming the dull ache that had settled there. 'Why?' I managed finally.

'No matter,' Glenn said. 'Look, you know we're on your side, Mrs Condron,' she added. 'If things are getting out of control for you, we want to get you help.'

'It's too late,' I said again. 'Just leave me alone now.'

'That's not really going to be your choice,' Glenn said. 'You'll be charged with assault over this morning at the very least, never mind the recklessness of laying out poison in a play area. I suspect you'll have to seek mental health support. Even if you're not required to, I think you need to anyway.'

'My mental health is fine,' I said, but without conviction.

'There's no shame in taking help when it's offered,' she said. 'It can't hurt.'

'Yes, it can,' I said.

Chapter Forty-Seven

Philip returned to a meeting the following month and, again, we found ourselves in the wine bar. I'd not told him about the birds or the arrest, simply that I had struggled mentally after Ellie and had sought help. My previous police caution meant that the police had pressed charges, though perhaps because they did not wish to bring Ellie's mother before the courts at the same time her stepfather was on trial for the images he'd had on the laptop, the agreement was reached that I would undergo counselling. None of this did I tell him. To his mind, I'd simply recovered on my own, and I felt a fraud in his esteem.

I bought the coffee this time and we sat at the window. Since we'd first met, perhaps due to the circumstances of the meeting, he'd called me Mrs Condron, despite the fact I was a few years younger than him. Since he'd started attending the meetings, he called me nothing, and I realised we'd never really been introduced.

'You know, I never knew your full name,' I said, sitting. 'I knew you were Philip from your name badge the first time we met, but that's about it.'

'Brooks,' he said. 'Philip Brooks.'

'Dora,' I said. 'Pandora, actually, but I don't use the full name.'

'Pandora?' he repeated. 'Why not? It's a nice name.'

'You try having people think you were named after someone who unleashed hell onto the world,' I laughed. 'No, thanks.'

'Were you not?'

'No. My dad worked away from home quite a bit. Looking back now, I think it was how my parents' marriage survived, to be honest, because when they were together it was a nightmare. On one trip, apparently, he brought my mum back a piece of jewellery from this company that had opened in Denmark but wasn't here yet – Pandora. My mum thought it sounded really posh and unique so that's what she called me. She knew nothing about the other Pandora and her box.'

'I don't either,' Philip admitted. 'Not much anyway.'

'The gods were angry with the creator of man for giving man fire, so they made a woman for him,' I said, gesturing towards myself. 'And to trick man, they gave Pandora and her husband a wedding gift of a chest they weren't allowed to open.'

'What was the point of that?'

'It's like putting a Wet Paint sign on something. Of course you're going to touch it. Anyway, the story is Pandora couldn't control her curiosity, opened the box and unleashed disease and war and death onto the world.'

'It wasn't really her fault, though, was it?' Philip laughed. 'I mean we've all done it, unleashed hell.'

I laughed with him, but felt weighed down even as I did.

'Absolutely,' I said. 'The gods tricked her, giving her something she had to look in to.'

'So she's to blame for all the bad in the world. Typical woman,' Philip joked, adding, 'I'm kidding of course,' in case I had doubted his intent.

'People forget that the last thing she released was hope, though,' I said. 'Anyway, someone told me the name means "all gifts" but I don't think it suits me.'

'That's not bad,' Philip said. 'My name means horse lover, apparently. There's part of the country where that's a crime!'

I laughed, enjoying the levity of the moment. 'I'd think that's a crime most places,' I said. 'When I was a kid, the others in school called me Banana because I couldn't quite say my own name clearly.'

I thought of Ellie, of the nickname she'd endured, of the way our stories had repeated, as if I had passed it on to her with her birth. The thought caught me unawares.

'Then I changed it to Dora,' I explained, holding the image of Ellie even as I spoke, trying to live with her spectre there, just beyond me. 'Eamon used to take the mick out of me about it.'

'Eamon?'

'My ex-husband,' I said. 'He called me Dora the Dormouse because I was so timid.'

'Timid? You?'

I nodded, a little surprised at his tone.

'You're the least timid person I know,' he said.

'Really?'

'I'll never forget you standing in the middle of traffic, that paint pot in your hand. You were ferocious looking. Sure, look at you now, running this group. You've found so much good to help others out of all your pain. You've found hope in hell.'

I blushed a little at the compliment. 'Thank you,' I said.

'Your ex-husband sounds like a bit of an idiot, though.'

'I'll not argue with you there,' I said. 'What about your wife? What was she called?'

The question seemed to stun him a little and he sat back slightly in his chair.

'I'm sorry,' I said. 'I didn't mean to – it's just, sometimes people are almost afraid to ask about the person who's gone because they're afraid it'll make you think about them, when in fact—'

'You're thinking about them most of the time anyway,' Philip said, nodding. 'You're right. Kate. She was called Kate.'

'What was she like?'

'She was sweet, kind. We didn't have a perfect marriage or anything, but she was a good person. She'd a son when we married, so I always felt a little like a third wheel, but I didn't mind that.'

'I sometimes think Eamon felt that way,' I said. 'I didn't mean for him to.'

'Nor did Kate. Then, when we lost him, she just fell apart.'

'My God,' I said. 'I'm so sorry. What happened?'

Philip shrugged. 'He was a good lad,' he said. 'He got in with the wrong crowd. You'd know all about it,' he added and for the first time, I felt the slow creep of dread stirring in the pit of my stomach.

'Me?'

Philip nodded. 'He got into trouble with Leo Ward and his boy. He owed them money.'

'What was his name?'

'Adam, I think. Nicola was the sister who was friends with your young girl.'

'No,' I said, feeling my throat constrict. 'Your son's name.'

'Mark,' he said. 'He kept his mum's name: Mark Dean.'

Chapter Forty-Eight

I thought I would be sick and had to excuse myself to go to the bathroom. Did he know? Was that why he'd come to the support group? But there was no way he could, not unless Leo Ward had said something. But why would he? He was the one who had actually killed Dean.

I'd missed the search for the youth in the weeks after his disappearance, being in recovery myself. Once or twice since then, despite my best intentions, I'd googled his name and read the news reports online, searching subtext for any hint that the police knew what had happened to him. I'd made myself stop eventually, realising it was like reopening a healing wound. As a result, I'd not read about his mother's death. If I'd read about Philip in any of the stories, the name would not have meant anything to me anyway, before now.

And yet now, out of nowhere, Philip had appeared at my group. It couldn't be a coincidence.

When I went back to the table, he'd ordered two refills.

'I hope you don't mind,' he said.

'I can't really stay,' I said. 'I've an appointment.'

He seemed genuinely crestfallen at the comment and I felt instantly guilty. What was I going home to? My days had become a form of passing time, ticking off hours and days but feeling always as if I was waiting for something. Perhaps this was what I had been waiting for: a final reckoning.

'Maybe I can manage a quick cup,' I said, and sat again.

He smiled so sincerely, I found myself questioning whether it had been a coincidence after all.

'Look, Dora,' he said. 'I want to be honest with you. I did know that you were running the group that first night I came; I wanted to see you.'

I felt my pulse race again, felt suddenly constricted by the table leg, wedged against my chair, making easy escape impossible.

'Why?' I managed.

'Because you know what I'm going through, I suppose,' he said. 'You know what it's like to lose someone and not to find them. To live with that uncertainty.'

'What do you think happened to him?' I asked, realising that having not might appear suspicious.

'He got himself into trouble,' Philip said.

I feigned shock, hoped it was convincing.

'His mother never gave up hope; after he went missing, we were looking everywhere but no one had seen him. Then these eyewitnesses started spotting him in London, Manchester, Glasgow, all over. That was nearly worse: on the one hand you'd the hope he was still alive but on the other, it drove his mother almost mad to think that he'd just left her without saying, that he thought so little of her that he couldn't call. She'd always suffered with her nerves anyway, but that just tipped her over the edge. I came back from work one day and she was lying in the bed . . .' His voice grew thick and he stopped for a moment. 'She'd taken an overdose.'

'I'm so sorry, Philip,' I said. And I was. Whatever the child had done to Ellie, I felt sorry for the suffering his mother had endured, that Philip had endured. Neither of them had deserved it.

I thought my heart was going to burst in my chest, so rapidly was it beating. I could hear the thudding of my pulse in my ears, could feel its beat in my temples. I felt a need to confess, to seek absolution for what I had done.

'Like I say, he was a good lad. He'd got into a bit of trouble now and again, but nothing really bad. But he got into drugs, and that led to debt. And that led to theft. So, by the time he went missing, the cops didn't really care too much. There was a sense he deserved what he got. But he was just a youngster, you know. He was the light of his mother's life.'

I felt my own guilt balloon inside me, but I could not tell him. He took some pride in the fact his stepson had not been that bad: what would it do to him for me to reveal that that same son had killed my child? That he was a rapist, a murderer. It would be like killing him all over, if I killed the memory of him, the *idea* of him, that Philip had created. Or at least, that was what I told myself. I settled myself, tried to steady my breathing.

'So, why did you want to speak to me?'

'This is a little awkward,' Philip said. 'I don't want to bring back up bad memories for you. But Mark was involved with the Wards. He owed them money along with quite a few other people. I'd given him what I could, but he just kept going into debt and then asking his mum for more.

Eventually, I got sick of it. I told him we weren't giving him any more.'

His eyes flushed with tears and I could see how raw the memory was, how ashamed he felt.

'He started stealing from us. First from his mother's purse and then from my wallet. So, eventually, I . . . I threw him out,' he said, finally. 'I thought it was for the best, to make him stand on his own feet.'

'And then he never came back?' I guessed.

He nodded. 'I don't think his mum ever really forgave me,' Philip said. 'After he went, we were never the same again. But I was still blindsided by her death,' he added, and a tear slipped loose and ran down his cheek.

I reached across and laid my hand on his, because I knew how he felt, because I knew that I had caused it and because I knew I could not tell him the truth but needed to do something to let him know he was not alone.

He laid his other hand on top of mine, briefly, then sat back and wiped his eyes. 'I'm sorry,' he said. 'I shouldn't be landing you with this. You have enough to deal with.'

'It's fine,' I said, and wanted to mean it. 'You were there for me on my worst days. It's only fair for me to repay that.'

'It's silly now, when I say it, but I suppose I hoped you might be able to help me,' Philip said. 'Tell me whatever you knew about Ward and his son and Ellie. Anything that might help me find Mark. It's clutching at straws, I know.'

'But sometimes that's all there is to stop from drowning,' I said. 'I know.'

I tried to think as unemotionally as possible. He didn't seem to suspect that I'd had anything to do with his son, yet inevitably if he looked closely enough, he would find me there.

'It won't bring her back,' I said.

'I know. But I thought finding him would be enough to help give Kate some peace. Or at least let me feel like I'd finally done the right thing and brought him back home again.'

It wouldn't. I knew that now. But what could I say? That his son had died a murderer, a rapist? That knowing would make him feel worse, not better?

The last thing Pandora released was hope. How could I steal it from him, along with his son?

Chapter Forty-Nine

The following day, I went down to Madge's to get some things. I was surprised as I came back up the street to see Amy. She'd gone to university the year after Ellie disappeared and I'd not seen her much since. I knew Brenda was still across the street, saw her occasionally in passing, but we had not spoken since the night I was attacked.

Amy saw me and waved across, then walked over the roadway to meet me outside my own house. A young man around the same age as her, whom I took to be her boyfriend, followed behind. She'd aged in a way, her features filled out a little, her confidence built through her experience of being away from home, I suspected.

'Mrs Condron,' she said. 'How are you?'

'You need to call me Dora, love,' I said. 'You're too old to call me Mrs and I'm too young to be called it!'

She laughed, lightly and without affectation. 'This is Robert,' she said, indicating the man, who smiled and extended his hand in greeting.

'Good to meet you,' he said.

'And you,' I said. I returned his smile, then looked to Amy. 'It's lovely to see you, Amy. How's university going?'

'Great,' she said. 'I'm in my final year now. Almost finished. I've been accepted onto a teaching course for next year, then I'll need to start looking for a job.'

'That's brilliant, love,' I said and felt an immediate pang, a remorse for the future that Ellie did not have a chance to live. In another life, she too would be at college. She too would be maturing into as fine a woman as Amy.

'And how's everything across the way?'

Amy rolled her eyes a little. 'Oh, you know. Mum's selling up the house. I'm up today to gather up my things. Robert's giving me a hand shifting my stuff.'

'She's moving?'

Amy nodded. 'Now that Eamon's out, I think she's afraid he'll keep turning up on her doorstep. She's moving to get away from him.'

'Eamon's out?' I'd not known, had assumed the police would tell me when he was due for release.

'I'm sorry,' Amy said. 'I thought you'd know.'

I shook my head. 'Why should I, I suppose?'

Amy nodded, but seemed to regret having come across to me. 'I didn't mean to upset you,' she said. 'I thought maybe you'd have heard.'

'You're not upsetting me, love,' I said, and placed my hand on her arm. 'How's your dad doing?'

'You know what? He's great. He'd a tough run of it after everything but he's out the other side and he's happy.'

'I'm delighted to hear it,' I said. 'I mean it. Your dad deserves every happiness. As do you, love.'

Amy smiled. 'Look, I best get back. I just wanted to say hello. See how things are.'

'Things are okay,' I said. 'I'm getting there.'

She smiled once more and then embraced me. She did not feel like Ellie in my arms anymore, did not remind me of her, but rather of what she might have been. But even then, that was not quite right, for Amy had a scent and shape and a future all of her own.

That evening, I found myself wondering how things might have turned out for Ellie. Would she have gone to university too? Would she have become a teacher? An artist? Who would she have ended up dating?

It seemed so unfair to me that there was a life unlived, a future unfulfilled for Ellie. I didn't begrudge Amy a moment of happiness – far from it, for she was a great girl – but I did resent the fates that had decided Ellie would not get a chance to do the same.

And I mourned once more all the future moments, milestones, that I might have marked with her and which I too had lost when she was taken from me.

Chapter Fifty

Despite my intentions to the opposite, Philip and I saw more of each other over the following weeks. He'd asked for my number that evening and I could think of no good reason not to give it to him that would not insult him. Whatever his son had done, he was a different man and was no more responsible for Mark Dean's actions than I had been for Eamon's behaviour.

He called me the day after I'd spoken with Amy and asked if I wanted to go for a walk. We met at the football pitches and did several laps of the surrounding pathway.

'I wanted to say sorry about the other night,' Philip began. 'I didn't mean to bring things up for you. It wasn't fair.'

'It's fine,' I said. 'I didn't mind.'

The truth was, it had reopened that part of my life, forced me to look at it again. I'd dreamed about Mark Dean. In the dream, I'd been watching as Ward shot him. Dean had stared at me, his last look frozen long after the shot had fired, a look of accusation, of recognition. But his face was not his own, but Philip's, and more than accusation or recognition, there was disappointment.

'I'd wanted to come to your group for a while,' he said. 'To speak to you about it, but, to be honest, I was ashamed.'

'Ashamed?'

He nodded, not looking at me. 'I've not been totally honest with you,' he said, and I felt both dread at what he was about to say and a degree of relief that his seeming dishonesty might mitigate my own and leave us even. 'Mark was at the forest the night your Ellie vanished.'

I swallowed, dryly, working hard to remain impassive.

'I think he might have stolen her bag.'

I feigned surprise. 'Really?'

Philip nodded, still keeping his head bowed a little as we walked. 'He came home that evening with more money than he'd left with. Kate was tidying his room the next day and lifted his trousers for washing. She found it in his pocket. We were keeping an eye on him; he'd been in trouble before and we were trying to keep him away from drugs and that. When she found the money, we questioned him about it and he said he found it. Then, when the story about your daughter appeared on the news with the description of her, he confessed to me that he'd found her bag and taken the money from it. I didn't believe him, of course, always expecting the worst. One of his mates told me the next day they'd found it in the woods as they were leaving and had dumped it in a bin along the road home. I'm sorry.'

'He stole her bag,' I said. 'Was that all he said?'

He looked at me now. 'Yes. He said they didn't know who she was or where to find her so figured they could keep it. I think he only told us because he was afraid they'd find his prints or something on the bag and get the wrong idea. He'd probably never have said anything otherwise. I made him go to the police to tell them where he found it and where he left it afterwards, in case it held up the search or misdirected them or something. In fairness to him, he held his hand up and admitted taking the money.'

I remembered Glenn had said the boy who took the bag had been brought in by his father. I also knew, though, that Mark Dean had done more than find Ellie's bag and while Philip was trying to be honest with me, I could not reciprocate, for to do so would be to shatter whatever little pride he had taken in his stepson for confessing to theft.

'Your wife didn't notice anything else about his clothes? No blood?'

He looked at me, aghast, as he realised the implication in what I had asked.

'God, no,' he said. 'Nothing like that. Mark was troubled, but he wasn't violent. We'd have known. His mother would have known.'

Perhaps, but I wondered whether she would have covered for him, even if she had found blood. Admitting to taking the bag might have been sufficient to keep the police off his back, the assumption that such honesty made him trustworthy. Would I have lied for my child? Covered for them when I found evidence of something they had done and could not undo? I thought that I might. If his wife had loved her son so deeply that she could not live without him, might she have covered up for him in that? And what did it mean that she could not live without her child, but I was still alive?

I found my thoughts spiralling downward as I considered whether her death had been a form of unwitting rebuke to my surviving. I had survived to find the truth about Ellie, I told myself. But, if I believed that I had already found that truth back when Leo Ward killed Mark Dean, then what now? Why was I still here? Did a part of me harbour the suspicion that perhaps Dean had not been responsible? No – to face that would require accepting that I had allowed an innocent child to die, had killed Philip's wife with my actions, had devastated his life despite his showing me nothing but kindness. I could not think that way, could not allow myself to follow that train of thought any further.

'Are you okay?' Philip asked and I realised I'd not spoken for some stretch. 'I'm so sorry. I should have been straight with you from the start.'

'It's okay,' I said. 'You did the right thing.'

'I just . . . I felt so guilty at the time that maybe what he'd done meant you'd not got your daughter back. I couldn't imagine then what that would be like, the not knowing what happened, the never knowing. I couldn't get my head around it. But now I do. I suppose there's some sort of justice in that. Kate couldn't take it, though – the uncertainty.'

I glanced at him then, wondering if he *knew*. What did he have to feel guilty about in comparison with what I knew, what I had done?

'I let her down,' he said. 'I let Kate down.'

'No, you didn't,' I said, but he shook his head.

'She told me that herself,' he said. '"Remember that poor woman, her out stopping traffic to find her child, and what are you doing?" she'd said. She thought you were a hero.'

I blushed. 'Stopping traffic wasn't my finest moment,' I said.

'Are you kidding? I thought you were so brave, facing down the Wards. The rest of the town was afraid of them and there you were, like a warrior. I wished I was that brave, but I couldn't be. And I knew that, secretly, Kate was disappointed in me.'

I felt sick then, realising that just as I had taken his honesty, his decency, as an unwitting rebuke for what I had done, his wife's death as a rebuke for my survival, he had taken my slow breakdown after Ellie went as a rebuke of his lack of one.

'I'm sorry, Philip,' I said. 'I didn't see myself as a warrior. I was just desperate and had no one else to turn to. If my husband had been half the man I thought he was, I'd not have done any of that.'

'But you were right,' he said. 'You've managed to find some peace despite not finding Ellie.'

In the weeks after I spoke with Glenn, when she'd warned me that I would have to accept help or face charges, I was removed from Black Lake twice.

I'd tried to dry out on my own, dumping all the wine in the house and telling myself I would not buy any more. I managed for three days before the agitation that shivered through me grew so intense that I could not stop myself from running to Madge's and buying two bottles. I savoured the first glass, telling myself I could control it, could make one glass suffice for the evening. Opening the second bottle, about an hour later, I called a taxi and was dropped off at the lake. I'd imagined being close to the place would bring me closer to Ellie. Glenn had refused to dredge the lake once more, it having already been searched. I told myself that the lake itself would become a sort of grave, somewhere for me to go and sit and be close to Ellie's resting place. And so I'd sat beside it, drinking the second bottle, convincing myself that I felt comfort in the place, in the proximity to Ellie. But I did not feel it, did not get a sense of her nearness.

I got the idea then, sitting there, that she had become one with the water, that she had dissolved into it and become part of it, that to be close to her, I needed to join with her, let the water touch my skin, become part of me and me a part of it, that it would be some form of communion between us both. I took off my trainers and socks and jeans and walked into the lake, standing waist deep, baptising myself with the blessed water of my child.

And for a moment, I told myself that I felt her close to me.

A man walking his dog rounded the bend in the lake and shouted to me. It was cold, the water chilled, the winter sky heavy above us and thick with coming sleet. The air was still and grey and I tried to pretend that I had vanished, dissolved into the water with Ellie.

But he saw me, called to me and, when I would not come out, came into the water after me to help me out, thinking me stuck.

Ashamed and half angry at his intrusion, I allowed him to lead me out, took my clothes and accepted the offer of a taxi fare home.

That evening, I sat in Ellie's room, trying to feel that closeness which I'd felt in the lake. I was shivering, the chill of the water only then registering as I sobered a little and the headache bloomed behind my eyes.

I cuddled Leo to me, tried to find Ellie's scent from him, but it was beyond my grasp now. On the wall were pictures and postcards that had meant something to her: a child's face, disfigured on one side; a woman on a boat. Among them an image stood out now: a painting of a woman lying in water, her hands outstretched, flowers around her as she floated. *Ophelia*, it was called. I remembered her story from one of the classes I'd sat in on when I was still working, remembered she'd lain in the water until her clothes had weighed her down.

The next morning, I went to Madge's early and bought a few bottles, then took the bus out to Old Farm Road and walked up to the lake. There, I drank to my lost child, spoke to her, told her how I missed her, what I had done to try to find her, what I had seen done on her behalf. Then, when the act no longer held any fear for me, I walked into the water. I lay down in it as Ophelia had done and waited for my clothes to soak up the lake water and pull me under.

It was not an attempt to die; I can see that now. I wanted to be close to Ellie, to feel her with me, in me, once more, as once she had been. I stared at the sky, felt the cold numb my body to the point that chill became heat, the sounds of the quarry dulled by the water in my ears. It was a moment of peace.

Then I heard a thrashing, felt someone grab at me. I fought back, trying to get them to leave me, trying to push them from me. Only when I was pulled out did I realise that it was a group of teenagers, taking a day off school, who'd seen me and come in after me.

I watched as two of them tried to resuscitate the friend who'd been the one to jump in to save me. I watched him vomit dirty water onto the ground, felt the relief flood me as his ragged breaths tore at the silence.

When the ambulance arrived, they contacted the police.

They gave me no choice.

They saved me.

For what?

Chapter Fifty-One

I did not feel comfortable yet inviting Philip back to the house so, at the end of our walk, we parted company at the car park with the promise that we would meet again soon. I thanked him too for his honesty; I could tell how difficult it had been for him to admit that his son had taken Ellie's bag and, in different circumstances, I might have been more shocked by the admission. But I knew all about his son already, knew all that he had done.

I was walking back up to the house when I saw a car drive past me on its way up the street. I was almost certain that the face which peered out at me as it passed was Eamon's. Sure enough, he was parked outside the house by the time I arrived.

I took my time unlocking the door, not wanting him to see that I was flustered, disguising the shake in my hand as I struggled to fit the key in the lock. I heard the car door slam shut as I opened the house door and knew he'd be in before I could close it.

He'd changed since last I'd seen him. I knew he'd been sentenced to three years, though half on licence, so I suspected he'd only recently been released. He was a little heavier than I remembered, carrying most of it around his waist.

'Dora,' he said as I turned at the door.

He waited on the pathway, as if sharing my uncertainty at what we should do next.

'You may come in,' I said.

We sat in the kitchen and I made tea. I could see him taking in the room, as if checking whether I'd changed anything in his absence.

'How was it?' I asked, setting out two mugs on the table and turning again to get milk and sugar.

'Inside? It was what you'd expect.'

'I'm not sure what I expect,' I said.

'Boring, mostly,' he said. 'After the initial few months. Passing time that never seems to pass. Occupying yourself with TV and books. Trying to find something to give the day purpose.'

'Sounds like life here, too.'

'You were welcome to swap places anytime,' he said. 'We were segregated from the others.'

'We' I took to mean sex offenders. 'For your safety or theirs?'

'People don't treat you well when you're accused of being a nonce.'

'You weren't accused,' I said.

He took a second, smiled, bit back on whatever he wanted to say.

'I see you moved on with your life,' he said instead.

'Moved on?'

'A new man on the scene. How long has that been going on?'

I guessed he must have been watching us down at the football pitch track, for it was not visible from the roadway.

'Were you following me?'

'I spotted the two of you,' he said, affecting nonchalance.

'He's a friend. He lost his son around the same time I lost Ellie.'

'We. We lost her.'

'She was never yours to lose, Eamon. You made sure of that when you started spying on her.'

Again, I got a sense that he was holding back, and I realised I was antagonising him. I assumed a condition of his release was that he was to avoid any further contact with the police. Perhaps he was afraid I'd report him if he lost his temper.

'I'm glad you're seeing someone else,' he said.

'I'm not—'

He held up a hand to silence me. 'I don't care,' he said. 'Our marriage was done long before you had me put away. It took the stretch for me to see it clearly, but it's true.'

In spite of how I felt about it, it pained me to hear him say it. I had thought we were doing okay. In retrospect I could see that I had not been particularly happy with Eamon in the end, but nor had I been so unhappy as to do anything about it. Besides, everything that had happened since had put it into perspective.

'Why are you here, then?' I asked.

'I want a divorce.'

Something in me was saddened by the request, even as I had expected it, indeed would have sought one myself once

I knew he was out again. Still, leaving seemed easier than being left, allowing the perception of choice.

'That's fine,' I said. 'I agree.'

'It will have certain implications,' he said.

'Like what?'

He gestured around him. 'We both own this house. I need to sell my half of it.'

The comment shocked me. I'd not considered for a second that my house might be at risk, partly because, once Eamon went inside, I became secure in it, in its safety, in its memories. In the absence of a grave, this had become Ellie's mausoleum.

'I don't know if I have the money to buy it off you,' I said.

He shrugged. 'That's not my problem, Dora.'

'You can't throw me out on the street. This was Ellie's house. This was the last place I saw her.'

He presented his two hands, palms upwards, towards me, a benign smile on his face. 'Again, that's not my problem. Until I can get a job, I need to find somewhere to live. Do you want me moving back in here?'

'No.'

'Well, then,' he said. 'I need the equity on this place to buy somewhere of my own. Ask your new boyfriend to buy somewhere for you.'

'He's not my boyfriend.'

'Well, get on your back and you never know your luck. That's what you did with me.'

I ignored the remark. 'I can't sell up, Eamon,' I said. 'Please. I need to stay here.'

He shook his head. 'Fuck him like you fucked me,' he seethed. 'And did you ever fuck me, handing that laptop over to the cops!'

The mood of the room had suddenly darkened. I was aware of every sound, the drip and hiss of the water in the kettle, the sounds of the cars in the roadway beyond, the shout of a child on the common. I felt myself tense, felt my grip tighten on my mug.

'I didn't ask you to look at those pictures,' I said.

'All those mornings when you pretended you were asleep. All those nights going to bed early to avoid doing what a wife is meant to do. What did you think would happen?'

'Don't blame me for what you did,' I said. 'They were children.'

'They weren't children,' he snapped. 'They were old enough.'

'You're a pig,' I said.

Before I could react, he threw his cup of tea over me. I had barely time to react when he was out of his seat, lurching over me where I sat, his face inches from mine, his lips flecked with spit.

'Watch your mouth,' he said.

Slowly, I took from my pocket the small peeling knife I'd lifted from the kitchen drawer when making tea for us both and pressed it into the soft swell of skin beneath his chin.

'Get back from me,' I said, standing now and, in the movement, forcing him to have to back away from me as I adjusted my grip. I could see the shock, his eyes wide and staring. Finally, I relieved the pressure and stepped away from him, leaving a little distance in case he reacted. 'And get out of my house.'

I could tell he didn't know what to do. 'You're a nutcase,' he said. 'I heard you'd cracked up, had to be pulled out of the quarry.'

'Get out, Eamon,' I managed.

He pulled his coat from the back of the chair where he'd been sitting. 'I'm not done with the house, Dora. I need my half of it. If you want to buy it, that's fine. But I've no job now because of you landing me in it, so I need the money.'

'I'll be waiting for you whatever time you come back,' I said, indicating the knife I still held.

'A fucking nutcase,' he repeated as he turned and left the kitchen.

'I'm no dormouse anymore,' I called after him.

Only when I heard the slam of the front door did I allow myself to relax a little.

Chapter Fifty-Two

All evening, I thought about Philip. I enjoyed his company, despite the fact that the thing that united us most was loss. And I respected his honesty with me, particularly in telling me about his son. A suspicion that he knew what had happened to his son and was playing me, to see whether I would confess, had been building since that first evening, but I tried to ignore it. In all my dealings with him, since first Ellie went missing, he had been decent and had treated me with kindness. I felt an urge to repay that in kind.

I convinced myself that I was not telling him the truth about what had happened because to do so would involve telling him the truth about his son, a truth I felt he would rather not know. But I could, I decided, try to find his son for him, so that he might find some peace.

There was only one person who could help me with that.

I'd seen, in the local press, a story the year before. I was still attending sessions with my doctor by that stage, though not with the same frequency or intensity as after the incident at Black Lake. On her advice, and partly because of the medication I was taking, I'd stopped drinking. What I'd done at Black Lake had put other people at risk, had put children at risk. It was not right.

I'd decided to walk down to Madge's and to tell her that I was staying sober. I knew that, if I decided on impulse to drink, I would go to Madge's shop to buy alcohol. I hoped that, by explaining my intention to stay sober, she would refuse to serve me when or if that time came. I'd worked there and Madge knew me; I'd no concerns about sharing this with her.

She brought me into the back of the shop and made us both tea while we chatted. It was quiet and the entrance to the storeroom was right behind the counter so that, if she saw a customer come in on the CCTV display, she could step out to serve them. It was the first time I'd spoken to Madge, properly, in some time, and I'd been enjoying the normalcy of the conversation as I built to make my request.

During one moment, when a customer came in and Madge went to serve them, I distracted myself by flicking through a copy of the local paper, which Madge had been reading earlier. On page five there was a story about a new club opening in the city. A single image dominated the story: the new owner, holding a bottle of champagne, as if presenting it to the camera. I recognised him immediately, the trim frame, the greying hair, the beard.

In that moment, I felt dread begin to flame in the pit of my stomach. I felt lightheaded and could not catch my breath. The air in the room was suddenly metallic with the smell of blood, the mouldiness of straw, the sweetness of aftershave. I breathed through my mouth to avoid smelling it and felt like I was gasping. My hands felt sticky and when I looked at them, although I could see they were clean, I had an overwhelming sensation that they were badged with blood, my fingers tacky as I rubbed one hand against the other. Unbidden, I saw flashes of Mark Dean, his head hanging low, bound to the chair opposite me.

I'd not had such an experience before, that sense of the past overlaying the present, so I was left for some time afterwards uncertain which was which. I had the most aggressive headache, a pain that throbbed in my temple and made me want to cry out.

When Madge returned, I made my excuses, telling her I wasn't well, and rushed home, checking constantly to see if Mark Dean was following me along the pavement, even as I knew how absurd that thought was.

My doctor explained to me later that I'd suffered a flashback. I told her some of the detail, though left out the part about Mark Dean and the blood and instead told her I had seen Ellie. She asked if anything in particular had triggered it. I'd lied, and said no, but I knew it had been seeing Leo Ward again.

I thought of that story then because it meant that I knew now where to find Ward: his new club. I hoped that, *choosing* to see him now rather than doing so unprepared as had been the case then, I would not have a repeat experience of the flashback.

It had been a while since I'd been in a club; Eamon and I stopped going soon after we married, Eamon reasoning that the only reason a man goes to a club is to get a woman and, now having one, there was no further point in going. He couldn't understand that I just wanted to dance, told me that he didn't like other men watching me when I did, didn't like how I paraded myself around in front of them. In my naivety, I'd taken his jealousy as a compliment of sorts rather than control. And so, we'd stopped clubbing. I couldn't even remember the last time I'd danced.

Now, the club was a very different experience during the day. What in my memory had been exciting and full of promise at night was, in daylight, tawdry and a little mechanical.

I'd come in through a single open door to the side of the club, through which a delivery man was moving back and forth carrying crates of drinks. Once inside, I'd followed the corridor past various office doors, before finally making my way out into the main bar area. There, a young man was standing behind the bar, working at the till. It took me a moment to recognise him; the last time I'd seen him had been as he'd driven past me, his car covered in paint.

'You're Adam,' I said. 'Can I see your father?'

At the sound of my voice he looked up in shock, having clearly not heard me coming in. He stared at me a moment, then his expression changed as he worked out how he knew me. He swallowed, stuttering before he spoke. 'You . . . you're not meant to be in here.'

'But I am,' I said. 'I need to see your father.'

'He's not . . .' He lifted the phone behind the bar and waited. He stared at me the whole time, his mouth slightly open, his chest heaving. I recognised his response, knew it to be fear. 'Dad,' he said. 'Come down here . . . Come down here. There's someone here.'

He hung up, clumsily, the receiver clattering off the hook and he had to bend to lift it, all the time trying not to take his eyes off me.

'You knew my daughter,' I said. 'Isn't that right?'

'You're not meant to . . . You're . . .' He looked wildly from me towards a door set into the wall to my right through which, I assumed, he was hoping his father might appear.

'I'm not meant to what?' I asked. 'Talk to you?'

'I knew her,' he said, then. 'I . . . She was a friend of Nicki's.'

'How is Nicki?'

'Nicki?' he asked and even from where I was standing, I could see his expression change. 'Nicki's—'

The door opposite opened and Ward stepped out. As soon as he saw me, he stopped. 'What are you doing here?'

'I wanted to speak to you.'

'I've nothing to say to you,' he said, turning to leave.

'We both know that's not true,' I said. 'I just need to talk.'

He paused then, looking first at me, then at his son. 'You okay, Adam?'

The young man nodded.

'Come on then,' he said, presumably to me.

He led me up to his office, an enclosed room upstairs without an external window. It did have a mirrored one which overlooked the bar below and provided part of a view of the dance floor, though I noted he could not have seen where I had stood.

'What is it?' he asked, turning and leaning against his desk and leaving me standing.

'I need to ask a favour.'

'*You* want to ask me a favour?'

I nodded. 'I want to know where Mark Dean is buried.'

Ward visibly tensed at the mention of the youth's name. He regarded me coolly, then raised his chin a little as he gestured towards me. 'Are you wearing a wire or something?'

'A wire?'

'If you're recording this, it's entrapment.'

I didn't fully understand what he was saying, though guessed he thought I was there on behalf of the police.

'After all, if the gun that killed him ever turned up, I suspect your fingerprints would be all over it.'

'I know that,' I said, staying calm despite myself. 'I'm not trying to trap you. I want him returned to his father.'

'Philip Brooks?'

I nodded. 'You know him?'

'You started something,' Ward said. 'When Mark went missing, he arrived at my door, looking to find out if I knew where he was.'

'You didn't tell him,' I said.

'I'm not stupid,' Ward said. 'Dean was in debt to so many people, the list looking to kill him was as long as your arm.'

'Why would you kill someone who owed you money?' I asked. 'Surely better for them to be alive and able to repay it.'

Ward shrugged. 'Either way, I can't tell you where he is,' he said. 'If he's found, they'll be able to trace him back to one of us.'

'I want him to know where his son is,' I said.

'Well, he's not going to,' Ward snapped. 'I'm not putting myself in jail, no matter what kind of death wish you have going.'

'Where's your daughter?' I asked. 'Nicki?'

Ward's expression changed again, hardening further. 'What?'

'Adam was about to say something downstairs, about Nicki.'

'Don't talk about them as if you know them.'

'Where's your daughter?'

'She's in Australia, with her mother, if you must know.'

'Why?'

'Because of people like you,' Ward snapped. 'It's none of your business why. You'd have been better minding your own daughter instead of worrying about mine.'

The comment was unnecessarily cruel and unwarranted in the circumstances and I wondered why he was so riled by me to lash out the way he did.

'The man lost his wife and his son,' I said. 'He needs peace. Finding his son might bring him that.'

'We've all lost people,' Ward snapped. 'You just have to get on with it. Suck it up and move on. If he can't do that, maybe he should just top himself and be done with it.'

'He's a good man.'

'We're all good people,' Ward said.

'We're not,' I said. 'Not after what we did to Mark Dean.'

'Are you looking to confess?' Ward asked, leaning forward now. 'Is that what this is? A guilty conscience?'

'If I'd known how it would end up, I'd never have asked you to find him,' I said. 'I didn't mean for anyone else to get hurt.'

'Bullshit. You knew exactly what you were asking. You wanted someone to pay for your kid. I don't even think it mattered to you who they were, so long as someone paid. You can't go back now.'

'I'm not looking to go back. We've hurt that man in ways he doesn't deserve. I caused that by what I started. I want to bring him some peace too – some hope.'

'Well, you can't,' Ward said. 'And before that change of heart sends you running to the police, remember it's your prints all over the gun that killed him.'

'I'm not afraid of the police,' I said. 'Jail would be no different from the life I'm living now anyway.'

'There are worse things than jail.'

'You think I'm afraid of dying?' I laughed. 'The chance to see Ellie again? It wouldn't cause me a second thought. I've nothing left that I'd be afraid of leaving.'

'No one mentioned killing *you*.'

It took me a second to thread out the implication in what he said.

'Philip?'

'We've all lost things, but we've also all got something we don't want to lose, too,' Ward said. 'You need to remember that.'

He stood then, moved behind his desk and dropped heavily into his chair. 'You can find your own way back out,' he said. 'And if I see you again, or I hear you're still asking questions about things that should be dropped, I will kill you.'

I suspected he planned to kill me anyway, even if I never bothered him again. I believe that now.

Chapter Fifty-Three

I found myself on edge that evening, wary of every car that passed, every creak and groan of the house. I wondered when Ward would send someone to deal with me, knew he would not do it himself.

As I lay in bed, almost on the cusp of sleep, I felt my stomach seem to twist all of a sudden, smelt again, as if on a breeze, the ferric scent of blood. I had the thought, which I could not shake, that my hands were bloody once more. I could feel the sensation, building, beginning to layer itself over my reality. I got out of bed and went into Ellie's room.

My doctor had taught me a technique she'd called grounding, where I had to take something that connected to my sense of reality, something that was physically distinct from the memory which was imposing itself, so that I might be able to maintain my sense of the present moment. My first thought was of Leo, Ellie's teddy. I hugged him into me as I climbed into her bed, between the sheets, no longer wanting it to be a museum piece, but wishing to be with her, to know that some infinitesimal part of her was pressed against me where I lay.

I woke around eight, feeling at ease in a way I could not fully explain.

* * *

During breakfast, I glanced out of the kitchen window to see someone standing at the rear of the house. My immediate instinct was that it was someone Ward had sent, and I felt both a growing panic and a sense of acceptance simultaneously. I went to the drawer and took out the small knife with which I had threatened Eamon and put it in my dressing-gown pocket. Then I banged on the window.

The man was dressed in a suit and was taking pictures of the rear of the house on his phone. He looked up and acknowledged me with a wave when he heard my knocking.

'Can I help you?' I called, opening the window.

'Sorry,' he said. 'I thought the house was empty,' he added, as if this explained his behaviour. 'Your husband asked us to value the property for you.'

'What?'

'I'm with Greene's Estate Agents,' he said. 'Your husband said you were looking to sell. I'm just doing a quick look around to give you a price.'

'I'm not selling,' I said. 'And he's not my husband.'

I closed the window and sat again, but when I looked out a moment or two later, he was still there, at the front of the house now, taking his pictures.

Philip had invited me to join him for a walk that day so I'd showered and got changed in preparation for it. The truth was, I was looking forward to spending the day with him. Our conversations had moved on a little from our shared experiences of grief, but even when they didn't move beyond that, there was comfort in sharing it with someone who understood. I knew I should have felt nothing but guilt at the way in which I was deceiving him, but I genuinely believed I was protecting him from the truth that he would not want to know.

I was sitting in the living room, waiting for him to arrive, when a car pulled up outside and Glenn got out.

I wondered if perhaps Ward had contacted her, made a complaint about my being at his club, though I could see no good reason why he would have done so. It was in his best interests to keep the police as far away from what connected us as possible.

I went out and opened the door to meet her. She stalled a second when she saw me, then smiled grimly and nodded. 'Mrs Condron. Can I come in?'

I could tell from her whole demeanour that something was wrong, and I could feel my own panic beginning to stir.

'What's happened?' I asked, stepping back as an invitation for her to come in.

'It's best if we talk inside,' she said, and I had that sense of déjà vu, of all those times before she'd uttered that line, moving past me and into the living room even as I followed her. She stood at the fireplace and waited until I had taken a seat on the sofa. I knew the routine now. Or so I thought.

The room felt suddenly close and stuffy, the seat on which I sat too soft to support me. I had a sensation of falling and felt like I was going to be sick.

'What is it?' I asked.

Glenn looked at me. 'We took a call yesterday afternoon,' she began. 'Regarding the possible location of human remains. A team was tasked with investigating. About an hour ago, they found those remains.'

'What?' My head was spinning, the formality of her language obscuring her meaning for me in that moment. I reached out and gripped the arm of the sofa to steady myself.

'We've found a body,' she said.

Chapter Fifty-Four

'Is it Ellie?' I asked, for I wondered, in light of my visit to Ward, whether he might have had second thoughts and told them where Mark Dean was buried.

Glenn nodded, grimly. 'It's a little early to tell,' she said, 'but we believe it might be. We need to source her dental records. Can you tell me who her dentist was?'

'The practice on Main Street,' I said.

Glenn nodded her thanks. 'I don't know much at the moment, but I thought you should be told before the media start reporting it. Is there anything you'd like to ask me?'

There was a knock at the door, three light taps. I went out and answered it. Philip stood at the step.

'Have you visitors?' he asked, nodding towards the car. 'I can come later.'

In that moment, I wanted him there, wanted the company of someone who would understand the conflict of emotions I was feeling; relief and gratitude, sadness with anger that it had taken so long to find her, hope that it was her and her long journey home was complete.

'It's the police,' I said. 'They think they've found Ellie. Come in.'

'I shouldn't,' he said, the pain in his own eyes evident. 'This is private.'

'I'd like you to,' I said. 'But I'd understand if—'

He stepped up and placed his hand on my back. 'I'm here with you,' he said, then followed me into the living room.

Glenn looked surprised to see him. 'Mr Brooks,' she said when he came in, looking at me quizzically.

'Sergeant,' he said, and for the first time I guessed that Glenn must have been promoted in the time since first I met her. 'That's good news, eh, Dora?' he said, sitting next to me. 'But sad, too.'

I nodded. 'How did she . . .?'

Glenn shrugged. 'We don't know yet,' she said. 'We'll have to run tox tests to see if that shows anything. At the moment there's no obvious cause of death.'

'What about her skull?' I asked, surprised by her comment into saying more than I intended. 'Is it not damaged?'

Glenn shook her head. 'Not that I could see. Why?'

I was aware of Philip looking at me and I could not explain why I had asked the question. Mark Dean had said he struck her on the head with a rock. That would surely have caused damage to her skull.

'It might not be her,' I said.

Glenn nodded. 'It might not. But, based on the state of the remains, the stage of decomposition, and the physical description we had of Ellie, you need to prepare yourself for the very high likelihood that it is your daughter, Mrs Condron. I'm sorry.'

I struggled to reconcile my varying thoughts. I longed for it to be Ellie even as I desperately hoped that it would not be for that would end, once and for all, my nocturnal fantasy that she was alive and happy somewhere. But if it was her, and her skull had not been damaged, why did Dean say that he had struck her?

And as I replayed my memories of that evening, it struck me for the first time that Dean had not admitted it to me. It was Ward who had told me that Dean had said that. Dean had simply nodded his agreement.

'Where did you find her?' Philip asked, perhaps believing me too shocked to be able to ask for myself and having missed Glenn already tell me.

'Rowan Wood.'

'Where?' I asked. I'd assumed she'd been recovered from Black Lake and had not thought to ask.

'Rowan Wood,' Glenn said, nodding, as if she was confirming a long-held suspicion for me.

'Wasn't that searched when she went missing?' Philip asked.

Glenn nodded. 'We searched huge areas of it. But it is over five hundred acres of woodland. The area where we recovered the remains today is in the next county, some distance from where we think Ellie went missing.'

How could it have been Rowan Wood? Dean had said she was in Black Lake.

'How would they have taken her there?'

'It's too long to walk, especially carrying remains,' Glenn said. 'We assume she must have been transported in a vehicle of some sort. The area where the remains were located is near the A5.'

Near where her bag was found, near where the Old Farm Road meets the A5, where Adam Ward's stolen car was found. The location could still mean Mark Dean had been involved. But the absence of wounding to the head still worried me. Perhaps it had damaged her brain, but not her skull, I told myself. Perhaps it wasn't her at all. That would make more sense. It wasn't her; the police were wrong.

'Can I see her?'

Glenn looked from Philip to me when I spoke.

'I'm not sure that would be a good idea, Dora,' she said. 'It might be best for you to remember her as she was. There are some things you don't need to have to carry with you.'

'Why did you start looking there?' Philip asked and I could hear, in his voice, the slightest inflection of hope that, if Ellie had been found after all this time, so too might his son.

'We were tipped off,' Glenn said. 'Someone phoned a local reporter at the *Herald* and told her. She contacted us then.'

'Who?'

Glenn glanced at me, perhaps wondering how much she could reveal.

'Ann McBride,' she said.

Chapter Fifty-Five

I called McBride and asked her to meet me in The Boston Tea Party, the café where I had met Ward three years previous. She didn't ask why I wanted to meet with her, so I suspected she knew.

Philip had sat with me for an hour or so after Glenn had left, partly to support me but also, I think, partly to work out how he himself felt, or might feel, if he were in my position.

'It must be a relief,' he'd said. 'Knowing that you've got her home, finally.'

'A bit,' I said. 'There's a strange sadness too.'

'Of course,' he said. 'We always hope they're still alive somewhere. There's always hope until the remains are found. Hope's the last thing to go.'

I'd nodded, but that hadn't been it. After Ellie went, and Eamon went, my life had changed in almost every way. I'd lived this reality, this version of my life, for three years now. I'd become used to it, in a way – not because I enjoyed it, but because it became normal, a habit. And habit was a crutch. Now that Ellie was found, now that Dean had paid for what he did, I had a sense that there was nothing left for me to do. So long as Ellie had been missing, her very absence had conferred on me a sense of purpose, a reason to be here.

Finding her had, in a strange way, bereft me of my very purpose. It was the end of things. And so, my relief at her being found was tempered by the gnawing awareness that without the need to find her now, I had nothing left to live for.

After a while, perhaps he realised that I needed to be left on my own, for he said he would go home and call on me later to see how I was. Glenn had promised to let me know as soon as possible whether the remains were confirmed to be Ellie's. I, in turn, had promised to let Philip know when I heard.

Once he left, I had time to think about all that Glenn had said. The timing of the tip-off was the thing that most registered with me. I'd visited Leo Ward: he and his son were the only people who knew I'd been there, and within hours someone had called in the location of Ellie's body. Had it been the father, perhaps keen to get me off his back once and for all? Had I been wrong in thinking he would try to kill me and, instead, he'd reasoned that with Ellie back, I'd be satisfied? Or had it been Adam Ward, perhaps prompted by guilt? I'd recognised the look in his face when he saw me in the club – it was simple fear.

One of them had phoned in the tip-off; it would be too much of a coincidence for it not to be. And whoever had called it in had known where Ellie was buried. And it wasn't in Black Lake. I suspected I knew which of them it was who had called it in: I just didn't know why.

I was there almost twenty minutes by the time McBride walked into the café.

'Sorry,' she said when she arrived. 'Busy day.'

I could imagine. She was, after all, no longer just covering the story but now, by virtue of the tip-off call, part of it. By teatime, she'd have appeared on several of the national channels and papers, recounting her role in it all.

'How are you?' she asked as she sat, then looked around for someone to place an order.

'It's strange,' I said. 'I'm in limbo again, waiting for final confirmation.'

'Have they not confirmed it's Ellie yet, then?'

I shook my head. 'But Sergeant Glenn seems fairly certain.'

'The person who made the call was pretty specific. They did say it was where we'd find "Ellie Condron", not just "a body".'

'Who was it? The person who called?'

McBride shrugged. 'They didn't give a name. They called the newsroom, asked to speak to me. "Ellie Condron's body is buried at the far side of Rowan Wood," they said. Then they gave me more detailed directions on how to find her. I called the police straight away, of course.'

I had wondered whether McBride hadn't been tempted to follow the directions herself on the off-chance she might find Ellie, but clearly not.

'Was the caller male?'

'Mrs Condron,' she said. 'I can't tell you that.'

'Why not? Surely the police asked?'

She accepted this with a nod. 'I don't think it would do you any good,' she said. 'Driving yourself mad a— trying to figure out who it could have been.'

'I'm not going to drive myself mad again,' I said, completing the statement that had died in her mouth. 'She's my girl. You don't have a right to decide what I should or shouldn't know about her.'

Even as I said it, I was aware of the hypocrisy involved, for that was exactly what I had done with Philip and his son.

'It was a male voice,' McBride said finally. 'It was muffled though, as if he was speaking through material or something.'

'Young or old?'

'Mrs Condron, I . . .' She looked around her again. One of the waitresses, thinking she was wishing now to order, approached and McBride shook her head. She clearly wasn't planning on sitting long after all, realising now the reason I'd wanted to meet her.

'I know who called you,' I said. 'It was either the father or the son. I suspect you'd be able to tell the difference, even with a cloth over their mouth. Tell me this, and I will make sure that you get the whole story. Every part of it.'

That got her attention. 'What story?'

'I need to know, was it the father or the son? Then I'll tell you.'

She angled her head a little as if considering whether I was bluffing.

'It was a younger voice,' she said after a moment. 'I don't know who it was, but it was a younger voice. He sounded emotional.'

'Thank you,' I said. It made sense. The father would never have had a reason to return Ellie to me. What I couldn't understand was, why would the son? Was he confessing to something? Had guilt eaten at him for so long, these past three years, that he felt he had no choice but to confess?

And with that, I was aware of the guilt gnawing inside me since first Glenn had appeared this morning. Had I been complicit in killing someone who was innocent of my daughter's death? And how could I not tell Philip the truth?

McBride stared across the table at me, expectantly. 'Well?'

'Well, what?'

'You said you'd tell me the whole story.'

'And I will,' I said. 'When it's finished.'

Chapter Fifty-Six

There was little I could do until I knew for certain that the remains found in the woods were Ellie's. Waiting for that call seemed interminable, the minutes stretching to hours in such a way that I felt sure I would not be able to cope. I played out each scenario in my head, over and over, trying to decide which was worse: that she had been found or that she hadn't. In my imagination, I greeted both pieces of news with an outburst of emotion that I could not control – one caused by grief, one by frustration.

In reality, when Glenn finally called round at about eleven thirty that evening, I did neither.

I could already tell from her expression as she came up the driveway that they had identified the remains as Ellie's. I opened the door and allowed her in, followed her into the living room and sat and listened while she explained how the dental records had confirmed it. I nodded, once more feeling as if I were outside myself, viewing this exchange at a distance.

'I'm sorry, Dora,' Glenn said. 'But I'm relieved that after all this time, we were finally able to bring her home to you.'

'Thank you,' I said. I'd a tissue wadded in my hand, in the expectation that I would need it. I played with it now, not able to look Glenn square in the face.

'How did she die?'

'We believe she was strangled,' Glenn said. 'There's evidence that the hyoid bone in the throat is broken.'

'Could a blow to the head have done that?'

Glenn paused a moment, regarded me carefully. 'Why do you keep asking this, Dora?'

'Donal Kelly said something about it,' I lied. 'I just wondered if he'd been right about anything.'

She shook her head. 'No. There's nothing to suggest she was struck on the head. He was wrong about that, he was wrong about Black Lake. He's a fraud.'

I nodded. 'Had she been . . .?' I couldn't find the words to finish the sentence. Clearly though, it was not the first time Glenn had been in this position.

'We don't know, I'm afraid,' she said. 'Some of her clothing was missing – her top and her bra – although we knew that from when she first went missing when we found bits of it burnt, so there may have been a sexual element to it. The . . . the condition of her remains makes it difficult to be sure.'

'Thank you,' I said. 'For being honest. And for finding her.'

Glenn acknowledged the comment with a brief nod. 'I'm sorry it took this long. We can, at least, now start looking for forensic evidence, which might help us find the person who did it.'

'I know who did it,' I said. 'Adam Ward phoned in the tip-off.'

'How do you know that?' Glenn asked in a manner in which I could not tell if she had been aware that it was him or not.

'I spoke with Ann McBride.'

'She told us she didn't recognise the caller.'

'It had to be either the father or the son. She said the voice sounded younger.'

'Why did it have to be one of those two?'

'It could only have been. It was the son's car found burnt out on Old Farm Road, it was the father's rave. The sister, Nicola, has left to go to Australia.'

'Who told you that?'

'Ward himself. I went to see him the day before last.'

Glenn shook her head. 'Dora, you need to step back and let us do our jobs. You can't be heading all around town accusing people of things. You're going to get hurt, or get someone else hurt.'

'You've told me nothing,' I said. 'Nothing. You only found her because Adam Ward phoned in her whereabouts, otherwise we'd still be sitting here, not knowing. And that only happened because I went and spoke to him. Because of me.'

Glenn straightened in her seat now and I could see that she was hurt by what I had said. After all this time, she probably felt she had managed to bring Ellie home and now I was taking the credit from her.

'Where's Stevens, or whatever his name was? The detective who was handling this case. Would he not have thought he should come and tell me this himself?'

'DS Andrews was transferred two years back,' Glenn said. 'I was promoted to sergeant and took over as SIO on this case. I told you that, back then. When I visited you in the hospital.'

A vague memory developed of the bed, Glenn sitting next to it, her voice echoing in the room while I tried to grasp her words, as if plucking them from the air. I had forgotten that completely and could not even be sure if the memory I had now was accurate or simply one I'd created at her suggestion.

'I've done my best,' she said softly. 'I want to get to the truth, but the thing is, when you start on one of these cases, when you open it up and look inside, so much stuff comes out, so much bad stuff. And you have to sort through it first and that takes time. All the secrets no one wanted revealed, all the dishonesty and deceit. All of that needs to be dealt with, too. Hopefully, when you get through all that, all the lies and hurt, you find the truth at the bottom.'

'Hope,' I said. 'Pandora found hope at the bottom of the box. That was the last thing left.'

Glenn looked at me, bewildered. 'Well, maybe finding Ellie will bring you some hope that you can begin to live again.'

'Perhaps,' I said. In reality, I knew that I could not move on while whoever had hurt Ellie was still unpunished and while Philip was still left in the limbo from which I had finally been released. I'd promised to call him, but my own feelings of guilt were so strong, I knew I would not.

'Leo Ward lied to you, by the way. Nicki Ward is not in Australia,' Glenn said. 'She's in Riverside Care Home. She attempted suicide last year; she's never recovered from it.'

It was only when Glenn had left that I finally cried, with grief, with shame, with relief, with guilt, with fear, with anger. A release of all of the gifts with which we were blessed and cursed.

Chapter Fifty-Seven

I knew Riverside Care Home. It was an upmarket private facility, situated, as the name suggested, on the curve of the river, in its own grounds. I took a taxi out the following afternoon, just after lunch, to visit Nicola Ward.

I don't know why I went to see her. It seemed right to do so. She had been with Ellie in her final hours and I felt sure that she knew more about what had happened than she let on. Her attempt to take her own life convinced me of that more than ever. I hoped she might tell me the truth now, now that Ellie had been found.

I had to ask which was her room at the reception desk. The nurse behind the desk stared at me and I could tell she was trying to place how she knew me.

'My daughter was a good friend of Nicola's,' I explained. 'When I heard she wasn't well, I thought I should visit on her behalf.' I raised the bunch of carnations I held in my hand as a signal of my good intent.

She nodded. 'She's in room three,' she said.

I was not prepared for the state in which the girl lay. She was unconscious, connected via wires and tubes to various pieces of machinery. Her breathing was mechanical, a slow steady rhythm that did not vary once the entire time I stood there. Selfishly, I felt gutted. I'd hoped she might be able to tell me something, but she was beyond that now. And, beneath my disappointment, lay a deeper, wider sadness.

Her features were young and soft and kind. I could see why Ellie had found her attractive, for there was, behind all the machinery, a beautiful young woman whose life had been destroyed. I found myself staring at her, captivated by her, imagining seeing her as Ellie had seen her.

A nurse came into the room and instantly apologised. 'Sorry, I can come back.'

'It's fine,' I said. 'I'm going.'

'It's difficult to see, isn't it?' she said, putting a supportive hand on my arm and I realised then that I was crying. 'She's such a lovely girl, too. Aren't you, darling?' she added, addressing Nicki.

'Will she recover?'

The nurse shrugged lightly. 'We have to hope, don't we? Shall I put those in water for you?'

I nodded and handed the flowers to her, then turned and looked again at the young woman lying in the bed. I'd expected when I saw her that I would feel anger or antagonism, but I felt none. Whatever had happened in Rowan Wood the night Ellie went, the night she died, had cost so many people so much.

I reached out and placed my hand on hers.

'What are you doing?'

I turned at the voice. Adam Ward stood in the doorway.

'You shouldn't be in here. Who let you in here?' he asked, turning to see if any of the staff were nearby.

'I'm sorry,' I said. 'I thought maybe . . . I thought it might make some sense to me.'

'What? My sister in a coma? That would make sense?'

I shook my head. 'I don't know what I was expecting,' I said.

'Did you come to gloat?'

The vehemence in the comment surprised me.

'No. I hoped she might speak to me. I didn't know about . . . about any of this,' I said, gesturing towards the machinery that kept the young girl alive. 'I think Ellie loved your sister. I felt I owed it to her to come and see her. And I suppose I hoped that, if she had shared those feelings for Ellie, she might have helped me find out the truth about what happened to her that night.'

It was not what he'd been expecting, and I could see his shoulders drop a little, his defences lower.

'Thank you for returning Ellie to me,' I said. 'I know it was you.'

He tried to pantomime confusion, but it was not convincing.

'I see you and your father and the next day someone calls in a tip-off. I spoke with Ann McBride. She said the voice was young.'

I could see the flush rising along his neck.

'It was you. Why? Guilt?'

'What?'

'These are lovely.' The nurse who'd taken the flowers arrived back with a small vase in which she'd placed them. When she saw the two of us she stopped. 'It's really only one visitor at a time, Adam,' she said. Clearly, he was a frequent visitor. I wondered why he had come without his father – and why his father had lied about what had happened to his daughter.

'I'm leaving,' I said. 'I'd just hoped to have a quick word with Adam here.'

The nurse nodded and smiled. 'A few minutes only, if you can,' she said.

I waited until she left, closing the door behind her. 'Why now?' I asked. 'Why call it in now?'

For a moment, I thought he was going to continue to deny it, but finally he nodded, his shoulders slumping a little as if in defeat.

'I saw you,' he said. 'You'd not given up, after three years. I felt so bad for you. And for Nicki. All the shit that happened because of that night to so many of us. It had to end sometime.'

'Did you kill Ellie?' I asked, expecting him to deny it but hoping that I might be able to tell whether or not he was lying.

Instead he slumped into the chair next to his sister and took her hand. 'I thought I had for long enough,' he said. 'But no. I didn't.'

'But you knew where she was buried?'

He nodded, shaking loose tears, which ran freely down his cheeks.

'Did you bury her?'

'I helped,' he said.

'Your father?'

A nod.

'Tell me.'

Chapter Fifty-Eight

'Nicki really liked Ellie,' he began. 'Like, they just clicked from the first time they met. They were so alike; Nicki is so sweet, so funny, but she's kind of shy, too. I think Ellie was like that. Anyway, Nicki asked her to come to the rave with us. I picked them up at the art college.'

I nodded. I knew all this already and while I didn't want to interrupt him in case he changed his mind about speaking to me, I was also aware that the nurse might return and tell me to leave.

'I was starting to sell some stuff then, herbal stuff and that, that I got through the head shops. I knew Dad was doing it anyway with harder stuff, so I didn't think he'd care.'

'Stuff?'

'Drugs.'

I nodded that he should continue. 'When Nicki and Ellie got into the car, I gave them something, some spice, just to get a buzz on. Raves are a nightmare if you're quiet. I didn't force them to take it; Nicki asked for some and then Ellie said she'd take some too. She'd had it before, she said.'

Instinctively, I wanted to correct him on that, but realised that perhaps she had and I simply hadn't known.

'I headed off and started selling and about an hour later Nicki came to me, freaking out. She'd taken a bad reaction to the stuff and was all over the place. She said Ellie had tried to kiss her and she'd freaked. They'd had a row and Ellie had run off into the woods. She was worried in case she got lost or fell into the river or something. It was night, like, and the lights flashing and that made it hard to work out where you were going unless you followed the markers we'd put in coming down from the car park. She'd headed in the opposite direction.'

He took a moment and rubbed his sister's hand with his thumb. 'The stupid thing is, Nicki really liked Ellie, like was into her like that, but she was tripping so bad she couldn't handle it.'

I said nothing, though the comment pained me even more than when I thought Ellie's feelings had not been requited. What might have happened if they had kissed? If this man had not given them spice?

'I went looking for her but couldn't find her anywhere. Like, I looked all over, but she wasn't about. She must have run off into the woods. I came back and told Nicki she'd be all right, that we'd find her when it was over, or that she'd appear somewhere once she'd calmed down and the spice had worn off.'

He paused, then got up and walked across to the window, on the opposite side of the room to me, where he leaned against the sill, his arms folded, his head lowered a little.

'About an hour after, I got a call from my dad. He needed me to bring the car around to the old gate.'

'Where's that?'

'It's a laneway down to a farmer's field. It brings you into the woods about halfway down. We'd used it once or twice when we'd had the raves deeper in the woods, but it was difficult to get at, so we'd moved them back closer to the main car park.'

I was sorry I asked and almost muttered an apology for breaking his train of thought.

'Anyway, Dad called and asked me to bring round the car. He told me to bring the spades with me. We always had them on site for burying cables and that, clearing away space for the decks and speakers. At the end of the night, we'd sometimes bury all the rubbish that was dropped too. Dad reckoned as long as the place wasn't left a complete mess, the cops would leave us alone and let him get on with things. And they did. But he asked for the car and I was sober 'cause I didn't use when I was selling. I didn't use much, to be honest. I saw all the melt-heads my dad had to deal with. So I lifted the spades and drove round. I didn't think anything of it, Dad was always having these schemes. I thought maybe he needed to dig up a stash that he'd buried out in the woods to sell. When I got there, to the laneway, he was waiting for me. He brought me down into the woods and that's . . . that's where I saw Ellie.'

He looked up at me now, his eyes reddened and shining. I did not speak, afraid to pull him from his memory of that evening.

'She was lying on the ground. Her top was missing and her bra. I asked Dad what had happened and he said she'd taken something and must have overdosed. He found her lying there. He said he'd come deeper into the woods to retrieve a stash and saw her wandering. When he spoke to her she started to be sick, all over herself. She'd taken something.'

He stopped again, his breath stuttering. 'I said that I'd given her spice and he bollocked me, told me it must have been that that killed her. I asked him why her top was off and he said she'd thrown up on it and he knew that there'd be traces of what she'd taken so he'd burned the top and bra. She'd blood on her face where he said she'd hurt herself, she'd taken a fit or something. He said we needed to get rid of her, that if the cops found her, it would link back to me, that I'd end up getting put away for it. I was a stupid bastard and he was saving my skin.'

He continued. 'So, we carried her up to my car. She was still warm. I thought she was still alive, I told him that, but she wasn't. Not really. She'd marks on her throat and I thought nothing of it, if she was having a fit, maybe she'd grabbed at herself or something, when she was choking. We were going to take her up to Black Lake, bury her up there, but, when we got there, there was a load of cars parked all around the place, people copping off with one another. So we went back to Rowan Wood, down at the far end and took her in there and buried her. I remembered when we went in, counting my steps, almost like Hansel and Gretel or something, so I wouldn't get lost myself. And we buried her there, eight hundred and thirty steps in. Six hundred and twenty along the path, two hundred and ten down towards the river where Dad said the ground was softer. I'll never forget eight hundred and thirty.'

It had been an accident? I didn't believe him, couldn't believe him that something as stupid as that had taken my daughter from me. What meaning was there to that?

'Why didn't you say before now?'

'I was afraid that I'd get into trouble,' he said. 'And Dad warned me. But I kind of knew, even then, it wasn't me. When Dad got into the car, he had scrape marks down his face, like he'd been scratched. I asked him what happened and he said he'd walked into tree branches in the dark, but . . .' He shook his head.

'So, we buried her, then Dad said we needed to destroy the car because she'd been in it. I drove him back to the main car park, he picked up his own with some petrol he kept for the generators, and then we drove up to Old Farm Road and burned out my car. He promised me he would buy me a new one. And he did.'

'Just like that.'

He nodded. 'Just like that.'

I stared at him, not knowing how to feel. He had given my daughter drugs, but she had asked for them, had chosen to take them. She'd not been forced. She'd made a decision. I desperately wanted to blame him, but knew that, in a sense, he was not to blame.

'Then,' he said, 'last year, Nicki came to me in a state. She'd been looking for some jewellery that had belonged to my mum that she'd left for her when she moved away. Mum went to Australia about ten years back with someone she met. Her and Dad hadn't been getting on for ages. They decided we would stay here until we finished school, then go over to her. But we knew that meant she didn't really want us over at all. Anyway, she'd left her engagement ring and wedding ring behind and Nicki went looking for them one day, just out of nosiness. She was going to ask Dad for them. She went hunting around his room and found this small metal box, about the size of a matchbox. There were different bits and pieces in it and she sifted through them. At the bottom, she found a necklace. She said it was Ellie's. A silver chain with a glass heart on it, all blue lines running through it.'

I stiffened, seeing again the necklace, Ellie, Venice, the heat, the light, us, smiling, happy, together.

'The chain was snapped, but she remembered Ellie wearing it the night she went missing,' Adam continued. 'Why would Dad have had her necklace in a box? She came and told me. She was in pieces, like totally breaking down. So I told her the truth, about what had happened that night. She blamed herself straight away. If she'd only kissed her, like she wanted to, none of it would have happened.'

He stopped again and his tears flowed more freely now.

'The next call I got was to say Nicki'd been found like this. She'd tried to hang herself and it hadn't worked enough to kill her, but enough to starve her brain of oxygen. She felt so guilty, like she was to blame, even back then. Before she knew. We both did, me and her. And then you'd been throwing paint on us and shouting at us in the street at the time. Nicki had said, even before she found the necklace, that people at college had stopped speaking to her. That people blamed her for what had happened. The same thing happened with me. I lost my job and had to work with Dad.'

'I'm sorry,' I said, because it seemed the right thing to say. I'd wanted answers, not to destroy so many people's lives. I'd looked for truth and instead had unleashed so much darkness.

'I'd have done what you did,' he said. 'I understand. Then I saw you the other day and I knew I had to say. This needed to be over.'

He stood then, his hands resting on the sill. 'I asked Dad about the necklace after you left. I told him Nicki had found it. He said he'd spotted it when we were burning out the car. That it must have snapped off and fallen in the boot. He'd brought it home and meant to get rid of it.'

'You don't believe him,' I said. It was clear from his tone.

He shook his head. 'I remember every moment of carrying her out of the woods. I remember looking at her neck, at the bruises, thinking I'd done that to her with whatever I'd given her. There was no necklace on her then. Dad had already taken it. And then he kept it, didn't dump it like he said he was going to. He kept it. Nicki is lying here like this, I've spent the past three years blaming myself for what happened, God knows what you've had to go through, and he let us all go through it. Look what he did to my sister.'

He gestured towards the bed and then he started to sob and he went to her, took her hand in his, knelt by her bed. I moved across to him and put my arms around him. Here, in this moment, this youth had given me the one thing I had needed most, no matter the cost to him, to his family. The truth. He had shown me what I needed to do.

'He kept it,' he sobbed, over and over. 'Like a souvenir.'

Chapter Fifty-Nine

I went back home. The house was empty, had been empty really since Ellie went. It had stopped being a home then, I realised, the day she left. And, with her return, with the truth now clear, I had no need for it anymore. She would not be returning to her room, would not lie again on that bed, press her face to the pillows, hold Leo in her sleep. The pictures on the wall would be seen no more, their value changed by the absence of the one who had so prized them.

I took them down, one by one. The picture of Ophelia, her hands outstretched, the garland of flowers around her as the water pulled her down. The Lady of Shallot, sitting at the prow of her boat, her candles almost burned down. All those doomed women. And then, between them, a picture postcard which I had seen time and again when in Ellie's room and which had meant nothing to me and so I'd dismissed it as just another piece of art she admired. It was the image of a child's face, one half of which had been painted naturally, the fine detail clear. The other half looked disfigured, but now, looking more closely, I could see that it was made up of the same colours of paint as the first half, but exaggerated, blue spilling across the pinks and greens. Clearly it had influenced her own self-portrait that I had seen that day in the art college, her face torn in two, revealing what lay beneath. As I took it down from the wall and placed it in a box, I read the name on the card: *Elpis* by Jenny Saville. *Elpis*. Hope.

Next, I moved around the room, gathering her most important things, the things she had on display, each a memento of a moment, a place. Our holidays together, a beach, Rowan Wood. I left Leo until last. I picked him up, held him to my face, inhaled the scent of his fur, kissed him. Then I placed him too in the box.

I went to my own room then and put the box beneath my bed, where I knew it would be when I needed it.

Finally, I phoned Eamon. I still had his number on my phone and guessed he was unlikely to have had a chance to change it. Sure enough, he answered on the second ring.

'Dora,' he said, a statement, readying for a fight.

'They've found her,' I said.

'I heard.'

I waited a beat. 'I thought you might have called.'

'I wanted to, but . . . I thought you wouldn't want me to. I didn't want to intrude; you told me she wasn't my daughter.'

I nodded. 'I did,' I said.

'I'm glad they found her,' he said. 'For you. You can bury her now. Have somewhere to go to be near her.'

'I won't need the house anymore,' I said. 'You can sell it. We can halve whatever it gets.'

There was silence for a moment, and I guessed he was suspicious of such a change of heart in light of our last conversation.

'Why?'

'Ellie's not coming home,' I said. 'I don't need it anymore.'

'You're not planning on doing something stupid, are you?' he asked with a soft laugh, as if embarrassed even asking. 'Are you, Dora?' he repeated, the concern in his voice evident.

'No,' I said. 'I'm going to try to do something smart for a change.'

Another silence. When he finally spoke again, his voice sounded thick and heavy. 'I'm sorry for everything, Dora,' he said. 'For the way everything turned out. I never intended for it to . . . you know.'

'Did she know? Ellie?'

'What about?'

'Any of it?'

There was a pause. 'I think she guessed about me and Brenda,' he said. 'She called to the house one evening looking for Amy and I was there.'

'She never told me,' I said.

'She probably didn't want to hurt you.'

'She didn't,' I said.

Chapter Sixty

Philip seemed surprised to see me when he opened the door. He blushed a little and, after inviting me in, apologised almost straight away for not having called me.

'The truth is,' he said, 'I was jealous. I know I shouldn't be, but I envied you getting Ellie back, even as I was delighted for you that you had.'

'I understand that,' I said. 'It's okay.'

'It's not,' he said. 'I should have just been happy for you.'

'We need to talk,' I said. 'About Mark.'

And so, we sat in his kitchen and I told him my whole story, from Ellie's disappearance until the killing of his son. Of Kelly and his promise of 'dark water', which fitted so neatly with Black Lake, and of the aftershave I smelt there, or at least imagined I had. I told him of Ward and of my holding the gun.

He sat in silence, stunned, broken. I wanted to gather the pieces of him and rebuild him, even as I knew that the only way I could do so was to reveal the very worst of me.

'You saw him killed,' he said, finally, when I had finished.

I nodded.

'You knew, all this time, and you said nothing?'

I nodded again, silenced by my shame.

'You saw what it did to me, to my wife, and said nothing. You let me confess about Mark, about the bag, about everything and you had chance after chance to say something.'

'I didn't want to hurt you,' I managed.

'Hurt me? What the fuck do you think has happened to me since? I'm *only* hurt. That's all there is here – hurt!' he said, jabbing at his own chest with his hand.

'I thought he'd killed Ellie,' I said. 'I didn't want to tell you that. I didn't want to take away from you whatever good memories you had of him.'

'You don't get to make that choice,' he shouted, rising now from his seat. For a second, I had flashes of Eamon, of my own father, and I instinctively winced. But he had stepped away from the table and moved back to the hob, as if trying to create distance between us, not to threaten me. 'You . . . you should have said. I had a right to know.'

'I didn't want to . . . I didn't want to take the final bit of hope from you. But then I realised it was wrong,' I added, standing myself now and approaching him. He held out his hands, warning me to stay back, so I stopped and stood before him.

'I watched my wife disappear after Mark vanished,' he said. 'I watched her die for months, every day, a little less and less of her here until by the time she took her own life, there was almost nothing left to take anyway. You could have stopped all that.'

'I was in hospital myself by then,' I said. 'I understand, Philip. I do. And I'm so sorry. I don't expect you to forgive me. I'm not looking for that. I wanted to give you a chance to live. I know now who killed Ellie. It was Leo Ward. And he killed Mark to take the blame off himself. He used me as cover. Just like he used his own kids as cover.'

'You're giving me a chance to live? Seriously? You know the version of the story you have is wrong,' he said. 'Pandora's box. She doesn't release hope last: she sealed the box before hope could escape. That's the final curse on mankind. The one thing that would let him endure all that suffering is locked from him. Because of Pandora.'

I nodded. 'I know that,' I said. 'But I prefer the other version. Why should Pandora be the villain? She didn't fill the box; it was filled for her. She was *made* to open it. And I didn't start this: Ward did when he killed my Ellie. But I will finish it.'

'I trusted you,' Philip said, his anger gone now. I felt all the worse for it, for the rawness of his hurt. 'I tried to help you.'

'You did,' I said. 'You were the only one. And I'm going to repay that. I'm going to the police to tell them what I did. What Ward did.'

Chapter Sixty-One

I called a taxi and headed straight to the police station. Glenn wasn't there and I had to wait in the reception for her to return. Sitting there, among the bustle and shouting, I felt, for the first time in over three years, a sense of peace. I knew now the truth, not just about Ellie, but about myself. I had spent so long silently blaming others for my choices. But this was my decision alone.

Glenn arrived just after eight p.m. She appeared from the door that led into the main body of the station, but did not invite me beyond the reception.

'My shift's almost done, Mrs Condron,' she said. 'Can this wait until morning?'

'No,' I said.

She must have misunderstood my intention, for she continued, 'I've nothing else to tell you yet, Mrs Condron. The toxicology reports will be a few weeks.'

'I know what happened to Ellie,' I said. 'And I know what happened to Mark Dean. I know who killed him.'

That caught her attention. 'Who?'

'Leo Ward,' I said.

I could see her expression change, the scepticism, as if she thought I'd regressed back to the state I'd been in after Ellie went.

'I was there,' I said.

'You saw him kill Mark Dean?'

I nodded.

'Seriously?'

She was conflicted, caught between curiosity and disbelief, aware perhaps that had she not looked out to see me she'd have been on her way home by now. In the end, as it always does, curiosity got the better of her.

And so, for the second time that evening, I told the story of the past three years. I told her everything, about Philip, about his wife, about my going to see Nicki Ward and speaking with Adam.

At the start she jotted down a few notes, perhaps in a display of interest, but soon she stopped writing and listened, not interrupting, not questioning. Just listening.

She shook her head when I finished.

'Is this the truth?' she asked.

'As best I know it,' I said.

'Why didn't you come to me?' she said. 'Mark Dean was never in the picture for what happened to Ellie. I told you we'd looked at him after he admitted taking the bag.'

'I wasn't thinking straight,' I said. 'I wanted someone to blame.'

'Did you really think he had done it?'

'I *wanted* to,' I said. 'At the time, I convinced myself that he had. He agreed with so much of what Ward said. It fitted so closely to what Kelly had said. I wanted to believe it was true. I thought it would let me move on.'

'And did it?'

'No. It made things worse.'

'I wondered where Philip Brooks came into it,' she said. 'When I saw him in your house the other day. Have you told him?'

I nodded.

'How did he take it?'

'As you'd imagine,' I said. 'I never set out to hurt anyone. I just wanted answers. I just needed to know what happened to my Ellie.'

'I understand that, Dora,' Glenn said. 'I do. God knows, I might have done the same thing myself if I'd been in your shoes. But you should have trusted me.'

'Trusted you? I'm on my own. No one. No family, no husband, no daughter. Did you not think I'd take help anywhere I could find it?'

Glenn shrugged. 'And the creeps came out of the woodwork, offering to help.'

'Like you said, you have to sift through all the crap before you get to the truth.'

'And this is the truth?'

'Do you not believe me?'

Glenn considered the question a moment and nodded. 'We'd figured it for either one or the other from day one,' she said. 'If we can find the necklace, we'll have the father for sure. By the sounds of it, the young lad may well give evidence against him because of what happened to Nicki.'

'Why did you tell me?' Something had just become clearer at the mention of her name. 'About Nicki. Why did you tell me she was in Riverside? Did you want me to go there?'

Glenn shook her head. 'God, Dora, of course not. I thought it would make you feel like Ward had paid a price, too. For it all.'

'He hasn't paid anything,' I said. 'His children did. Just as mine did. And Philip's.'

'Mark Dean was in deep with so many people. The rumour was he'd stolen a stash he found in Rowan Wood. I suspect Ward probably wanted him dead anyway. He just saw you as a chance to kill two birds with one stone. Maybe he thought you'd start telling people that Dean had been the killer and you'd leave him and his family alone. Take the heat off them a bit.'

'So what now?' I asked. Glenn had not commented on my role, nor on the likely punishment I would face.

'For you?'

'For everything.'

'We'll bring Ward in for questioning. Get a warrant and search his house for the necklace. Perhaps he'll have dumped it by now but, if he kept it that long, I think he'll want to have held on to it.'

'A souvenir, Adam said.'

'A trophy,' Glenn said, frowning. 'Something to help him relive the moment.'

'And me?'

Glenn shrugged. 'That'll be a decision for higher up. If you'd a clean record, they might have looked more favourably on things, but you've a few things there already. They may decide to charge you with being an accessory to murder.'

I nodded. It was as I had expected.

'I'm sorry, Dora.'

'Don't be,' I said. 'I'll finally have a chance to tell my story. To tell Ellie's story.'

'Of course, the fact you were hospitalised in the months after the killing might allow you to argue diminished responsibility. That's something your solicitor would need to help you with, though.'

'When will Ellie be ready? For me to bury her?'

'A few weeks more,' Glenn said.

'And will I get to bury her? Even with this?'

Glenn nodded. 'I promise you that,' she said. 'No matter what else happens, I'll promise you that.'

She went out soon after to have my statement typed up from the recording that she'd made, for me to sign. I felt lighter than I had done for three years, felt closer to the person I had once been. I didn't need to lie in Ellie's room, or to lie in Black Lake, to be near her. She was with me always, I realised, for in every moment of the past three years she had been at the centre of every thought I'd had, the reason for every action I took.

Just then, Glenn came back into the room, her two hands empty.

'There's a problem,' she said. 'Leo Ward has gone missing. His son just called it in.'

'Has he done a runner?' I asked, my heart sinking at the thought he had once more managed to avoid being held to account.

Glenn shook her head. 'His car is still at the house. There's blood in the hallway, according to the son. I've sent someone round to Philip Brooks' house. He's gone, too.'

'He's doing what his wife wanted him to do all along,' I said. 'He's going to recover his son and then avenge his death.'

'Someone's going to keep an eye on you here,' Glenn said. 'I'll be back when I can.'

'Let me come with you,' I said. 'I know where he is.'

'Then tell me.'

I shook my head. 'Take me with you. I'm the only person who knows what he's going through. I'm the only one who understands.'

'You stay in the car,' she said, finally.

Chapter Sixty-Two

There was only one place I could think they would have gone. Adam Ward had said his father's initial thought was to bury Ellie at Black Lake but there had been too many people around the evening she died. I thought it likely then that that would have been where he buried Mark Dean. If not there, then Rowan Wood.

I asked Glenn to allow me to sit in the front as we left the station, just as she had allowed me the day they took Eamon out of the house. It would let me avoid the humiliation of being seen being driven around in the back of the car, like a criminal. I did not wish to consider the fact that, to all intents and purposes, I was one.

The lake itself was still and, in the darkness, slick as oil and dark as its name suggested. The truth would be found near 'dark water', just as Kelly had said.

The roadway which encircled the water was in darkness too, there being no streetlamps this far from town. Glenn drove clockwise around its perimeter, the squad car that accompanied us driving counter-clockwise to speed up the search. At various spots along the road, parking or passing bays were spotted and it was to these that I paid most attention. I assumed they would have parked somewhere and then walked up into the trees that lay beyond the roadway, which is where it was most likely Mark would be buried. Either that, or he'd have been put into the water and they'd have parked along the water's edge.

The car lights caught the reflection of an animal's eyes as it darted across the road and into the scrub that ran alongside us. And then, just past it, I caught sight of the red reflective lights of the back of Philip's car, parked away from the lake.

'There,' I said.

Glenn pulled in behind Philip's car and radioed through her position. 'You're to stay here,' she said.

'I can't,' I said.

'Dora. If you've told Philip that you were there when Mark died, what's not to say he won't turn on you as well.'

I shrugged. 'I need to try,' I said. 'I caused him to do this. I need to try to stop it, too. To stop him, before he does something he can't undo. Please.'

Glenn stared at me a moment. I suspected she felt sorry for me, but I also think she knew that if anyone could appeal to him, if anyone could talk him down from what he was doing, it would be someone who had been there themselves. I only hoped we weren't too late.

'No,' she said. 'You stay here.' But then she got out and set off without locking the car. I followed her.

She moved off through the scrub, looking for them. I could see the torchlight bobbing up and down ahead of me as we moved through the scrubland. The ground was uneven, the air crisp and sharp with the smell of the dark water.

I counted my steps, just as Adam had done when he had walked into Rowan Wood with my daughter. At four hundred and seven, we spotted them.

Glenn's torchlight raked across the thin lines of the aspens, which seemed to shiver in the breeze. In the light, Philip's pale face stared back at us. Glenn stopped and focused the light more carefully. He stood with a pistol in his hand, Leo Ward standing next to him, his clothes muddied and marked with blood, which had clearly come from a wound he carried on his left cheek. He leaned on a shovel as he dug, his chest heaving with the exertion, his breath clouding above him.

'Mr Brooks,' Glenn called. 'Police. Put down the gun.'

Philip said something and Ward looked at him, but did not react. He spoke a second time and, with his foot, pushed at Ward who resumed digging again, though with little enthusiasm.

I moved past Glenn, into the light thrown off by her torch.

'Dora,' she cautioned, but did not stop me moving forward.

'Philip,' I said. 'You need to let him go.'

I stepped nearer to him now, only fifty yards or so from where they stood.

'Stay away. You . . . you caused this.'

'I know,' I said, taking another step. 'I did. And I'm so sorry. I didn't mean for any of this, I didn't mean for you to be hurt. You of all people. You were the only one who showed me any kindness; the only friend I had. I didn't mean it, Philip. I'm sorry that I hurt you. But let me help you now, please. Let me try to make up in some small way for what I did. What I've done.'

He snorted derisively. 'Hope.'

'Hope,' I said. 'Pandora didn't seal it away to stop mankind from having it. She kept it for us, so it would always be there. There's always hope. Even now. But just let him go.'

'I can't,' he said.

'You can. You've beaten him. You wanted Mark back and you'll get him back now. You don't need to do anything else.'

'And what about Kate? Will I get her back?'

'No,' I said. 'You won't.'

Glenn had moved closer behind me now, drew level with me. She did not have her gun drawn, though her attention was focused on the one in Philip's hand, which remained pointed at the space between himself and Ward, who had stopped digging again.

Philip looked at me and I could see that he was beaten. I recognised the look, knew the emptiness inside that he was trying to fill with anger. But that was not who he was.

'It's done,' I said. 'If you don't stop now, there's no hope left.'

'She's right,' Glenn said. 'You've done nothing wrong yet, Philip. Nothing anyone will want to charge you for. Let him go now, let us get your son back and let this bastard face the courts like he should.'

'And what do I do then?' Philip asked.

'Then you start to live again,' I said. 'You did what was right by Kate. You did what was right by Mark. You're the one good man I know,' I said, and realised I meant it, genuinely. 'You're the one decent person in all of this and I'm so sorry you got hurt. If I could take it all back, if I could drag back all the evil things that happened since Ellie died, I would. But I can't. After Mark died, after I thought it was over, I fell apart. I tried to drown myself. I ended up hospitalised. Doing what

I did didn't make me better. It made me worse. This won't bring you back to yourself, Philip. It'll leave you further from yourself than you've ever been.'

'I just want things to be the way there were,' he said, and I could see in the torchlight the shininess of his cheeks as he wept. 'I was happy.'

'And you will be again,' I said. 'Just not like this.'

'Then he gets away with it.'

He raised the gun now, pointed it directly at Ward, his arm muscles tautened as he gripped it tighter, his finger on the trigger. I knew that feeling, remembered it clearly: the power and powerlessness, simultaneously – the conflict, the sense that once pulled, once done, it could never be undone. The lid could not be closed again.

I shook my head. 'He's lost a child, just like you and me,' I said. 'In fact, I think he's lost both his children now, in every way that counts.'

Ward had stopped digging altogether now and had slumped to the ground, sitting in the shallow grave he had dug. I suspected he wasn't even sure if this was the right spot or not. Perhaps he'd simply been trying to buy time, hoping someone would come to save him.

'Stand up,' Philip shouted.

'No,' Ward said. 'If you're going to shoot me, shoot me.'

Philip glanced towards us, then back at Ward. He shifted his stance, as if readying himself.

'Get up,' Philip repeated, moving closer to him now and jabbing the gun at him.

Ward stood now and I could see his gaze fixed on the gun, perhaps trying to gauge whether Philip would actually shoot it, or perhaps trying to guess whether he might be able to disarm him.

'Please don't, Philip,' I said. 'We have to live with our loss. Why should he get away so easily?'

'He needs to pay!' Philip snapped, looking to me.

It was the distraction Ward had wanted. He grabbed at Philip's arm, wresting the gun from his grip, then raising it himself and pointing it at Philip.

The air exploded to life with a loud crack and Ward twisted as he slumped back against the mound of earth he'd dug.

Beside me, Glenn moved forward, her gun raised. The air was sharp with the smell of the shot.

Philip stumbled backwards, away from where Ward lay, gripping his shoulder which was now red with blood.

Glenn had reached him by that stage, bending to lift the gun he'd dropped while still training her own weapon on him. But Ward was beaten now.

I moved across to Philip and stood next to him, my hand on his arm as he regarded the scene in front of him with horror, as if only seeing it for the first time.

'Leo Ward,' Glenn said, standing over the prone figure now. 'You are under arrest on suspicion of the murders of Ellie Condron and Mark Dean. You do not have to say anything, but it may harm your defence if you do not mention when questioned something which you may later rely on in court. Anything you do say may be given in evidence.'

Behind her, the bobbing torchlights revealed the other officers coming to join her at Mark Dean's graveside.

Chapter Sixty-Three

Philip visited me several weeks later. I was still on remand, waiting for my first hearing. We sat together in the visitor's room.

'How is it?' he asked, looking around the room at the bustle of relationships, the chatter.

I shrugged. 'I've been in prison for three years already,' I said. 'It's nothing I've not already lived.'

He nodded, absently. I could tell he had something he needed to say and was working himself up to saying it.

'I wanted to thank you for telling me the truth,' he said. 'I know it can't have been easy.'

'You deserved to know it,' I said. 'You above everyone deserved some peace. I hope you find it.'

He shrugged as if embarrassed by the compliment.

'You knew you'd end up in here though,' he said.

I nodded. 'I've spent so long being told what to do by everyone else, there was something freeing about making my own choice, even if it was choosing this.'

'We found Mark,' he said.

I nodded. 'Glenn told me. And they found the gun Ward used. And Ellie's necklace. She has everything she needs now.'

'That's good,' he said. 'She told me that Ward would have killed Mark anyway. That he used you. It wasn't your fault.'

I nodded. 'That doesn't make it any easier, I'm sure.'

'It does, actually,' he said. 'I'm glad she told me. I'm sorry for blaming you.'

'I blamed myself anyway,' I said. 'But thank you.'

Irrespective of the outcome of the case, he had absolved me and that was more important than anything.

We sat in silence a moment and I could see he was working himself up to whatever it was he wanted to say.

'Does it get better? Eventually? I thought . . . I thought when I found him that it would right everything, that it would let me be me again. But it hasn't. I just feel so empty all the time.'

'You do,' I said. 'And then, things begin to appear again. You never lose that emptiness, but you learn to accommodate it a bit better. And then you meet people who help you carry it, too.'

'I hope so.'

'I'd like to help you carry it,' I said. 'After all you did for me. If you'd let me? When this is done.'

'I think I'd like that,' he said. 'Maybe we can help each other.'

I nodded. 'Maybe we can.'

After he'd left, I went back to my cell. Glenn had brought me some things from the house. I'd asked her to bring the picture of me and Ellie, the one of us smiling with our faces pressed together, taken in Venice, when we were happy. It was on the wall above my bed. Next to it was the one other picture from the box of Ellie's belongings that I had asked her for: *Elpis*, the child. She stared at me from the blood-red background, her face a revelation of all that we were: the conflict, the sadness, the joy, the hope. All the gifts of the gods. I touched her face with my fingertips and felt Ellie close by me.

Then I sat on the bed and lifted the paper and pencil I had requested and considered where to begin. The morning of Ellie's disappearance.

I had promised that I would tell McBride my story when I finished it. So, this is my testimony.

This is my tale.

Acknowledgements

Thanks to all those involved in helping this story on its journey from my desk to the bookstore shelf, especially the team at Constable. Special thanks to Krystyna Green, Beth Wright, Caitriona Row, Sean Garrehy, Amanda Keats and Joanne Gledhill.

My thanks, too, to bookshop workers and librarians everywhere who have recommended my book – or indeed any book – and so kept alive the tradition of sharing stories. It's a noble calling.

I'm hugely grateful to everyone who has ever bought, borrowed or read one of my books. Stories need readers in order to come alive and, in reading these words, you have brought my stories to life. Thank you sincerely.

Thanks to Dave Headley and Emily Glenister of DHH Literary Agency and to Emily Hickman of The Agency for all their work on my behalf.

Thanks to all my family and, in particular, to Carmel, Joe and Dermot for all their support through the years. And to my mum who, along with my beloved late father, taught us all a love of reading and the value of books.

Finally, my love and thanks to my wife, Tanya, and our kids, Ben, Tom, David and Lucy, for, well, everything.

Keep reading for
a sneak peek of

THE LAST CROSSING

The First Crossing

Chapter One

Martin Kelly cried for his mother before he died.

His face was glazed with tears, his mouth a grotesque O as first he pleaded for his life and, when it became clear that they would not listen to him, called for his mother. Stripped naked, he knelt in the grave they had already dug for him. The light of the torch Tony held caught the shiny skin of the scar on his lower abdomen where he'd had his appendix out, standing out against the lividity of the bruising he carried there, his phallus shrivelled amongst the dark of his pubis at the outer edges of the glare.

Tony had wanted to cover him up, give him his coat to offer him some dignity, but Hugh had refused. He was aware of Karen next to him, her breathing quick and shallow as she watched, the black plastic bag of Martin's clothes, which they had stripped from him, twisted in her grip.

Martin held out his bound hands in supplication, looking from one face to the next. 'It wasn't me,' he said. 'I didn't do it.'

'You're a liar,' Hugh spat.

'I'm not,' Martin sobbed. 'I swear on me mother, I'm not.'

'And you knew what would happen.'

It was then that Martin broke down, his body wracked with sobs that turned to retching. He vomited onto himself, half choking on it, the bile and saliva hanging in a lace from his chin to his chest. He made no effort to wipe it away.

'Fuck this,' Hugh said, moving forward, raising his pistol. 'Tell me mother—'

The shot reverberated through the trees, which came instantly alive, cacophonous, as a murder of crows took wing against the evening sky.

Martin twisted with the shot, his body thudding against the edge of the grave they had dug. Hugh moved across and, with his toe, pushed him down into the gaping space, before firing three more shots in quick succession, each one momentarily illuminating the still white body where it lay, the red wounds flowering as the blood unfurled with each shot.

'Get those clothes burned,' Hugh ordered, glancing at Karen. 'You,' he added, looking at Tony, 'grab a spade and get shovelling.'

It took them twenty minutes to fill in the grave, Hugh and Tony quickly shifting into an alternating rhythm while, in the distance, through the uniform ranks of the spruce trees, they could see Karen, her face illuminated by the flickering flames, burning Martin's clothes. The air, acrid with the smell of the fabric as it burnt, splintered with the crackle and hiss of the pine needles Karen had gathered up from the forest floor to kindle the blaze. When she was finished, they saw her dance on the embers, which sparked once more at her feet as she put the fire out and kicked a covering of leaves over the scorching.

In the distance, a low rumbling resolved itself into the roar of a plane taking off from Glasgow Airport and traversing the sky overhead, just above the clouds; the whine of its jet engines rising in pitch as the aircraft rose, building to a crescendo, before dissipating slowly into silence.

Tony wondered if any of those on board, glancing down, might see them about their business in the gloom. He felt his pulse throbbing in his ears, felt his own stomach twist and churn at the thought of what they had just done.

'Are you sure—?' he started, the first words either of them had spoken since taking up the shovels.

'We never talk of this again,' Hugh said. 'We never come back here again.'

Tony motioned to protest, but Hugh raised the spade in front of him. 'I'll fucking cleave your head in two if you don't stop. We did what we had to do. I'm no happier than you are about it, but he got what he deserved.'

As they gathered their stuff and left the clearing, Tony looked back once at the spot, the slight rise of the earth just visible, in the dying light of Hugh's retreating torch beam, through the fork of an oak, twisted with ivy. It took them almost an hour to pick their way back to the car, the journey through the trees made in silence.

Only once, as they crossed a stream that ran down through the woodland, bridged by a fallen tree trunk, did Tony stop and reach out a hand for Karen to help her across. She took his hand in hers, squeezed it a little in reassurance, held it a second longer than necessary after she reached the other bank.

* * *

They drove back to Glasgow that evening and dropped Hugh at the train station.

'I'll be in touch,' he said, as he left them. 'Go home and forget about the whole bloody business.'

They watched him shuffle his way into the station, sticking a hand in his pocket and pawing out a few coins to pass to the young fella squatted at the station entrance, a paper coffee cup his begging bowl.

'Where do you want me to leave you?' Tony asked.

'How about we get a bottle of something?' Karen suggested. 'There's an offie across the street.'

She arrived back with a bottle of Southern Comfort and two litres of Diet Coke. They drove to Karen's flat in Paisley. Once inside, they stripped off their clothes as Hugh had instructed and put them in a hot wash. They sat in front of the fire, wrapped in bed sheets, and drank half the Southern Comfort before Karen moved across and straddled Tony, her mouth sweet, her tongue cold in his mouth as she kissed him with an urgency, a hunger, which surprised him, even as she pulled the sheet off him and pushed him back onto the floor.

They made love there. Tony had the sense he was discovering her body anew in that moment, as if their proximity to death had somehow enflamed their desire to live, to breath, to feel. He tried to dispel from his mind the vision of Martin Kelly, kneeling in his grave, the thought that his body was cooling beneath the earth even as theirs blazed in a moment of climax.

They lay together, Tony's head resting on her chest, his hand on her stomach. He could hear the rapid beating of her heart begin to slow, and felt his own breathing synchronise with its rhythm. He imagined himself happy, imagined them together like this, somewhere at home, a Donegal winter wind blowing outside.

That was what he would remember in years to come, when he was both alone and lonely. This last time together. The heat of her body, the scent of her perfume, of her skin, the gentle lift and fall of her breast beneath him with each breath, the saltiness in his mouth as he raised his own head and kissed her, the light of the flames dancing across her flesh.